On the War Path

Michael Chatfield

Dawn Chapman

Maraukian War
Book 5

Chapter One

The Yard

Ark Orbit, Emarl System

10/3559

It had been over two years since the Luyten fleet had attacked the Emarl system. Their actions had brought the system and its people together.

The Yard was heavily damaged and unable to come out of its defensive mode.

With the mergers and the crews of the Yard working together, they had been able to repair the Yard and once again get it functional.

As this was going on, a second yard was created. This was the navy yard, with the express purpose of making military vessels.

With their newly trained staff and the mergers' abilities, building had progressed smoothly.

Trade had been established with the Union planets, with many freighters coming from all over to try to buy the highly advanced technology.

The Emarl system was the pearl of humanity, where miracles were made. The Victor Corporation fleet was operating throughout the colonies. The corporations were powerless to stop them.

Sol had turned into a system filled with civil war, with the Union watching to make sure that none of the war spilled over and affected the rest of the Union.

Maraukian barges were appearing across humanity's controlled systems. With them, more people were gaining weapons and overthrowing the corporations.

Jerome knew that Moretti's hand was in most of those dealings.

"VCF *Reclaimer* coming in from the Luyten system," Esamai said as Jerome looked over from his station to the main star map that showed the dozens of ships moving through the system.

"I don't think the Luyten Conglomerate was so happy with what we returned to them," Jerome said dryly.

They'd repatriated the Luyten Conglomerate forces that had attacked Emarl. These were the soldiers who had been ejected by their own captains into space.

Returning to Emarl, they were the only military force in-system.

With their gliders and strength, they were able to erase the Luyten Conglomerate and created a AI progressive system—again, Moretti's work in convincing them and getting the people to stand up and fight for their freedom.

Earth and Her Colonies only existed in name now. When returning to Emarl from three systems, many of the mega freighters would have thousands of people looking to gain Emarl citizenship, or attend the Emarl Skill Schools, which were now renowned through human-controlled space.

Jerome sat back in his chair a bit. "We've created the fastest merchant fleet in the entire Union and the fastest warships. I never thought we would have an entire system to call home." Jerome's eyes moved to Tyler, who was waddling around with something in his mouth.

Still, Jerome's smile was only faint.

Esamai moved from her desk to his, hugging him from behind, even with her large belly.

"It's fine to be upset," Esamai said, reading his mind.

Jerome rubbed her arm, but he knew that although she tried her best and sympathized, she didn't know what it meant to be on that front line, to be aboard a ship going to war. That tension filled the air and was a running undercurrent to everyone's day-to-day activities. He knew these things all too well; his guts turned over in guilt.

"They'll arrive in the Tok system in just a few weeks," Jerome said.

Esamai didn't say anything, just hugged him a bit tighter.

Jerome patted her arm and let out a deep breath. He turned around and pulled her into his lap.

"I'll break the chair!" she complained.

"Don't worry, Mark's heavy ass reinforced it." Jerome smiled.

Esamai pouted and pinched him as Jerome showed a sliver of a smile.

"All right, Mrs. Esamai Victor, what do you need me to do?"

"Production is up across the board; the Yard is back in operation and Charles's mega stage four forge is working overtime to create parts for the freighters. I've heard from the navy yard they've got four more warships which will be ready for testing over the next three months. Once completed, they'll be working on retail Praetor cannons and defensive missile systems. Everyone and their cousin is looking for more defensive weapon systems after the last four attacks by the Maraukians." Esamai's expression soured.

Jerome couldn't blame her. Sacremon had been turned into an uninhabited system, with the Maraukians clearing out the population and then burrowing into the planet.

If anyone stepped onto that planet, they would need to deal with the Maraukians surging out and killing them.

The Maraukians went into a kind of hibernation, but not before they replenished their numbers. Once the Maraukians took a planet, then it was nearly impossible to get rid of them.

Mintran of the old EHC was attacked as well, but with the Union's support and weapons, they were able to save about twenty percent of their population and regain control over their main planet. They had applied to be a member of the Union afterward and were going through a rapid period of growth as their population moved out to learn more and return home with their skills.

Some people from the Emarl system had even settled down there.

The systems Yui and Praeki had fallen under attack, but since Cassius returned to power, the entire Union had been overhauled, including the senate and all of the legions. There was no place for politics within the military ranks anymore.

They, too, had Sam, who elected people of the Union to take command over different areas.

"At least humanity is working together and we have more safeguards left in place," Jerome said.

"You mean the Shadow Legion turning into mergers and supporting Sam?" Esamai asked.

"It was a natural choice. This way, they get to actually live and they can cut out corruption before it's fully formed. With Sam, their actions are limited and with the others knowing what they are doing, it's a self-regulating group. To safeguard humanity—sounds like one hell of a complicated job."

"Thankfully we just have to deal with building ships!" Esamai moved, getting more comfortable in Jerome's lap. "How are the factories coming along? I haven't looked at them in a while."

"Good. Much faster than I expected," Jerome admitted. The holographic projector in the room dimmed the lights as the system appeared. The original station now had three rings around it. The Aegean Gardens orbited the planet and there were signs of another station being built around Tricticus's orbit.

Out from Tricticus, there were four stations being built. These were the factories that took in materials from the refineries, turned them into useful items, and sent them across the system or out to other human planets.

"With the factories, we were able to reclaim a lot of the Yard's real estate back for building ships. They're also building subsystems which even though we could build them here, it takes them less time to make them.

"The new forges that the engineering group from the Crucible were able to think up are really showing their abilities. The stations aren't even fully built, but they're already exporting forges to other ships and groups who need them."

"Seems we've got some good competitors!" Esamai smiled. Only one of the factories was owned by the Victor Corporation. The others were backed by different groups in the Emarl system, or had loans with the Victor Corporation or other financers in the Union.

From the beginning, they never wanted the Victor Corporation to control everything in the system. Finally, things were starting to grow organically as new businesses started to appear and the whole system was undergoing a massive, accelerated rate of improvement.

"The problem we're having, even with the mining efforts going on within the Ark and the asteroid belt, is the refineries are currently our choke point. With the loss of Refinery Three, we've been down in production a lot. With new refining processes and two grinders working full time, we should be reaching a state were our resources are meeting our needs, at least for a few weeks." Jerome sighed.

"It's a sign of progress!" Esamai tousled his hair.

Jerome grunted.

The grinders were basically massive vats of nanites. Asteroids were slowly placed in them and they seemed to dissolve, being broken apart by nanites and sorted. It was a slow process, but if the asteroid had a high purity of metals, it was faster than having to try to separate the metals out again and again through chemical processes.

"Johnny tells me everything is going well and that Refinery Three will be rebuilt and ready to start working," Esamai said.

"That's good. Felicia has been complaining about the number of raw materials she has and needs to get refined." Jerome laughed.

"Those two are certainly personalities." Esamai shook her head as Jerome grinned.

Tyler came around the corner of Jerome's desk and looked at Esamai and Jerome with confused eyes.

"Well, I think it's about time for lunch. Come on, boys," Esamai said. Jerome helped to get her upright.

He looked to the hologram in the middle of the room again. It couldn't be compared to the Emarl system just three years ago as ships moved constantly, from all corners of humanity's systems.

Still, he frowned as he thought of his friends who were hurtling toward the unknown, chasing down wherever that signal that controlled the Maraukians was coming from.

Chapter Two

The Core

Preena, Sharventi Home System

10/3559

Sharventi sat around a table, thirteen of them in total. All of them had bland looks on their faces as they sat. Identical to one another, their uniforms were all the same except for the marker on their shoulders.

One stood up from the masses. On his shoulder, a human male and female patch showed.

"Race four, named humans, has shown mass improvement over the past two years. It seems that a group within the human race was able to find our signal and are moving to an offensive position. It is the expectation of my department, based on human behavior, that the human fleet will attack and move forward to the fourth stage of the plan, advancing on the Sharventi communication centers that relay the signal to the Maraukian systems and fighters. Once they advance through these relay stations, they will reach the Sharventi home system and we can start with part five of the plan. Calling of the Black Guard." The Sharventi's eyes were dim.

None of them showed any excitement, fear, or anxiousness as they took in the information.

"Time till completion?" Operator Seven, overlooking the T'laks race, asked.

"One to two years," Operator Four said.

"Previous prediction models said a time window of eighty more years," Operator Eleven said.

"Yes, the predictive model has been updated. But even with its information, it seems unable to fully understand the path of the races, with twenty percent margin for error. The group called mergers, a subspecies of the humans and an advancement in their biological and mechanical machines, show an error rate of forty to forty-five percent when analyzing them with the predictive models."

"The degree of error is high. We will continue with focusing on completing the stages," Operator Seven said.

There was nothing more that needed to be said. They all knew the same information and had been groomed into these positions from birth.

Seeing there was no one else who needed to talk, they stood and departed.

Chapter Three

Refinery Three

Oort Cloud, Emarl System

10/3559

Johnny watched as the rebuilt and much better Refinery Three was almost ready to be brought back online. Leon and Misha waited at their consoles, ready to relay any and all information he wanted. The truth was Johnny just liked to feel like a starship captain and up here, with them, it felt as if he were.

"All systems are in the green," Misha reported in, as Johnny watched to see gaseous puffs shoot out from the station's four main funnels. One more than they were used to, but the upgrades had condensed their whole process, leaving them with lots of space to fill. Might as well push in another unit. It had been tight, but this would now be the largest out of all the refineries that he owned. And he knew the extra output would make Felicia happy, as well as all the new crews he could hire in.

Nothing made him happier as a business owner than being able to provide for everyone. Of course, for him it hadn't always been this way. Building what he had, had taken many years, and a lot of balls to do so.

Felicia's voice came across to him. "Everything all right down there?"

"Yes. Looks like we'll be able to take your loads as soon as the system's been fully checked over."

"Good. Getting tired of having to shift this stuff farther than I need to for a pay packet."

Johnny laughed and he noticed a slight shift in one of Misha's readings. He stepped closer toward her just as several lights started turning from green to red. "Section two is misfiring across the board."

Johnny waited as Leon started to act, giving out orders to those inside the unit. He watched on as unit leaders relayed them and his personnel's reactions kicked in. Misha matched Leon's instructions, making sure all the other team leaders were aware of the situation and they were ready to act if the reactions going on inside couldn't be stopped. In all the years he'd been doing this, Johnny had only ever seen one refinery have problems, only ever seen the damage one could do planetside when they went up.

Out here, everything was different. "We've lost it once. Have faith." Johnny pulled every bit of faith he thought he had and tried to push against it. Their luck was changing, he knew it; it had to be.

"Get me the team leader's view up if you can."

Johnny was soon watching the live feed from the man's NIAI, and hearing his orders as he gave them out. Misha looked confused, but looking up at him, Johnny mouthed for her, "He's got this under control. Don't worry."

And Johnny wasn't worried. He could see that he was doing his job and perfectly well. Around him, people moved and whirled, a perfect vision of perfective management.

"How are the stats?" Johnny asked.

"Decreasing back down. We'll be back in the green in no time."

Johnny smiled. This was a good thing to happen now: better for the system to have a couple of glitches now than when there were real goods going through. If it had been running and not testing, it could have been a huge payload wasted. One that he would still have to pay for without being able to deliver the refined product to someone else.

"Unit two will have to stay offline for a while, till we've completed some more checks," Leon said.

Johnny understood. Lives and money was at stake; there were no higher bets in this world.

***

Pela hadn't just watched the new refinery go up in smoke, but nearly. After their last escape from the Luyten fleet blasting it and her asteroid into pieces, Pela had really had enough of things going wrong. From that day, she'd vowed to continue to strive for the community around her and she'd worked damned hard to get where she was. Today, however, was her birthday and despite wanting to get in and get the loads on their way to the new refinery, she wanted to spend time with her boyfriend. It had taken awhile longer for Lucus to ask her out properly. Ashaeed really had been jealous but he was two years younger than her. Lucus was two years older and no matter how much she thought of Ashaeed, she didn't quite see him the way he wanted her too.

"What's it like to be twenty-one?" Lucus came up behind her and wrapped his arms around her waist.

Pela didn't answer right away because it felt weird. She'd known it was coming, and it should have been a big day for her, but this felt so very wrong with everything going on about them as it had and was doing.

"It feels good," she said. "Besides, you promised me some Vermolt chocolate cake from the main station. I do hope you managed to keep that promise."

Lucus chuckled and nibbled her ear. "I have another surprise for you," he whispered.

Pela squirmed around in his grip. "What?"

He smiled but just winked at her instead, then he held out a keycard.

"What is this?" She took it from him and looked it over. There was a small number on the bottom left: Apartment 206.

"I thought it was about time we did something for us, that was right for us."

Pela swallowed. "You're asking me to move out of the dorms, right?"

Lucus nodded. "Yes. With this promotion for me, for us, I think it's about time we stepped away from the others a little. Give us more time to be together."

Pela leaned in and kissed him.

"I know how much you like being a part of the crew, but I want more time with you."

Pela watched as fire rose up the side of his neck. "Ah, you mean you want sex every night and not every once in a blue moon..."

"You know I'm not like that. I..."

Pela continued to laugh and pulled him in closer. "Of course I'll move in with you. Sounds wonderful. But," she said, "I still want that chocolate cake."

Lucus eased off her and took her hand in his. "Then let's go check it out. A full-sized chocolate cake is in the fridge just for you."

"*Gondi?*" Pela asked. "*Weight check?*"

"*Weight has declined in the last couple of weeks. But is still within parameters.*"

Pela frowned to herself. No matter how much she seemed to eat, sometimes it was a constant battle.

When Lucus realized she'd stopped walking, he turned to her. "What's wrong?"

"You think I'm ill, don't you? Just like Doctor McKay did a few years ago."

A slight frown crossed his face. "I don't think today's the right day for this conversation."

Pela's anger rose. "There's never going to be a right time for it." Pela could see him squirm almost as her anger rose all the more. "I eat everything I'm given. I eat everything you all ask me to." Tears started to fall then and Lucus pulled her to him, wrapping her up once more.

"Hey, hey, this is supposed to be a happy day."

"I can't eat any more than you're giving me. I'm not throwing it away. I'm not hiding it. I swear."

"Gondi looks after you and so do we, but something isn't right. I don't know why, but your metabolism switches so much, no one can predict what you're burning. Even the NIAIs are having trouble."

Pela looked up into his eyes. "So, I am sick?"

"*All vitals and checks are normal.*" Gondi replied to this in her ear.

"We've booked you back in with Doctor McKay in a few days. She will get to the bottom of it."

Pela looked away and out into the vastness of nothing. She didn't want to go back. If she had to, she'd eat the whole darn chocolate cake today.

Chapter Four

SLS Steady

Tok System

11/3559

Captain Lucy Khwan moved with her patrol group around the Tok system. It was one of the systems farthest from the center of humanity.

Though, in the last year, it had seen a massive growth as ships and personnel were shifted to the system.

Once it was revealed there was a signal controlling the Maraukians, Cassius moved into talks with the mergers to coordinate an offensive to find out where this signal was coming from and destroy it. If they could stop the Maraukians getting orders and being told how to build ships, then it was possible they could enter a time of peace, clearing out the remaining planets which held human populations on them and then dealing with the planet-bound Maraukians.

With the emperor back in command, the Union had been quickly reorganized, with the new systems put in place to assure that the system wouldn't fall into depravity again. Business had exploded as defensive structures, stations, ships, and weapons were supplied to systems across the Union.

Lucy Khwan had been promoted three times since the purge of the Union, leading to her position as a small patrol commander.

"Transit signal found!" Reoul, her sensors officer, said.

"On screen. Joas, inform Admiral Nessa," Khwan snapped off as she looked at the information coming in through her NIAI.

A moment later, a ship appeared. Then another and another; dozens started to transit into real-space and store their Alcubierre drives away.

"Identification codes have been confirmed. It's the Emarl fleet," Reoul said.

Khwan looked to Joas.

"Relaying to higher, Captain," Joas said.

Khwan smiled and relaxed.

"Continue on patrol route." Khwan snuck a glance at the Emarl Navy.

At the center, there were ten troop transports and fifteen supply ships. They were joined by twenty carriers and battleships, with the *Moby* riding among them all.

She looked over the *Moby*. It wasn't the first time she'd looked at the mysterious ship. It had grown again.

The old-style carrier had been heavily upgraded and not even the space legion knew what the full capabilities of the ship were.

The mergers had proved one thing: they weren't to be underestimated and they were not an opponent one wanted to fight.

The crew of the *Moby* was made up of mergers only. There were mergers serving on other ships but the fact was the *Moby*'s abilities, although they were survivable for the mergers, if someone was a human, there was a high risk of being severely or critically injured.

The *Moby* was meant to lead the way, with the Vanguard, RSDs, tanks, and artillery coming in support to clear an area for the remaining troopers to land and assist the merger ground forces.

There was something powerful that gripped Khwan as she saw those sixty-six ships moving in formation for the interior of the Tok system.

This would be their platform to launch their offensive.

Khwan felt a sour taste in her mouth. While they were heading out toward war, the legion was still in a defensive posture, holding what they had.

Still, it felt good they were moving in the right direction finally. Things were actually happening instead of it all becoming stagnant.

Chapter Five

ENS Homeland

Tok System

11/3559

The fleet made an impressive sight as it moved toward the deployment station near the Oort Cloud of the system.

"Looks like they've been following your exploits, Admiral," Rasalov said as information appeared on the main screen.

"Now, now, Rasalov. Play nice." Admiral Hall smiled.

"Got flight details for the fleet. Sending them out," Yeltsin said.

The others in the command center were used to Admiral Hall and his command staff's ways. Their history was long and they'd been with one another longer than they'd been with some of their significant others.

"We're all clear within a few light-minutes," Rasalov updated.

"Good. Now, Guy, you look like you want to ask me something by the way your board is lighting up?"

"The supply ships want to go and scavenge some asteroids." Guy sighed.

"Let them." Hall sighed, feeling as if he was letting puppies off their leashes. The supply ships were always focused on having the most amount of materials onboard so they could resupply the fleet as needed.

"I wonder if they know there's going to be asteroids in other systems?" Rasalov asked.

"Eh." Celik shrugged from his place at weapons.

"We've been okayed for sensor buoy uplink. Connecting you now, Rasalov."

"Nice!" Rasalov turned his attention to his station and forwarded all of the sensor information to Admiral Hall.

He looked out over the system. There hadn't been much here just a few years ago; the system was inhabited and had a fighting force as well as a supply station for the space legion.

Upon learning about the signal and how it was close to the Tok system, Cassius had ordered the legion to set up a position there. They were seeding the area around the system and beyond with sensor buoys to try to understand what was going on.

The other system close to the system the signal was coming from was Sacremon. There was a sensor network there, but the system had been lost already so infrastructure had been placed in the systems nearest to it.

They'd also sent out scout ships, not like the *Phoenix* that Captain Chen used to command, to search the system Hip 10 30 39, where the signal was coming from.

It was heavily inhabited by Maraukians but the signal looked to originate from an asteroid belt.

For now, Hall pushed that to the side as he looked at the roving patrols and the different bases in the system as well as the defensive cannons and launchers which orbited the habitable moon of the system.

When he was listening to the hum of chatter and looking out over the star system, he was struck by the beauty of the system, the tranquility of those moving planets.

Even as he had fought his entire life, these planets had continued to spin around this blazing star, and they would continue to do so well after he had passed away.

They were fighting to survive, to try to reach further into that distance called time. He didn't know who he was fighting or why they were fighting humanity.

All he knew was where he needed to go.

Chapter Six

Emperor's Residence
Roma, Hellenic System
11/3559

Cassius had gotten used to reports being on the slower side of things, and it made him kick back today and relax. The sun shone in through the open windows and the breeze drifted in. Moving over to look out at the building around him, he'd finally decided that maybe it was time for him to step down. To let someone new take over. The thoughts whirled around in his head, but he'd still not gotten the courage to do so.

After the initial cleansing two years ago, it had taken some strength in voice and determination in the heart to start to bring things back to some semblance of order. Even backing in full the Shadow Legion's choices, the decision on whose lives to end thankfully not his. However, now, the more he thought about it, the better he felt. Roma had once again begun to thrive. Most of the Shadow Legion members had moved on. They'd trained with Moretti and become mergers to go mount the offense in the Tok system. Some had made the pact once more to defend Roma in her darkest days and had gone back into cryo. They would be there if ever needed in the future. That was their right to make that decision. What had surprised him was that Zedra wanted to stay awake. She was more than thorough with her work here, and he'd expected her to want to go back below.

The day she appointed her next-in-command to take her place, he'd found it strange. He'd asked her why, but he knew: the fire burning inside her to destroy the Maraukians. And he'd remembered reading about what happened to her family those many years ago. "Besides," she'd also smiled at him, "I might well live to see the Shadow Legion rise once again." Those who hadn't gone below then trained with her and Moretti. Cassius was interested in the process, and he visited their training grounds quite extensively at first. Just so he could get to know the ins and outs of the selection.

Today, he wanted to see the sun, walk in the gardens. Roma had been mostly rebuilt, not only in its leadership personnel but in its surrounding areas. The Aegean Gardens had gone but the practical need for them hadn't. So, while they'd had to outsource from other parts of the system, they internally started to rebuild a fully functioning growing station as well.

Cassius looked to the blue skies. It might not be anywhere near as helpful or the size of Nerva's gardens but it would get there in time.

"*Damus is waiting for you,*" his NIAI said.

This was an unexpected meeting that Damus sprung on him. Not very often did they get to meet face-to-face now. Damus was mostly out over the planet and into the system.

This time he'd asked for lunch, and Cassius felt it would be good to see each other.

He walked through his corridors and past room after room till he made his way out into the back gardens, cordoned off by the most beautiful shrubs, bushes, and flowers. He couldn't help but pause to stop and admire them.

Damus stood overlooking the greenery and the soft trickle of a pond drifted over. That was a new addition to the gardens, and it had been Zedra who wanted it.

"Good to see you, Damus," Cassius said as he approached.

But, when Damus turned, he didn't seem to think it was a good thing, but he dutifully respected his emperor and saluted, then smiled. "It's always good to see you, but I fear we might not have all good things to talk about."

Cassius had thought things had settled in a little too easy the last few months. Though attacks on certain systems by the Maraukians had increased, they were also ready for them. Not unlike previous years.

"What is it? Please, let's sit and discuss."

Damus sat down and picked up a glass of cool amber liquid. He drank deeply before he started. "We're not relaying any of this information over the net," he said. "The fact is we need to keep this as close to us as possible. While we put a plan of action together."

Damus passed over a device so Cassius could see a new threat. Though in his heart he already knew where they were coming, where he knew eventually they would stretch out to. The Hellenic system. It was not the only reason they'd kept most of their fleet here, but it was part of it. Even Mark had said that through Moretti. Once the Maraukians had hit enough of the smaller planets and stations, then it would turn to the next lot of largest populated areas.

That meant, in time, all would come to a head. "We're ready for this," Cassius said. "Mark's had us be prepared for this ever since they left here."

"Yes, we are, but our citizens are not. We need to tread very carefully here how we do things. Not to make their lives more stressful."

Cassius almost laughed at this. The lives of most Roma citizens weren't stressful anymore. A thriving working community. Those who wanted to serve the Union or train to become legionnaires had a good life.

"Do we know where they'll strike first?"

Damus nodded. "This is why I'm here. They're coming for Earth and Velia."

Cassius swallowed. "I can see why that might be a problem for some. No matter what, Earth is a legend that people never wanted to let go of."

"You mean except for Mark."

"He's probably one of few exceptions, yes. There are and always will be those who will fight for her, no matter the consequences."

"You think we should?"

"No. Though a lot of what is going on with Earth and Her Colonies isn't what we'd have liked and there are people against both the Union and Mark, there's not a lot we can do."

Damus crunched on some nuts.

"The Emarl Navy might have headed off at the wrong time." Cassius sighed.

Damus raised an eyebrow. "No, they might be the only ones who can stop them. It might be too late for most planets. The more the Maraukians seem to wage war, the quicker their growth in numbers. I hope Mark and the mergers can stop them at their source."

Chapter Seven

Wind Snapper

In Transit, Hellenic System

12/3559

Moretti hadn't thought he would be training anyone, but he didn't have much choice when the clean-up happened. He was the only merger in the Hellenic system and when things had settled, there was a need for more. With Charles's help across the net, he pulled together the resources to create a lab under the palace and to work with the Shadow Legion to get them to pass Mark's stringent tests.

At first, he thought no one would make it through. The Shadows had been through so much change, though, in their awakening months that there was a side note for potential with their testing.

Mark would never relax the rules or criteria, but they had extra time. It was the only way.

When Moretti had asked for the first to go through training to become mergers, it was of course Zedra. He'd gotten to know her much more in the leading months, and this was now no surprise. Her family, wiped out by the Maraukians, was the push for her to finally get her revenge and peace for their loss.

Now, looking out at views he had from the *Moby*, Moretti knew she was with the EN fleet, arriving in the Tok system. If he could ever be as proud of anyone, it would be his friends.

Thoughts drifted momentarily back to Sertoria in the nanite tank. He thought he'd been unconscious with her, but he hadn't. At first, the memories returning to him at that time were bad. He didn't want her to be a monster, nor did he want any other changes for himself, but when the process for her had taken a more bitter turn for the worse, she'd made the decision for him. She asked him to be let go. That was one of the hardest things he'd ever done. He'd lost over the years, just like everyone else, but Sertoria hurt the most. He didn't know whether he'd loved her; didn't know whether he could. But that was what bothered him, the what-if. Now those two years later, he'd had plenty of times to worry about the what-if. He couldn't worry about them anymore. The Shadow Legion, now mergers he'd helped to create, were off out in the depths of the universe with the one man he really knew now above all. He called Jerome brother, but Mark felt like more than family.

Around him were his most trusted people. Those he'd come in on the *Wind Snapper* with. A few had made the decision to join him as a merger, but the one person who had asked and he denied still stuck around: Cronus—Hael's son, and Mark's partner's brother. He wanted to become like his sister so he could help save the universe, but Moretti made the tests harder. He failed him on purpose. That young man was more than smart; he was sure he'd known it but had taken it in his stride, still striving to prove himself to Moretti and even his crew.

Moretti sat with Captain Shwab, and one of his other close members of the crew.

They'd all been witness to the transmission over to Damus and the rest came as no surprise. The Maraukians were attacking in much greater numbers now.

Mark's image appeared before them but it was strained and weak. It wasn't surprising; the actual distance between them was phenomenal. Moretti was hopeful they'd maintain contact throughout their engagement, but his gut told them the closer they got to the Maraukian's system, the more they'd lose him and be on their own.

Moretti didn't need to hear how Mark felt about Earth or Velia being attacked; he knew it from the inside. For those systems now, it was almost certainly over. Moretti wasn't sure whether the Union would help at all, or whether they should.

Chapter Eight

Royal Palace

Tricticus, Emarl System

12/3559

When the cleanse happened in the legion, there were also multiple hits on Tricticus. Moretti's men were deep inside the ruling government, seeing who might and who was planning to overthrow High King Hael and try anything to stop the mergers. Under extreme circumstances, Julieus Desialias returned back to his family for a little while, then he'd gone back out into the field under his father's orders to help one of their neighbors rebuild.

Now back at the Royal Palace, things felt very different. He'd known some of the groups in Gtrul were bad, but the truth of the matter had shocked him. They weren't just bad; they were rotten to the core. The day his best friend turned on those he thought were his friends and pulled the trigger on them, stuck with him most nights. Nightmares plagued him for all the wrong reasons. He had turned to his friend, watched the look in his eyes as he actually contemplated killing the first prince of Tricticus. Seeing that gun aimed at his chest, the thoughts that he wanted him to pull the trigger, really hit home.

"You're not even going to try to stop me?"

And he hadn't. He would have accepted that punishment for all the things he'd done, trying to impress the wrong people. Thinking back on it now, he'd realized that was his wake-up call. It was only a day later and from out there in the distant galaxies, he'd gotten a message from Cronus, and for the first time he'd actually listened. He'd listened and he'd gone home.

"Everything all right?" Thia said as he poked his dinner about the plate.

"Sorry, Mother. Just a lot on my mind."

Hael had taken the twins up to bed, and was no doubt reading them stories from their favorite book.

Thia picked up the bottle of wine sitting in an ice bucket. "Come with me. We'll have a drink outside and talk."

Julieus looked away, but picked up his glass. "That would be lovely."

It was nice out, and being home had taught him a lot. He'd missed not only his mother, whom he adored like most young men, but he'd missed seeing his new little sister and brother. When they'd seen him for the first time, it broke his heart. "Dada, who dat?"

Now he'd had some time to contemplate the last few years of his life and what he'd been trying to do.

"What's going on?" Thia poured him a glass full of wine.

"What makes you think something is going on?"

"I can see it in your face, the conflicted look. What happened in Gtrul?"

When he looked toward her, there was something in her eyes that he'd not seen before and he finally found himself talking. Honestly talking. "I was playing them off. It was not a game to be messing about in, but I was trying to protect my brother and my family."

"It went wrong?"

Julieus thought about not telling her, not spoiling the illusion she had of him. But he found the wine had loosened his tongue up some, and the details started to come out.

Thia just listened. Most of it she already knew and she just agreed with him in all the right places.

"Then," he said, "after all of that, I came home."

Thia nodded. She wasn't going to push him too much, but she also wanted her son to stay around. "We have a lot to do here," she said. "There's some hard times ahead for us, for all of the Emarl system."

This confused him. Emarl was more than thriving, with people and resources he'd never imagined before. Julieus looked to her. "I don't understand?"

"You've not been privy to the information, because we wanted you to talk to us first." Hael stepped up behind him and placed a hand on his shoulder.

Julieus tried not to flinch, but the fact was they'd never really shared any kind of closeness, not since Cronus had been born. Those details he'd remembered from that very early age. "And you'll tell me now?" he asked, feeling some kind of hope rise inside him. Maybe he'd not broken or lost all their trust.

"The Maraukians are heading back here, and you're one of our greatest assets out there."

Julieus swallowed. The attacks the first time had been horrendous. He didn't want to see that again. That amount of death had almost broken him too. Then his sister had gone off to become one of those things...a merger. She'd sacrificed herself for nothing, in his eyes.

"We know how you feel," Thia said. "We feel the same. We hope they won't get to Tricticus again. If you don't want to join the fight, we'd understand."

"Do we have long?"

"Long enough to move defenses around the farthest points in the system so we can strike while there's any chance of bleeding them in space. If they try to get farther in, our defenses are much better. We believe they'll come in fast, hit what they can, and head straight for us once more."

"So you want me to fight in space?"

"No, no," his father said. "We need you on the ground here, helping to manage the cities and new human settlements."

Julieus saw it for what it was. "That olive branch is poking me in the eye." He could see they both wanted this for him.

"You'll take the position as the legate over our smaller cities?"

The hope in Hael's eyes brought about in him the strangest feeling of wanting to make his father proud. Julieus stood and in the traditional way of his people, he saluted his king. "Yes, sir. It would be my honor to serve you there."

Hael smiled. "I had no doubts, son."

Julieus, however, had many doubts he could lead against an invasion. He'd watched all the vids; he'd seen all the training his friends had gone through to move to become mergers with Mark. He'd toyed with it, but he also got the message from Ava: "No." That was it—that was all she'd had to say to him, to his brother and to their father. "If you let them do this, I'll hunt you down myself." That had been the threat he'd overheard while she was still in Tricticus the first time with him, the lead merger—Mark Victor.

Julieus pushed the thoughts aside. He'd do anything he could for his father and he'd regain his position within the new Emarl Navy.

Chapter Nine

ENS Homeland

Tok System, En Route to the Hip 10 30 39 System

12/3559

"Refueling complete. We're full on raw supplies as well as ammunition and consumables," Captain Chen said, Admiral Hall's now second-in-command. He had thought about bringing him onto the *Homeland* but Chen made it clear he wouldn't leave the *Moby*.

Hall respected his stance and it also added a layer of protection. If Hall was killed, then Chen wouldn't be killed at the same time and he could take over the fight.

"So what you're saying is we've overstayed our welcome and it's time to leave," Hall joked.

"Well, we're already exiting the Oort Cloud. I don't think we can turn back now," Chen said.

"No, I don't think we can." Hall felt tired and old down to his bones. He took a deep breath as they moved closer and closer to the edge of the system.

"Two months," Chen said.

"Two months until we know the true face of our enemy. Hopefully we can start getting some damn answers," Hall said.

Chen nodded.

Chapter Ten

Emperor's Residence

Roma, Hellenic System

12/3559

Cassius had started to get word from Earth, not just reports. It was a slaughter.

Even with the fight against the Maraukians going on, the people of Earth were still fighting one another, trying to gain a better position.

Could they win? He was not sure. What he wanted to do was make sure if they hit any of his planets, they were heavily defended and ready for it.

Waiting on any word from the Emarl Navy was tough. Sleep didn't come easy and if he took stimulants to help him through the day, it had a knock-on effect when he wanted to rest. So, running on next to nothing was the only way to go.

Damus had stayed nearby, working the newly appointed legatus from the Shadow Legion. This man had single-handedly infiltrated and took down one of the largest opponents in the space fleet while the cleanse was executed. Admiral Nessa commanded all of their space legion forces.

It had undergone a massive change. There had been so many political dissidents in her ranks that the new space legion was looking rather skinny.

The Emarl system had helped out with creating systems that would allow them to operate their current fleets and ships with less personnel. It wasn't ideal but needs must.

There was an active recruiting campaign going on and although they were up to seventy percent of their previous strength, they had less forces. But their coordination was much higher than previously.

Still, with all of these people, Cassius found that as the emperor, he was lacking.

He called Damus as he was waiting in a clean-looking facility, his guards around him.

"What is it?" Damus asked. They were close and they didn't waste time on things like formalities.

"Does having an NIAI hurt?"

To run the defense and whole of the Hellenic system better, and to have instant information when the Maraukians attacked properly, he thought it was a must now.

"It's more overwhelming than anything else," Damus said after a few seconds.

"Well, looks like I'll be able to get in touch much easier from now on."

"Great, more random calls." Damus snorted.

"Well, I'll let you get back to it." Cassius laughed awkwardly, realizing that he was probably taking his top general away from something that was actually important.

Damus cut the channel as a medic walked toward Cassius. He looked around at the royal medical bay.

He frowned and then looked at the emperor. "One NIAI?"

"Right here," Cassius said.

"Good. We're going to knock you out. Once you wake up, you'll have an annoying voice in the back of your skull for the rest of your life. Arm?" The man was brusque and quick.

Cassius held out his arm. Quickly, he was given an injection. He closed his eyes and opened them again, looking at the man, who was pulling out the needle. "So, when does it start?" Cassius asked.

"Already done." The man gestured to his arm.

There was now a silver band there, molded to his arm.

"*Integration complete.*" A modular monotone voice sounded in his mind. It sounded as if it were just talking right next to him. He looked around but no one had said anything.

"Takes some time getting used to, but even in older patients it's pretty quick." The medic cleared up the last of his equipment and then turned to leave.

"*Do you wish to choose a name for me?*" the voice asked.

He had been thinking of names for the NIAI ever since he made the decision to get one.

"*Portia.*"

"*There is an incoming link up already waiting for you,*" Portia said.

No rest for the wicked, or emperors.

Cassius sighed.

"*It doesn't seem so. There are more information streams coming in that I can make available to you. We should set up your communication settings first,*" Portia recommended.

Chapter Eleven

EMFC Promise

In Transit to Aegean Gardens, Emarl System

1/3560

Captain Austen watched as his pilot maneuvered in close to their drop-off points. Their cargo was so very precious to the people: reinforcements for their spatial city walls. Their lands at the moment were protected but needed to be ready if the Maraukians came down.

He'd watched as they'd been loaded and was sure that the shipment had extras, more so than he was asked to carry earlier this morning. He'd asked to see the cargo hold and there were indeed several items that had been pushed on.

Now they were approaching the gardens and his thoughts turned to Moretti. "I'll be in my room," he informed his comms officer. "Unless it's a Maraukian invasion, I don't want to be disturbed."

With the door closed behind him, Austen sucked in a breath and opened his comms to Moretti.

"You at the gardens already?" Moretti asked.

"Yes. *Promise* is still receiving upgrades. Some decent tech coming in from the Ark and the science teams there. They've done nothing but hype up what they want to do to the enemy if they get a chance."

Moretti answered this. "I'm really hoping they don't get a chance there. Emarl might have better weapons than we have here, but those Maraukians are not an easy kill. Keep them at bay as much as you can, and when they're in range of any defensive RSDs, for heaven's sake throw everything you've got at the bastards."

"Thanks for the concern, M," Austen said. "We're dropping off and moving to the outer limits. We've been tasked to meet with the other EMFCs beyond the Oort Cloud and wait their insertion. Both mining and growing facilities are our priority to protect or deflect them away from, if that be the case."

"Not too sure I like the sound of that," M replied.

Austen knew this was because there were a lot of his people on these ships. "M, we've been at war for much more than the years here. These alien creatures don't fight as dirty as humans. They have immense armor and capabilities, but they're not thinking creatures."

"Then you'd better outthink them." M smiled.

Austen nodded. "I will, don't you worry. They're not getting past me."

"Don't be doing anything stupid now either," M said. "We need you and those ships."

"The crew here can fly RSDs off like the best of them. I don't plan on getting close enough for other tactics, but if we have to, there's enough rail cannons and missile bays to light them up here as well."

"Keep me posted on the drop, and when you're back in the system for patrol, we may need to use you for some more transport missions, as soon as we get some ideas what's heading your way. Are you all right in carrying some prototype missiles for the RSDs?"

Austen raised an eyebrow. "Not a problem, M. We're here to help. If it's coming from the Ark, then it sounds good to me. Just don't tell me they can blow my ship to smithereens, all right?"

"We're putting them up around the system. There's a good few already in place, but these are more powerful upgrades."

"Consider it done."

M cut the line and Austen eased back in his chair. The transporting goods and troopers didn't bother him, and neither did laying down his life in the line of duty.

Chapter Twelve

Watchtower

Tiel City, Tricticus

Emarl System

2/3560

The main crew leaders were controlling this meeting. That meant Sun, because she was directly under Dominguez and Phillips, Trina and Donny as they were both main gang heads, and Enzo Lamm, and Timothy Johns. Phillips should have been the overseer, but he was at present keeping himself on the top side of the tower to deal with the ship relays and other emergencies as they seemed to keep popping up. This was strange for Sun. Despite what was going on, he could have delegated personnel for that and met with the legate; it seemed he didn't want to. At least not yet. So she would make any excuse she needed to keep the legate from suspecting too much, even if it were saying he was caught out in a shuttle during a storm.

This also meant Sun was the head of the table and the others would follow her lead. After General Dominguez had left, there was the chain of command to fall back on, and they would.

They were waiting on Legate Desialias and his entourage of escorting commanders. They were late. Not just late, but annoyingly so. Julieus hadn't even sent them a message as to why. Sun had looked over all their files. The men under Julieus were battle worn; some had fought the Maraukians the first time around and others were newbies. Just like the legate and his position overseeing everything here. Sun might have been new to the whole travel in space and set up a new planet thing, but she wasn't new at organizing defense against incoming problems. That meant those of the human kind as well as any other enemy that would be beating down their doors.

Julieus seemed to come with a high-end warning label and yet no one actually did the warning. The men under him were capable of doing things without his guidance; that was a good thing. Sun started the meeting and called for attention where the new tanks and equipment they'd been loaned would be better placed. She pulled up the images of the surrounding city, its defense walls, and then placements for fallback positions and safety zones.

Running these through with those at the table, she was getting nods of approval and they'd all but settled on who else they could call upon if needed. The idea that the new or partly trained mergers might be joining them scared Sun. She'd seen them fight; on their side or not, these men and women were beyond being warriors. With everyone in agreement and the meeting almost about to end, Sun relayed the orders to the waiting men and women to where they'd deploy, and confirmation came back as they started to move out.

That was when the meeting room door opened, and in walked the legate with three other men in tow.

Sun stood to greet them, and she then proceeded to introduce the people around her.

"Thank you, Major Sun. These are Tribunus Tullius and Iovia." He noticed the 3D holo on the table and immediately moved to study it. "This isn't what we've been discussing in regard to deployment of the tanks or the other pieces of equipment." He raised an eyebrow to Sun. "What's going on?"

Sun replied, "I was not aware of any of your intended defense positions. You are," she checked the time, "two hours late to the meeting, and the orders have already been given."

"Then retract them, while we go over things again!" Legate Desialias said.

Keeping hold of the young man's gaze, Sun never wavered. "Take a few minutes to study the lay of the land, and the new positions of the Bellona and then we'll discuss retracting my orders."

Sun could see the young man squirm. He was trying to assert his leadership but in the worst way possible. His face flushed, and yet instead of doing what his body was saying, he seemed to swallow his anger, and move to the table. Then he started to process what was before him. Sun knew he was also using his NIAI for confirmation and he finally turned to her.

"Good call, Major," was all he said on the subject. "Might I suggest we start off once more." This time he held out a hand for her to shake instead of the usual military greeting.

Sun took his hand and shook it. "Pleasure to meet you, Legate."

Chapter Thirteen

ENS Moby

Hip 10 30 39 System

2/3560

The *Moby* came out of transit as everyone was focused on the sensors and seeing what was inside the system. They had all downloaded and assimilated the reports from the scout ships, but seeing it secondhand and seeing it for themselves was two totally different concepts.

"Welcome to the Hip system," Chen said, his voice carrying to all of the linked-in mergers.

Mark and the leaders of the military arm of the mergers were all around a command table that showed them a holographic representation of the system.

There was the sixth planet in the system that had shipyards across the plants, building the different parts of a Maraukian insertion barge as Maraukians covered the planet.

Their attention wasn't focused on the planet but a remote section of the system's only asteroid belt. This was where the signal was originating from.

They didn't try to hide their presence as they charged toward the asteroid belt, their sensors cranked up as the fleet altered its course on a least-time journey to the asteroid belt and the station that hid there.

"Looks like we found it," Ava said.

The others didn't say anything but Mark could feel their agreement through the net.

"The operational plan hasn't changed. We need more information on this unknown threat. For that, we need to get people on that rock. The Vanguard regiment is up for this. We'll be going in on drop-ships, with RSDs providing cover. We've got sixteen days until we reach the asteroid belt. Make sure your people are rested and ready." Mark looked at the familiar faces.

Mark had once again became a major as he commanded over a complete regiment of mergers.

He saw their cold eyes turn hot. Finally, they would be on the leading edge of the blade, attacking the enemy instead of waiting for the Maraukians to attack them.

Ava and Mark looked at each other and shared a small smile.

Damn if she isn't stubborn. Reminds me of Alexis. Tyler and I always needed stronger women to restrain us, Mark thought ruefully. The loss of his brother and sister-in-law still weighed on him, but he couldn't help but smile sadly at the memories they had together.

It was a lifetime together, a life that felt as if it had been forever ago.

He was sad to be losing the connection of time to the events of being in the Earth Military Force. Even if he wanted to forget, he couldn't now as a merger. It was one of the things he was thankful for, but one that also kept him awake and led him to a much darker place, where he met with the souls he had known and lost.

Ava had carved out a place in his heart and he was helpless to stop her.

He no longer had thoughts of pushing her away, just the constant fear of losing her.

It wasn't easy loving someone who was on the front lines next to him.

It made them embrace every moment they had.

Chapter Fourteen

Roma, Hellenic System

Streets

2/3560

Moretti walked through the streets of Roma with many thoughts inside his mind. There was a lot going on, a lot to juggle and people he needed to see. Heading into the city quarters, he was meeting with one of his advisors, someone who had stayed undercover from the cleanse, and someone he needed to coordinate with. They also didn't have an NIAI or links to the net. This posed some difficulty for quite a lot of the men and women he used across the galaxies. Something as simple as getting or keeping in touch with them could be hard work. This, however, was a mounting problem over in Emarl that he needed a close eye on.

The local market was in full swing. It was good to see the local people to Roma behaving like they should. Selling their goods and wares in the most vibrant way possible. The stalls were filled with fresh fruits, vegetables, and hand-stitched clothing. Soft aromas of the freshly baked breads and delicacies from the region invaded his nostrils. It hadn't quite been the same for him as a merger. He really missed food. It was great to be able to just digest what you needed with the nanites' help, but sitting down to a real meal had become a chore. His mind and body worked better at higher speeds; slowing himself down was grating on his nerves.

The man he was looking for was up ahead, but Moretti made sure he stopped at a couple of stalls to buy goods. Even if he wouldn't use them, he would pass them on to someone as he left the market.

He walked up to the stall where his contact stood, looking over a jacket. "That won't fit you." Moretti laughed.

Vel's green eyes met his with a smile tugging his lips. "I might be a fair few years older than you, Mr. Moretti. It seems you've been packing on some weight, too, by the looks of things."

Moretti flexed his arms. In the warmth of the sun, he'd removed his own jacket and now was thankfully down to just a shirt.

Vel put the jacket he was looking at down, much to the annoyance of the vendor. "I'll listen to him, sorry. Not quite my size." And then he moved away, with Moretti beside him. "Hungry?"

Moretti neither agreed or disagreed with him, but he let Vel lead the way and take him into a side bar, where he ordered two breakfasts and drinks. When they at least had a strong cup of coffee in their hands, Vel finally looked him over. "You hide it well." He twirled the cup in his hands before taking a sip. "But how long have I known you, M?"

"Many years, and no, I don't suppose I could hide it from those who really knew me before..."

"You mean before the Maraukians came into the world?"

"The bane of everything, but yes, I guess so."

Vel had taken off across the galaxies in the opposite direction he'd gone in, and finding him here in Roma had been a bit of good luck.

"So," he asked when there was food in front of them. "What is it you want from me?"

"I need a message getting through to one of our oldest friends. He came through with the Earth shipment and I believe the last I heard, he was also closest to Dominguez."

"Alex Venti?" Vel asked.

Moretti picked up the coffee mug and savored the flavor. With a nod, he looked to Vel, gauging his expressions and mannerisms in a much different light. Usually reading his men was one of the things he was very proud of. Now, with the added senses and workings of his NIAI and now the fact he was a merger, he saw the man differently. *Was he being played himself?*

Moretti waited for Vel to say something else, but he held back, just enough for Moretti to actually have to speak again. He didn't.

"Why don't you contact him yourself? You used to be good friends."

Moretti looked away. There weren't many people along the years that he'd had crossed words with, but with Phillips it had been different. Phillips hadn't originally been born on Earth; he was as fresh off Masoul as Moretti was himself. But, Phillips had other ideas on where he wanted to be and the intel he'd wanted to gather. He'd almost vanished off Moretti's map until he'd had a conversation with Dominguez one day and he'd been in the background. Of course, under a new name now, and one that hadn't crossed Moretti's NIAI before: Andrew Phillips.

"The message?"

Moretti passed him a chip. "There's information on there that only he can see, understand?"

Vel smiled and put the chip away. "You don't need to tell this ole man his job. But you do need to tell me more about what *you* are now."

Chapter Fifteen

Drop-ship 314

Inner Hip 10 30 39 System

3/3560

Yu, Young, and Bobbie checked over their stations once again. They were all nervous. With the asteroid, it was better for them to use the drop-ships instead of the drop pods, or Hell Hammers as they'd come to be known.

"They've got to know we're in-system by now and we haven't hidden that we're going right at them," Bobbie said, voicing what they were all thinking.

"Don't try and understand aliens. They're aliens, after all," Young said.

Yu took her advice to heart. It was an off-hand comment on one hand, but it was also true. They didn't know who the commander behind the Maraukians was. They didn't know why they had attacked humanity and they didn't know how they thought, their tactics. All of it was confusing and not something they could resolve easily.

"All drop-ships, prepare to launch." Chen's voice was heard in all of the flight crew's heads as they focused their efforts.

The massive carrier doors started to open slowly, revealing the star-studded scene at the end of their acceleration rail.

The fleet was relatively close together but there was no way for them to see one another with their naked eyes.

"Looking good on navigation plan." Yu checked the plot again as Young updated the flight profile.

He saw the RSDs, ready and waiting.

Their goal was simple: defend the drop-ships and cover them on their trip to the surface of the asteroid.

"Well, looks like time for another ride," Mark said.

Yu and Young looked at each other and smiled.

"Seems like you're always lost on some rock or looking to get somewhere fast. Would you please pick a place that isn't having a fireworks demonstration every time?" Bobbie complained.

Yu smiled and shook his head as he sat back into his seat and checked his harness, waiting for the next order that would launch them down the acceleration rails.

"What can I say? I'm a dangerous man!" Mark joked.

"Maybe with a spoon. Do you remember that eating contest on our way back to Earth?" Young reminisced.

"Hah! Mark broke a plate with a spoon and stabbed it into the mess table! I nearly forgot," Bobbie said as Mark groaned.

"They didn't give you silverware for three months," Yu joined in.

"How am I supposed to train people when I've got a magenta-colored plastic sporknife!" Mark said.

"Sporknife?" Young sounded interested.

"There was a serrated edge on the side so I could cut. You ever tried to cut something with a sporknife? I bet even Charles wouldn't know how to," Mark said with a faint sense of pride.

"I have yet to meet a full-grown man proud of his exploits with a sporknife," Bobbie said, amazed by Mark's thick skin.

"Rare talent," Mark agreed.

The others couldn't help but laugh.

"Lunch in ten seconds!"

"Did he just say lunch?" Young asked Yu.

"Think the A in launch took the day off," Yu muttered back.

"Oh, yeah he's not going to live that one down," Bobbie laughed.

"*Launch* in five!" the flight commander said. Clearly Bobbie and Yu weren't the only ones who had noticed their slip-up.

The acceleration rail fired up and the drop-ship shot out of the ship.

"Fuuuuuucckkk," Mark grunted.

"Woo-hoo!" Bobbie said in contrast, throwing his hands up so he was pinned against the wall.

The acceleration stopped as Yu merged with the ship and Young.

The drop-ship became an extension of themselves as they moved into a flight pattern, with other drop-ships following in behind them and the RSDs providing cover.

After a few minutes, all of the drop-ships were out of the *Moby* and headed for the asteroid base under the cover of the RSDs.

All of the drop-ship's crews were linked together, ready to react to the asteroid base if it showed any sign of being a threat.

They advanced forward quickly, wanting to get to the asteroid before anything happened.

They didn't push up to their full speed as they'd need to cut their velocity in order to get the Vanguard onto the asteroid.

They bounced back signals to one another and they moved around erratically to make it harder to target them. The RSD's cannons twitched around, focused on different points on the asteroid.

"Five minutes out," Young relayed to the Vanguard who were with them. All of the Vanguard were already merged, linked to the ships and to one another.

Yu felt a chill down his back. The thing that was the weirdest about the Vanguard was the sense of stillness that came with them. There was never wasted motion and when they were waiting to go into battle, they were utterly silent.

"Power fluctuations!"

"Weapon systems firing!"

The drop-ship's cannons opened up as four RSDs in a straight line just disappeared.

"Light focused weaponry!" The mergers combined all of their information, analyzing their attack.

"Use missiles to create screen for targeting sensors." Young came up with a solution as missiles shot out from the RSDs and the drop-ships. The mergers directly took control over the RSDs as their reactions were faster.

"RSDs, move in to take out those laser installations!" Yu, in charge of all flight assets, ordered.

Another slew of RSDs were destroyed and a drop-ship was hit. A three-foot-wide hole appeared in the ship as the laser weapon lanced through the drop-ship. The drop-ship's momentum carried it forward, the beam of light cutting through the ship.

"Two point one five eight three second burst," the pilot of the ship responded in a cold tone.

"Hits almost instantaneous," Bobbie summarized. The missiles started exploding, but not before seven more of the laser weapons lashed out, taking out some sixteen more RSDs and destroying two drop-ships.

"It seems they understand the threat of the drop-ships," Yu said.

"Once landing on the surface, stay grounded. Those weapon systems won't be able to depress enough to attack you," Mark told Yu directly.

"All drop-ships, hold on landing area. Do not lift off again once you've dropped off your payload."

The missiles had created a screen, allowing them to see the laser interacting with it and weakening their attacks.

"Missile launches!" Young caught them as missile systems were revealed and started shooting toward the incoming fleet at a high acceleration.

"Linked defensive fire." With Yu's words, the cargo masters all linked together, using the weapons of their drop-ships to cover one another and try to destroy the incoming missiles.

The RSD's AI was slogging away, spitting out rounds. More ships were destroyed. One second, they were on one another's wing; the next, they had a hole burned through their core systems, or a missile had torn them apart.

Even the effects of being near the explosions were devastating as the different ships were bucking and awing as their structures were placed under incredible stress.

***

Mark gritted his teeth. He kept anything he wanted to say to himself unless it was vitally important. A second's lapse of judgement could mean the ship went up in a fireball.

They were being thrown to and fro with the missiles. Yu increased their acceleration to get them on the asteroid faster and out of the line of fire.

Mark heard the rattle as a side of the combat shuttle was torn apart, eight Vanguard gone in a second. The drop-ship started to skew wildly as it had lost several engines before it corrected on what it had remaining, coming in on at an odd angle.

The ramp started to lower and some hatches started to open on one side. The Vanguard came up to standing, ready to be launched. They kicked their feet, breaking open the hatches in some cases.

Mark tore off his harness with his strength and moved from the front of the craft toward the rear, using handholds along the way. Through the broken section of the hull, he could see Armageddon as battle raged on, the asteroid's systems decorating the skies with the drop-ships and RSDs being torn apart.

Missiles were destroyed on both sides and ignited over ships and defenses alike.

Mark steadied himself as his M20 snapped up.

The drop-ship dived. With the ramp now being above Mark, his aim was steady as he fired at the locking mechanism on the drop-ship.

The metal around the mechanism holed; flashes of sparks appeared.

A Vanguard ripped off his harness and grabbed onto the drop-ship's side; they were flung to the side as the drop-ship twisted itself around. The Vanguard paused and then slammed their foot into the ramp. It started to give way, with the metal twisting.

Mark moved to the other side and forced his foot into the ramp as well.

The ramp gave way and was tossed backward, flipping away.

Mergers with broken hatches broke out of their harnesses and magnetically locked themselves to the shuttle.

"One minute!" Young yelled to the Vanguard people. The ship shook badly. The strain and the missing section was taking its toll; the entire drop-ship was groaning.

Mark and the other Vanguard, seeing the weaknesses, put out their nanites, repairing what they could. The structural member next to Mark started to give way. If it did, then the roof would be peeled back like a tin can.

Mark let out a roar and grabbed onto the two sections. Nanites poured from his hands and worked to repair the structural member as Mark held it together.

The ship's acceleration nearly hit zero as Yu brought them in toward the asteroid.

"Fuck! Brace!" Yu yelled.

The drop-ship slammed into the asteroid, spewing up dust and debris. They bounced once; the thrusters pushed them into the crater on the asteroid that Yu had picked. They blasted through rock outcroppings. A wing was torn off and the drop-ship spun before stopping before a wall.

Even attached magnetically, some of them were tossed loose, taking sections of the drop-ship with them as they ricochet into other parts.

Mark looked out of where the ramp had been and was jacked up on a strange angle.

"All right, let's move." Mark moved out of the shuttle and checked the area as Sarah updated information on the closest possible point to enter the asteroid base and also information on where other drop-ships had landed.

"What's the orders, top?" Dominguez asked. She was across the asteroid but safe.

"We get our people together, find out just how big this base is, map it all out, then we go in," Mark said.

"Understood," Dominguez said.

Mark was using gravity clamps to keep him secure to the asteroid.

The Vanguard had fanned out, covering the crashed drop-ship.

There were a few wounded but they were already starting to heal themselves. Other than those who had been ripped away by the close missile, they were okay.

Mark looked above. The sky seemed to be filled with explosions as RSDs continued to cover the incoming drop-ships.

Chapter Sixteen

Asteroid Base

Inner Hip 10 30 39 System

3/3560

Mark let the nanites pack his lip before he spat into the nanite film inside.

The release of nicotine and chemicals allowed his mind to calm down. He felt a familiar shake through his body as it mixed with the combat chemicals that were still coursing through his body when the shuttle had crashed.

The regiment had formed up. Nine drop-ships hadn't made it to the asteroid. Two hundred and seventy-three mergers, flight crew, and Vanguard.

Mark pressed his chew tighter, simulating the grating feeling that came with chewing tobacco. The pain didn't affect him. He let out a sigh and he wiped the face of his helmet with his hand.

There would be time later. Now—now he had to focus, to carry out the mission.

"All right," Mark said, pulling himself together.

"What's the plan?" Dominguez asked from beside him.

Mark looked over the information once again.

The facility was in a crater of the asteroid. Around it, there were multiple laser weapons that had lanced through the landing forces.

Once getting on the ground, he'd pulled them into a defensive posture while sending out sensor devices so they might learn all of the secrets of the asteroid.

There was only one entrance into the asteroid base. At least it looked that way. They had not only been using exterior sensors but sensors that used impacts on the asteroid's surface so they were able to see the facilities through the ground.

Mark called all of his leadership and shared with them a hologram of the asteroid base.

"All right, the asteroid base is bigger than on the surface. It also has the high ground, with all those laser cannons. If we go up to their front door, they're just going to cut us down. Thankfully, with the asteroid base being so large, they're close to the surface in several points." Mark highlighted different points on the map as well as symbols next to them, denoting what areas the companies and platoons would be operating in.

"From these eight different points, I want to gain access to the asteroid base. Phantom Lord regiment will be lead on the assault. Devil Divers, you are a secondary reaction force. You will reinforce the Phantom Lords as they move through the base. Don't worry—you'll get your shot at these bastards too."

"We're fighting in close quarters. Remember, anything that looks important, get it covered in nanites. Anything that looks dangerous, kill it," Dominguez said, backing Mark.

"Get your people organized. You've got ten minutes," Mark said.

Green lights appeared and the line went dead as the different officers and their warrants set to work.

Mark spat out into his nanite film.

Dominguez sat down next to him, making motions with her hands as if she were lighting a cigarette. A simulated cigarette appeared to her, complete with the nicotine buzz, as they sat there for a few minutes.

"Fuck." Mark sounded tired. He was an old man. He'd lost so many that he no longer had the energy to try to distract himself from the losses.

Dominguez let out a breath. "Fuck," she agreed.

Mark checked his weapons and spat out into his nanite layer again.

Dominguez grunted but got to her feet as well.

The section with them looked to them in question.

"All right, Sergeant. Let's get to the rally point. Everyone watches for anything. If it looks like a threat, put it down. Keep an eye out for friendlies," Mark said.

"You heard the major," the sergeant said as everyone got themselves sorted out, checking their weapons and ready to move forward.

Mark led the way. Staying low, he started to cross the crater, his M20s deployed. He got to the lip of the crater and looked over for any threats. "All right, cover me."

Dominguez and a private looked in two different directions, looking for anything that might be out there, ready.

Mark ran and jumped. Using his gravity systems and his momentum, he shot across the open ground and fell into another crater. "Good here." Mark got himself up and covered a direction as well.

"Two by two," the sergeant said.

Two at a time ran and jumped over to the new crater. They dove into the new crater.

"Move it," Mark said, to Dominguez and the private. They were the only ones left.

They rushed over and moved through the crater on the other side.

It was annoying. The craters were large, thankfully, so the mergers used the low gravity, their flight systems, and their strength to cross it all in one bound.

Between craters, they covered one another or ran as fast as possible to try to limit any exposure.

***

Evan had pushed out his people to the sides of the crater, where they were making entrance. The Vanguard were all over the asteroid. At the center of their position, a pile of nanites was eating through the crater.

The mergers ducked as their sensors went off, alerting them to an incoming round that sparked off the side of the crater.

"Fuckers!" Fussli yelled.

More rounds started to land around the mergers as they ducked into cover.

"Where the fuck is it coming from? Anyone got eyes on?" Evan yelled out.

"Think I've got them!" A merger's twin M20s fired as Evan checked were the rounds were landing.

A hill, four kilometers or so away, was dotted with dust as the M20 rounds sparked off the ground.

His sensors picked up energy spikes as more rounds struck around the crater.

"Get some fucking fire on them!" Evan yelled.

Three more Vanguard oriented themselves and fired on the hill.

"Good hits." Rachel surveyed the battlefield and checked on the Vanguard in the crater.

"Vanguard Actual, this is Phantom Actual. Taking fire from snipers. Grid tree one, eight, seven, six, one, nine. Seven, location linked," Evan reported.

"Phantom Actual, this is Vanguard Actual. Can you flank?" Mark asked.

Evan surveyed the map again. "Too exposed at this time. They've got the high ground." Evan shifted so he was farther out of range.

He instantly ran calculations on his support options. His lightning missiles were an option, but the gravity of the asteroid was negligible, greatly reducing their kinetic energy. "Do we have RSD support?"

"Phantom Actual, if you are able to lase it, we can get AD round on target," Mark said.

"Understood. Marking. Will lase in once payload is ready," Evan said.

"Shaw is hit!" one of the corporals called out.

A flash of pain and fear filled the regiment net. Evan clamped it down, trying to make sure it didn't bleed over to everyone.

Evan saw the corporal pulling Shaw back from the front line.

"*I'm sorry, sorry,*" Shaw said, feeling as though she had let them down, making them have to care for her, angered at her weakness.

Baz took control of the situation and pushed more people into the position they'd occupied. Elgi got a hold of Shaw and his battle buddy got to work on Shaw to save her life.

"*I'm sorry,*" Shaw said as a corporal got to work on her.

"You don't have anything to be sorry for," Drekt, her fireteam partner, said, his voice filled with emotions.

Another net was connected to Evan.

"Phantom Actual, this is RSD command. Payload is ready and armed. Waiting on your lase," the officer said.

"Understood. Marking position. Hold one," Evan said, changing channels.

"Fussli, get me a fucking lase on that hill!" Evan yelled out.

"Sir!"

Fussli had one of his sections that was firing on the hill, suppressing the enemy there, lase the target.

"Phantom Actual, lase is good. Payload away," the RSD command's officer said.

"Bomb drop!" Evan called out.

A few moments later, the area denial anti-matter missile from the belly of a RSD holding outside of the asteroid base's range landed.

A pillar of dust shot up, accompanied by a brief flash. The asteroid shook with the impact and the wave of pressure.

"Good bombs," Evan said. The bomb drop had been right on target.

At the same time, Evan felt Shaw no longer connected to the net. He gritted his teeth and concentrated on his job, her words ringing in his head and pulling on his heart and soul.

"Phantom Actual, this is ENS *Moby*. Sensor readings show no signs of life in the area," Liang said in Evan's ear. They were the Vanguard's link to the rest of the fleet and their sensors.

Right now, the asteroid was rotating slowly so the fleet would only get short periods where they could survey what was going on in the different areas of operation where the Vanguard were located.

RSDs and seeders were moving around the asteroid, creating a network of sensor buoys so that the enemy's movements would all be seen.

"ENS *Moby,* appreciate the update. Phantom Actual out." Evan let out a breath and had his nanites put some gum in his mouth. He chewed on it, trying to get his nerves down.

"How is Shaw?" Evan asked Elgi.

"Gone." Elgi's voice was terse and forthright.

Evan's lips pressed together. His guts twisted. Seconds and inches—that was the difference between life and death.

Shaw was-*had been*, a mother to a fourteen-year-old girl and a twelve-year-old boy and had a wife. She'd left the legion to join the Emarl military and directly gone the route of Vanguard merger, wanting to create a better place for her children, no matter the cost.

It hadn't even really hit Evan.

"All right, everyone keep a watch on your arcs! We don't know how they got out of their little hole, so keep your eyes peeled," Evan said.

"Merge," Mark called over the leadership channel. All lieutenants and higher, excluding warrants, merged together.

Mark directly uploaded a file on the sensor information on their targets.

The first image of the enemy started to appear.

"*They have twelve lower limbs that are similar to an octopus' limbs. They have a torso connected to larger and stronger limbs, with a brain sack at the top and bug-like eyes to see in more directions. Basically, like two octopi stacked on top of each other, with bug eyes for greater visibility on top,*" Mark added to the video.

"*Ugly fucks,*" Waters spat.

"*Bobbleheads,*" Fussli agreed.

No one disagreed.

"*Looks like they're using upgraded coil guns, much more lethal than the Maraukians. Has the same effect as the Maraukian guns against legionnaire armor with our own Pluto armor,*" Ava said.

That chilled everyone's mood.

Their armor was the best humanity had to offer, but it looked as if it was only just able to help against this new weapon.

"*How long until we gain access to the enemy base?*" Mark asked.

"*Fastest, eight minutes; slowest, fifteen,*" Ava reported.

"*Fastest, six; slowest, twenty-one,*" Evan said.

"*Let's hit them all at the same time—twenty-five minutes. I want all areas to be completed and we pour in. Don't give them time to focus their strength in on one area,*" Mark said.

Evan acknowledged Mark's orders.

"*See to it.*" Mark clicked off the net and all of them stopped being merged to one another. Only a few seconds had passed.

"Twenty-five minutes—we make entrance into the enemy base. Make it so," Evan ordered the section leaders and second lieutenants under his command, who were focused on digging through the crater and breaching the asteroid base.

The nanites slowed down the rate they burrowed through the crater and started spreading out, increasing the breach size. Evan nodded in agreement.

"Contact!" Hahn called out as his location was now under fire from more of the octopi.

Evan saw the signs of fire on his sensors but it was eerily silent, making him look around with nervous eyes.

The Vanguard scanned everything and anything, trying to make sure they didn't get surprised again. But with the crater-pockmarked asteroid with its hills, rises, and cliffs, it was impossible to see everything.

Dancing on the edge of the blade. Evan shook himself. He couldn't think on Shaw's loss; he had to focus on the mission. Afterward he would deal with the guilt and loss.

***

The twenty-five-minute marker was reached. Charges went off across the asteroid, opening up the asteroid base.

Air rushed out. The Vanguard, on the other side, moved forward through the pressure of the air, using their gravity-clamped boots to enter the base.

A bobblehead, as they'd been called by Fussli, shot out through the breach Ava was watching.

A mono-blade lashed out, cutting them in two.

"Capture that corpse," Ava said to a section commander outside the breach. They grabbed the corpse and brought it down to the ground. The mergers ran scans across the corpse, sending everything higher.

"Contact!" Ava saw the breaching teams brought the enemy under fire.

The bobblehead's reactions were fast; those who hadn't been hurled around or out of the base fired back.

The Vanguard spread out quickly, going through doors and hatches. Their strength allowed them to ignore the explosive decompression. Vanguard members were injured or killed in the exchange of fire as the Vanguard fought to control where they had gained entrance to the asteroid base.

The halls weren't square but octagonal and although there were familiar elements, like ladders on the walls, the writing didn't make sense and the different systems were foreign.

Ava rushed in behind the third section. The Vanguard had pressed outward in every direction but it looked as if they'd kicked up a hornet's nest. Bobbleheads rushed in from all over the place as M20s, coil guns, and missiles crossed between the two groups.

Ava fired down the hall as Vanguard before her suppressed the bobbleheads.

She entered some large room that had Vanguard rushing out in different directions through doorways that had been cut through the walls with mono-blades.

"First section, push out on the right flank. We've got energy signatures coming from there! Second, hold the breach and cover those coming in. Third, I want you moving down through the base. Try to get under these fuckers!" Ava switched to Polwell.

"Establish a casualty collection point in this room here." Ava marked out a larger room that had been secured near the breach.

"Ma'am!" Polwell said, getting organized.

"All right. Four section, let's push forward and toward the center of this base!" she ordered the section commander.

"Yes, ma'am," Sergeant Ludwinsky replied.

"Let's seize the initiative here, people!" Ava yelled as her different sections moved forward. The first platoon of Alpha company had fully entered the base, with second platoon coming in right behind them.

Ava was tagging behind fourth section. At the front, she heard weapons fire. She wanted to be up there, but she was needed to coordinate.

"Second Lieutenant Urisi, get some of your tech-minded people on these different systems and start pushing information out to the engineering group on the *Moby*. If we can control the base's systems, then we own the battlefield," Ava said.

"Ma'am," Urisi agreed as half of his platoon had pushed into the base.

Rounds started to come through a wall at Ava and the section she was attached to. She dropped to the ground and fired back through the wall. Her rounds punched through the wall easily.

"Posey! Open up that wall!" Sergeant Hammond, the section commander, yelled.

"Sarge!" Posey rushed forward, pulled out a blade and stabbed it into the wall, cutting out a large sphere before coil gun rounds pierced the wall and hit Posey.

He dropped to the ground, his confusion replaced with pain and fear.

Corporal Richmond let out a yell and rushed the wall. He slammed through it at full tilt. Targets appeared on everyone's NI-AIs.

Master Corporal July rushed after Richmond. Ava followed after them. Only if they could put the bobbleheads under fire could Posey get treatment.

The three of them came out shooting. Richmond took a round in the leg and crumbled. With his training, instead of being confused with being shot, he threw himself to the side so that he wouldn't get in the way of his buddies.

July came out, firing on the fuckers that had brought Richmond down, who was fighting and got his leg working again by using the suit's motors.

Ava came out behind July and saw the room.

It was a long corridor, with air locks at either side.

Bobbleheads lay on the ground. Ava stood behind Richmond; the two of them covered one direction as July covered the other.

Ava took down a bobblehead and scanned. Breathing heavily, she looked for more targets but nothing appeared.

Posey's shock and fear filled the net before it disappeared.

Ava didn't need to ask Kela anything. Posey was dead.

Ava could feel Richmond's anger: at himself, at the bobbleheads. He'd done all he could to save his friend but it was useless. The doubts started kicking in when Ava grabbed his pull tab.

"Get up and moving!"

Sergeant Hammond was out of the room next. "Fung, Xiter! Get me a door here! The rest of you, stack up and prepare to advance! Second platoon's third section is moving to reinforce us!"

The rest of the section filled out and started to advance down the corridor while Fung and Xiter pulled out a shaped charge and put it on the opposite wall, offset from the hole they had come through.

"Second platoon third section, coming in!" Sergeant Lowel moved in. His people slotted in and moved to assist first platoon's fourth section seamlessly.

"Captain Desialias, we've secured the breach. We're expanding it right now," the first platoon's second section's master corporal said. Their sergeant had been hit with the rest of the section; three more were wounded but they were still in the fight.

"Good. Move to assist Warrant Polwell." Ava didn't know the situation there so she would leave it up to Polwell to move them out to try to take more of the asteroid base, or keep them as helpers.

Ava gave up her position and started to check on how things were going.

She sighed in relief as she saw that Charlie Company, under Lieutenant Quina's command, had entered close to some power systems. They'd hit lightning-fast through three breaches. They controlled the power station and they were advancing into other areas that seemed to hold systems that were key to keeping the asteroid base running.

The engineering teams on the *Moby* were poring over information; Quina was destroying anything that looked important with nanites, allowing them to get a good reading from the items, and completely taking them out of commission.

Already the engineering people were starting to send back information to the forces on the ground.

Six of the eight locations for the breaches had a firm foothold.

She got bursts of reports telling her of wounded.

The Phantom Lords' Bravo Company was having a savage fight as they fought through what seemed to be a living area.

There had been no attempts at communication from the bobbleheads. The Emarl fleet had been trying continuously and now, as the mergers started to take over systems, they were modifying their signals and sending them right through the bobbleheads' systems.

"Fuck! Laousher is hit!"

If they wanna fight, they can fucking have it. Ava's anger built as she saw so many good people being wounded and dying around her.

She might just be a few hundred meters away, but it felt like miles. She could only rely on what came over the net to know what was going on.

Now they were inside the base and they'd established entrances, things were going easier. They moved section by section, moving up and down levels with holes they'd cut through the base.

They removed sensors that the engineering group had identified, but the bobbleheads could see where they were advancing and they were trying to hold out different locations that led into the center of the base.

Although the base was large, there wasn't too many of the bobbleheads, only about three hundred to five hundred. With three times that number, the Vanguard—although they might be taking losses—could push forward.

It was cold and callous math but in war, nothing was simple or kind.

***

Mark was looking over the battle. He had given the overarching plans of what he wanted to accomplish and his people were carrying it out.

It was his job to keep the two regiments in his division connected and use them both to accomplish his goals.

Reams of information was fed from the asteroid base to the waiting fleet that hung around the asteroid base, clear of the laser cannons around the raised area of the asteroid base.

Information came back but at a much slower pace. The coding for the systems was complicated and it would take time to try to understand and then get control. Then there was no knowing what the firewalls were even like.

They'd at least identified some different kinds of machines, so they could destroy other systems, and they had taken power and air systems offline, denying the enemy these resources.

As they shut down more of these systems, the enemy wasn't able to know their positions in real-time and their home field advantage started to weaken.

The Vanguard pushed onward, fighting door by door, hatch by hatch.

They'd cut or blast their way through different walls, ceilings, and floors to flank or attack the enemy they'd pinned down in another direction, or get supporting forces to surround and destroy them.

"That should be the final power system," Charles said. All of the lights that had been dimly lit in the base changed to emergency. The lighting was odd but to the Vanguard, it seemed as if it was a bright, sunny day, clear and easy to see everything.

"We've reached the command center." Lieutenant Quina had been on Gilese and after joining the Vanguard, he'd quickly risen to his current rank through his previous command history and his attitude.

His company would follow him into hell.

Mark wanted to be there when they made entry but knew it would just pause their advance and momentum. "All right, crack it open and take out their command systems."

"Yes, sir," Quina said.

Mark watched as two platoons surrounded the command center of the asteroid base. Another was pushed out ahead to cover them in case more of the bobbleheads tried to hit them in the ass.

Mark watched through a private's eyes as their hands were raised, pointed at a hatch as cutting charges were laid on it by another merger.

"Three!" The private ran toward the hatch, his speed increasing quickly. "Two, one!"

Cutting charges went off. The door shot inward, as did the private. They jumped low, almost on the floor as their gravity systems took over. Their sensors were going full blast as they entered an octagon-shaped room. They fired as targets appeared. More Vanguard rushed in from other directions.

The bobbleheads' fire focused on their targets, without the crazed or anxious spraying that Mark was expecting.

M20s from multiple directions tore them apart as four people were hit by the rounds.

Those first in were joined by more and more Vanguard. They quickly checked over the command center. All of the bobbleheads were dead but Mark's eye picked up on something. He went back in his internal memory.

"Kovyas, check on this guy," Mark said, wanting to confirm the blurry image that had jostled his mind.

Kovyas sent someone to the location Mark wanted. They linked to Mark and he frowned.

On the bobblehead's uniform, there was a patch. It was covered in glowing blood, but he could make out the human male and female images on the badge.

"The fuck?" Mark said to himself.

"Thanks, Corporal," Mark said to the person who was looking over the area.

Mark could look in on it later. Of the four injured, two of them were badly wounded but they would be fine with time. The other two were walking wounded, repairing their armor already.

Mark's attention turned to the Phantom Lords working under Evan. They were advancing past the command center and pushing toward the surface of the asteroid base.

Chapter Seventeen

The Core

Sharventi Home System

3/3560

"Four Alpha's commander has been killed. Four Bravo is readying itself for the incoming human element," Operator Four's computer system informed him in a monotone voice.

"They have been faster than expected, with their tactics outside of the prediction model. Send a message to the prediction unit. I want them to adapt the prediction models for just this merger subrace to clear up the error prediction rate," Operator Four said.

"Message sent. Do you have orders for the remaining Four Alpha forces?" the computer asked.

"They should continue to fight to their abilities. If the humans see they're not fighting with their full potential, they might be confused." Operator Four Alpha was talking about the death of hundreds of his race that listened to his orders.

From when they had been born, they'd been assigned these jobs. They only followed the orders of their commander, without emotions. They only followed the orders passed down from their oldest records: to recover their emotions, no matter the cost.

Dying—they didn't understand the fear and finality that humans would; they just saw it as something which happened. A process that was part of life.

Operator Four looked over the preparations laid down by Four Bravo. It would be the final outpost before the human race was led to the Sharventi home system.

Everything was within what the plan hoped for. The issue was the prediction models weren't able to understand what the mergers would do.

As they were still abiding with what the plan hoped for, Operator Four didn't pay that much attention to it.

The feed to Four Alpha was cut off.

"Report to the other operators, that the fourth race has been able to defeat the Alpha outpost. It is unknown if they have been able to interpret the information located inside, including the modified history of our race from the perspective of the other three races that made up the Boundless Council with our ancestors." Operator Four stood up as time for nutritional supplements had come.

He moved out of his office and stepped into a line of other Sharventi that were moving through the Core offices to gather food.

There was only the sound of their suckers on the floor as they moved like mechanical machines.

The day for them to regain their emotions was coming but all of them continued on with nothing new, numb to the world.

Chapter Eighteen

Asteroid Base

Inner Hip 10 30 39 System

3/3560

"What are we looking at?" Mark asked as he entered the command center. The dead bobbleheads had been moved to the side. The Devil Diver regiment was moving in patrols under Ava's careful watch while Evan's Phantom Lords were securing everything they had found of interest and scanning through the information they had.

With the processing speed of the mergers working together, both those in the asteroid base and those on the *Moby*, their gains weren't small.

"Charles can explain it." Evan nodded to the side, where Charles appeared in holographic form. He was still on the *Moby* and working even with the hologram connecting them.

"We've cracked what looks to be the Sharventi's language. Well, I think they're called that." Charles shrugged.

"Have we shut down the signal?" Mark asked. That was his biggest goal.

"Yes, but we have a bigger problem." Charles took a deep breath and actually stopped working on other items.

Mark spat dip spit onto the command center's floor. He didn't think he was going to like what Charles had to say.

"When we shut down the signal, we were looking for the signal on our scanners across all of humanity's systems. Another signal has reached out. It sent a new order." Charles paused while everyone was focused on him in the command center.

"The Maraukians are moving, at a greater speed. Also, we've seen they've sent orders to other systems we don't know of. Using this relay station and the reaction of the Maraukians, it looks like the Sharventi have increased their attacks."

"Where did the signal come from?"

"System Gl 829, nearly thirteen light-years away. Specifically, a moon of an ice planet," Charles said.

Mark didn't think it would be this easy, anyway. He tapped down his chew and spat on the floor.

"Looks like we're going to Gl 829," Dominguez said, walking up to Mark.

"Yeah," Mark said, not happy about it, his face hard.

"Captain Miles, police all of the data. Make copies of everything here, then ready charges for this place. When we're clear, we'll blow this shit hole back into just floating rock." Mark looked to Evan.

"Sir." Evan nodded.

Mark looked around at the mergers. They'd lost people; now they were all throwing themselves into work, or thinking about those losses.

"We're not done, but when we are, there won't be any more of these Sharventi left to threaten humanity." Mark looked at the people in the room.

They looked back at him. Mark's body tightened and the anger grew as he saw that same anger in their eyes.

They killed our people. For that, we'll destroy them. This kind of feeling was powerful, like a force. It would make them run through a hail of bullets.

This was the strength they drew on as they defied the odds and ran to help their buddies.

Mark lived through those moments as each merger died, the pain as it twisted him up inside. He nodded and spat on the ground again.

These were his soldiers, his warriors; they would charge into death for him, for one another. That kind of feeling couldn't be described. Mark felt attached to them all, as if each of them contained a part of his soul and hopes. Seeing them gone, he could only wish they'd been able to live full lives, to change the universe.

They didn't make it but their memories lived on. Already they had been laid to rest with Sam, where their impression would care for humanity till the very end.

"Ninety minutes and we're off this rock. Get to work." With Mark's words, they once again moved into motion.

Mark opened a channel to Yu. "How are we looking for pickup?"

"The rest of the fleet is moving to assist in picking us up. The supply ships and the carriers are making replacement drop-ships and RSDs. Hall has moved out supply ships under cover of battleships to mine the asteroid belt," Yu said.

"Right. I want to start moving the dead and wounded out as soon as possible."

"I can get the drop-ships on the asteroid moving. First lift in fifteen," Yu said. Once they'd taken the base, he'd headed back in order to get a new drop-ship.

"Got it." Mark cut the channel and then opened another to the *Homeland*.

"Major." Liang's voice came across the channel.

"Hall there?" Mark asked.

"Passing you up," Liang said.

"Mark?" Hall asked.

"Did Charles tell you yet?" Mark asked.

"Nope."

"Looks like this is just a relay station. As this signal stopped, another one kicked off. Looks like it sent orders to other Maraukian planets. Charles has all of the information. Our next target is in the Gl 829 system, thirteen light-years away or nearly four parsecs," Mark said.

"Shit. I'll get the info from Charles and get a new plot for Gl 829 sorted out," Hall said.

"Understood, Admiral."

Hall cut the channel as Mark started to go through the information he had.

"Looks like someone has started to decode the Sharventi language," Dominguez said from Mark's side. "These Sharventi are some serious fucked up."

Mark shared a look with Dominguez.

"Fuck," He spat on the floor and opened the information she'd sent to him.

He might not like it, but he couldn't get away from it.

Chapter Nineteen

The Yard

Tricticus, Emarl System

4/3560

The alarm went off through the night and roused both Jerome and Esamai.

He quickly pulled on his armor and checked for his side arm.

Esamai was looking at him, bleary-eyed as she took in his appearance. "What?"

"Maraukians spotted outside of the Emarl system. This is not a drill. All military personnel and volunteers are to report to their respective ready positions," a voice said through the entirety of the Yard.

Jerome closed his mouth as Esamai looked at him with wide eyes.

"We just do what we've trained," Jerome said.

Esamai's panic quickly disappeared as Tyler was crying in his crib. Esamai got up and made for Jerome, stopping him before he left. "Look after yourself and remember to eat." She kissed him and checked his armor.

"I will." Jerome smiled. With that, he was off and through the hatch.

Jerome quickly reached the Yard, finding Trina, Dominguez's old second-in-command. He had pulled her to help him at the Yard, where they were coordinating the defenses of the Ark and Tricticus.

"What's the situation?"

"We have four insertion barges heading in for the system. They transferred in just minutes ago. They're aimed toward Tricticus." Trina had been on watch. While they were waiting, one of them was always awake while the other was asleep.

"How long will it take for them to reach the planet?"

"Eighteen days," a sensors officer yelled out.

"All right, I want a plot on their course." Jerome looked right back at the sensors officer.

"Understood." They and the people around him bent to their work.

"The rest of the system?" Jerome asked.

"They've all been alerted," Trina said.

"Good."

"Incoming call from the Hellenic system," a communications officer said.

"To my chair!" Jerome replied.

Moments later, he was greeted with Cassius's face. "Getting used to the NIAI?" Jerome asked.

"Yes. I wish I'd done it sooner. How is the situation there?"

"Four insertion barges bearing in on Tricticus. We are refining down their plot now." Jerome's tone was brisk and businesslike.

This was the situation he was in; he'd been in shitty ones before and his old training and thoughts came back to him.

"They won't be able to crack the Emarl system, Emperor. Don't worry."

"Good luck," Cassius said.

Jerome nodded and cut the channel. He wouldn't need luck; he would use everything that he had to defend this system. This was his task given to him by Mark. He wouldn't let him down, or the people who were in the Emarl system.

"We have the new plot of the Maraukian force," the sensors operator said.

"On the main holo," Jerome said.

Quickly, an image of the Maraukian's flight plan appeared.

Jerome looked at it and quickly came to a decision. "Trina, send out an order to all of our available shipping. I want to have all of the ships to move to the Ark. They're to collect the defensive Praetor cannons and missile launchers from there and ship them to Tricticus's orbit. When there, they are to evacuate any and all who wish to move to the Ark.

"I want all working in the Crucible to go toward improving the defensive bunker system there. Contact Dodger and get his support on it," Jerome said.

"Yes, sir," Trina said, acknowledging her marching orders.

The Maraukian fleet wouldn't be coming near the Yard or the Ark. As such, the weapons there were useless. If he could put them at Tricticus, then it was more firepower to overwhelm and reduce the Maraukian numbers with.

Chapter Twenty

ENS Detector

Oort Cloud, Emarl System

5/3560

A lot had changed in the last couple of years and they had all been assigned to different ships. Their leadership and skill to train new recruits and teams much needed. Captain Kemp had expected to be called up for this latest mission though, with the new Emarl Navy off to find the perpetrators, they were the first defence for Emarl.

Standing with him and the new ENS *Detector*, in the now beefed-up and very battle ready EMFC *Sporadic* and *Fearless* were Captain Marcelle and Captain Janina Ramirez. On the other side of the system were the VCF *Fernix* with Captain Aaron Grild, and the VCF *Avenger*, with Captain Tracy Delmotte.

These ships may have been upgraded—they had almost new of everything and their crews were re-trained and just as ready as they'd ever been to fight any opponent—but most of them had only watched the vids of the Maraukians, and Kemp could sense the apprehension around them all.

"Captain," his comms officer said, "the others are requesting your audience at the meeting."

Kemp looked at him and stood. "Anything looks amiss out there," he addressed the whole of his bridge crew, "let us know."

When he sat down in his office to link in with the others in their respective places, he found the atmosphere a little more than tense. But although they knew he was there, they continued their conversations.

"We don't seem to be doing anything!" Ramirez stated.

"What do you want us to do?" Marcelle asked. "We can't go out any farther and leave Emarl open. Those ships can appear anywhere and head in, just like the Luyten Conglomerate did. Our best positions for covering the area are here. We can't do anything but wait."

"I'm fed up of fucking waiting," Ramirez said. "I need to be doing something."

Kemp understood her frustration. Like Marcelle, they were originally EMF troopers in respectable ranks. They went into cryo; they woke up; they fought. That was what they'd signed up for. This was very different than what they had been used to over their many years of service. Kemp listened to their exchanges for just a few moments longer before he stepped in.

"Quiet!"

They all looked at him, and he quickly regained control. "Getting all of you to agree on anything at the moment is impossible."

The others were silent.

"We have our orders. They might not be from Hall, or Ortiz, but they're from the next best man for the job, Jerome Victor. So, despite when and where we all come from, we're here to do one job, and that's the most important job I've ever had in my entire life. *We* are the force that will stop those alien bastards from landing on any planet here. *We* are the only force that has a chance. Let that sink in for just one moment. You might have been ground pounders, you might have led great battle against your enemies, but this one we all hope will be our last. The EN is in the aliens' home system. They're doing everything they possibly can to stop them at the source. They will have a fucking home to come back to, so help me God."

Kemp met each of their eyes, one by one. "Good. Now I have your attention, I need you to relay back to all those you command that the Maraukians have been spotted again and are about a week, maybe just over, out of our system."

The expressions on his captains' faces changed.

"This is it. We're not far from the battle. Instill what you need to get the job done. We are all they've got down there. No matter the defenses we think we have..." He paused. "I've never seen anything destroy like they do. The only way they'll get to a planet's surface here is over my own dead body, do you hear me?"

"Yes, sir," they all said.

"Then we're on amber alert. Make sure the watches are adhered to, that the men are rested and ready. It could happen at any time."

Kemp didn't wait for the next reply. He cut his link and his mind came back to the office around him.

None of them knew what the next few weeks would bring, but they sure as hell had to keep it together. If they needed a poke here and there, he would do it, or the flack when Ortiz and Hall returned wouldn't be worth living through.

Chapter Twenty-One

VCF Fernix

Oort Cloud, Emarl System

5/3560

Captain Grild was just about to put a forkful of chicken dinner into his open mouth—grabbing a bite to eat had been a nightmare recently—when the claxons sounded. He shot up just as soon as it registered; chicken dinner splattered the floor and then he was running. "What is it?" he asked his comms officer.

"They're heading this way, as we thought. Then towards the denser populations."

"Put me through to the ship, all stations."

He heard a ping in his ear as he kept up the pace back to the bridge. "General Quarters."

It was mere minutes before he reached the bridge, but the information from his NIAI was coming through and he was making sure he read it while the lift and sections of the ship all came together.

Stepping on the bridge, he made sure they were all attentive. Not one of them were off their stations and they were deep in battle plans. "Get me Captains Delmotte and Austen. We need to nail these bastards now."

It seemed Ramirez, Kemp, and Marcelle might not get a chance to get over here, but he hoped that it wasn't just down to them. He heard in his ear the words: "Don't panic; do as we planned. We'll be there as soon as possible."

But his racing heart gave way to his true feelings, and the lunch he'd been eating threatened to resurface.

"Prepare all RSDs to launch all missiles in their way. We'll hit them as hard as we can with our weapons before they get anywhere near us. As soon as we're in range, we will start taking them on. Engage all freighters, all weapons."

Grild watched as the Maraukian barges maneuvered into better positions.

"All turrets showing online, sir."

***

Grild backed up with Delmotte and Austen turned their ships to face the oncoming foes. This was it. They'd live to fight, or die to fight.

"We're getting readings they're going to launch."

Grild moved to his comms unit, pulling up and comming for Moretti. "They're here. About to engage the four barges. We'll be engaging in a few hours. If you can get word through to the EN in Tok or beyond, just thank them. We're more prepared for this than we'd ever be."

***

Moretti took the comm from Grild and then moved to call through to Cassius. "They're in Emarl. Ships to engage in the day."

Cassius's voice was calm. "Then let's pray for us, because we're not far behind them."

Moretti knew this and hoped that for all they had, Emarl could defeat their barges in space. Over the years, there had been few taken out, but they had been able to reduce the threats with each one that couldn't start invasion procedures.

Moretti then contacted Hael.

"We're watching from the palace," came his reply. "We have feeds from the ships as they will engage. And if they make it through, there are backup plans so that we hopefully have enough troopers on the ground to defend anywhere they hit."

"One big guessing game, though," he said. Which was really hard. How could they guess when there were people's lives at stake?

Chapter Twenty-Two

Mining Station Fourteen

Outskirts of Emarl

New Settlement

5/3560

Pela had heard there were Maraukian barges in the system but she didn't want to see them. She'd seen just as much of the vids as anyone else. Because if they came here and they were in high numbers and they decided to take out the refineries or even where she was in charge of mining, there would be no stopping them. Pela and Lucus had clear evac procedures just like before, but she hated the thought just like she hated it back then.

Lucus opened the door and came in with his usual smile. "Everything okay?"

Pela had been back to see the miners' doctor first, who had tried her best to understand some of her issues. But nothing seemed to be working. Her weight was still changing and she was having to eat more and more.

"What time are you to leave?" he asked.

"In about ten minutes. Aileen's coming with me."

Lucus pulled her up from their couch and held on to her tight. "Let me know as soon as you're out what they say. If they can't get to the bottom of it, I don't know who else can."

Pela had also thought the same. McKay was a Victor Corp doctor, who was helping set up medical facilities in and around the larger mining facilities. It had been many years since Pela had seen her face-to-face, but her doctors couldn't offer her any solutions to her supposed sickness. The hope was visiting with her original doctor from the VC that there might be some answers, or at least some way to help her.

The door pinged, and Pela answered it. Aileen was early.

Lucus opened it and let her in.

"Glad you're ready. Thought I'd have to drag your ass onto the shuttle, or away from him at least."

Pela forced a smile as Lucus pulled her back to him for more hugs. She neither wanted to go, nor wanted more tests. But to appease them all, she would.

"Who are you seeing?" Aileen asked as they walked out of the apartment blocks and toward the shuttle bay.

Pela didn't answer. She just wanted to get there, not talk about it all the way.

Aileen talked most of the way from the mining facilities, onto one of the rotating stations. The trip to the refinery would take the day, and then they'd spend a night over in a station hotel. Pela admitted she was looking forward to being with Aileen and to have some time away from work and Lucus.

"What's wrong?" Aileen asked.

Pela pondered this for quite some time. *Was there really anything wrong?*

"Working and living with someone really changes your perspective of everything," Pela finally admitted.

"Things with Lucus not that great?" Aileen turned to her, lowering her voice. "Is this why you've got problems with food?"

"No, it's not like that. Really, I am eating like a horse. You can ask Gondi."

Aileen went quiet for a moment. "I trust you, but what's going on with Lucus then?"

Pela knew she wouldn't tell him. She let out a sigh. "I just don't know. I think it's me, not him. I just feel like we're doing too much together."

"Have you tried talking to him?"

Pela looked away. "Sure, but it's almost like he doesn't want to listen."

Pela really didn't want to talk more about it. She had enough to think on, with her weight issues. There was no way she could fool her NIAI that she was eating when she wasn't, so she knew it wasn't intentional. Everything she was asked of, she did.

Aileen seemed to understand this and didn't ask any more questions. Instead, she started to talk about Remy and the things they were getting up to. This made Pela relax at least a little.

By the time they'd arrived at the main ship down to the planet, they had lunch, watched a film and then dozed off in their chairs while it headed on in.

Pela woke to the sounds they'd arrived. She was exhausted, and all the travel just made everything seem so much harder. The refinery, however, was alive and took her breath away.

***

"What time are you meeting the doctor?" Aileen asked once again.

Pela's mind whirred. She knew Gondi would make sure she didn't miss it, just like all her other parts through the day where she needed a break.

"*In a few hours*," Gondi answered inside her head.

"We have time for a coffee." Pela quickly strode off in the direction of a nice-looking café. Aileen followed.

The café was busy because so was the newly built-up area. Pela looked around carefully. Things in general looked like any other part of a mining station, but there were so many more people around she suddenly felt overwhelmed.

The clerk behind the counter took their order and made idle chitchat while making their drinks. "Different, isn't it," he said, "when you're a miner?"

Pela turned to look at him; his soft brown eyes stared back. He was a lot older than any of them combined, but his smile was genuine. "How'd you know?"

Skilled hands made her the perfect coffee and he just grinned. "When you've seen and talked to as many people as I have, you learn to spot the differences."

Pela took the drinks from him and paid. She wondered whether she really did look like a miner. "Hey, Aileen." She popped the tray down. "Do you think I look like a miner?"

Aileen proceeded to look her over and frowned. "Not really?"

Not really? Guess she'd have to take that...

Pela chose a seat so she could watch the wandering people. Outside the café, traders were busy selling their goods, and mechanical cleaners floated around, helping keep the place spotless. The refinery itself was a hub of working mechanics. This made her all the happier she'd chosen to live away from towns or cities on a planet. Planetside was so very different and her feelings so far were mixed. *Could she still classify a planet as home? What were her family doing now she'd been gone for so long?*

Aileen took hold of her hand and squeezed it. "What you thinking?"

Pela looked at her friend. "Sorry."

"Don't be sorry—just talk."

"Do you think I should see what my family are doing?"

Aileen shook her head. "That ship sailed a long time ago. You're never going back, so don't worry about them."

"I guess it's just the thoughts, the memories."

"Are any of those good memories?"

Pela thought back to when she met Rachel and the trouble she had afterward. "No."

"Then let's think more about your future."

Pela didn't want to think on that either, at least not just yet. "Let's get this doctor visit out of the way, then I'll think about what I want."

Aileen sipped her coffee and smiled. A big frothy lip appeared, which made Pela giggle. It was good to have these moments. Looking outside, life seemed to be just drifting on by. *I want more than this,* Pela thought. *Much more.*

It was Ashaeed's voice that echoed in her mind but he wasn't there: "You can do anything if you work hard."

The problem was, Pela was working hard.

Gondi pinged her. "*We must move if you're to make it in time for Doctor McKay.*"

Pela drank the rest of her coffee and they made their way through the bustle of people to the medical facility.

Chapter Twenty-Three

Tiel City, Headquarters
Tricticus, Emarl System
5/3560

Andrew Phillips knew today would be difficult. Overseeing the whole operation that was basically a full planetary rebuild had been intense for everyone in the management teams. The original gang members who had worked with them to save as many people from Earth as they could, now formed the network of new cities and governing bodies that had been built up. There was much that needed to be done, but he looked over the planet and its holograms of everything topside and inside the dirt and he was one of the proudest men alive.

It had been a bit of a shock to get a message from his colleague Moretti. Andrew had known he'd been working within the world of the VC for quite some time; he knew that one day they would cross paths. They always did.

He'd toyed with the message, not wanting to open it for fear of any repercussions. He didn't want his past digressions messing up his position here. Here on Tricticus he meant something and he was doing right by everyone who surrounded him.

When he finally opened the file, he read carefully. "You've done well for yourself, Alex. I'm contacting you today to pass on pertinent information that you may need in the coming months, if, as I believe it will happen, I want to protect the new planets and Dominguez's people as much as possible."

The rest of the message was simple. If King Desialias's son was to be the legate in charge of the forces near Tiel city, then he needed to contact a merger named Dodger from the Ark to bring the Vanguard in from the Crucible. Phillips thought about it for a moment. Dodger and the mergers there were only in training. Possibly some not merged. Then he read the last of the message. "Protect them, Alex. Use everything you've got. I'm trusting you."

Andrew pulled up the background info he had on Dodger, and a frown creased his brow. This merger was put in training because he'd started to show signs of PTSD. He read over them quickly and worried. If this was the only merger they trusted here, it came with a price. He pulled up the comms signature for Dodger, using the input codes Moretti had also included. As usual, he was top-notch in his intricate network of hierarchy and included inside his packet was one for Dodger. New orders, no doubt. After all, this merger was supposed to be a little short of psychotic. Phillips had his job cut out for him. Of all the places, these two guys would come, it had to be Tricticus.

The voice that came through from deep inside the Ark resounded around his room and the face of Daniel "Dodger" Reckhi appeared before him in a 3D holo.

Dodger was big, and Phillips raised an eyebrow. He'd met Mark and Ava only twice in the years they'd been in the system. Even tying Dominguez down for a few days had been a nightmare, but he wasn't giving up on her.

For a brief moment, he worried for her out in the Tok system and his thoughts drifted to their last meeting. The day she handed him watch over the cities, she had nothing but business in her eyes. It was obvious she didn't know whether she'd return; she'd laid everything out on the table for him to see. All their accounts, their assets—everything was now under his watch. Phillips had tried his best to keep her in his mind, to not flirt while she'd commed or visited with him. Since that night in the hospital, he'd not pushed himself on her anymore. But his feelings were deep. She'd been honest with him and it had hurt. Now she was gone and it hurt just the same.

"Good to meet you, I guess," Dodger said.

"I guess. Did you read what I pushed over?"

Dodger nodded. "We're coordinating now, and we'll be with you as soon as possible."

"You're good with this?"

Dodger's face was placid. No emotion came off him at all. "Orders are orders, Phillips. Even though you seem to have a more corporate position on Tricticus than military, your background is impressive."

Phillips raised an eyebrow. "What background might that be?"

"The true one. Moretti wouldn't 'not' give it to me."

They held each other in thought, and Phillips knew the merger would have a much better understanding of the man before him, probably even more so than he knew himself.

"So, I'm going to say to you the same. You're good with this?"

Phillips let out a small laugh and repeated, "Orders are orders."

"Pool all your defense plans and send them over. I'll review on my way to you. Then when we land, we'll meet with Julieus Desialias and see if he has anything else to offer us."

"Agreed. I'll forward it on now. I'll pass him the same info packet." No sooner had it gone, Dodger's image faded. "ETA thirty hours."

Chapter Twenty-Four

Medical Center

Refinery, Emarl

5/3560

The place itself was still being built. But the sheer beauty of the structures made Pela look up as she walked with Aileen toward the main doors.

Once inside, they were both greeted by a secretary at a stunning marblesque desk. She looked to the two of them and Pela placed her hand on the scanner so that she was ID'd in. "I'm sorry," she said. "But your friend will have to wait down here while you're escorted to see Doctor McKay."

"You'll be okay." Aileen gave her a shove. "I'll wait for you, relax, read some books and drink their coffee."

Pela frowned. Someone approached from the side, and waved her on. Pela could do nothing but follow. She wasn't a baby; she needn't have a friend there to hold her hand. She could do this. It just felt so scary.

The corridors were long, white, and really clean. The bots in here were constantly making the most of their skills. Pela followed one while it polished the shiny floor and then when she was at the doctor's door, she just knocked and waited to be called in.

Doctor McKay waited with another white-coated doctor, a man. "We've been expecting you. Come on in, sit."

Pela really didn't want to sit, but she edged in closer and perched on the end of the chair.

"This is Doctor Galin Vanko. He's joining me to assess my performance today with you and your specific case."

Pela looked to him. *He was assessing McKay? That didn't seem right.*

"Good to meet you, Pela." He nodded over at her, but still stayed a good distance. It looked to her as though he were reading notes as well as observing.

"So, I know I have all your relevant data from Gondi and the last few scans you had at the medical centers at the mining facility hospitals."

"Oh, did anything show up?" Pela asked, hopeful they already knew the results and what her problem was.

"Both scans were corrupted. Something is interfering with them, so that's why you've been sent back to me. We've a new scanner I'd like to use, and we can then take it from there. Would that be all right?"

Pela looked to the other doctor. "I can keep some clothes on, though, right?"

Dr. McKay nodded. "Of course. It will just see through them. Don't worry."

Pela tried to smile. "Okay."

"Before we do move to the tests, is there anything you can think of that exacerbated this?"

Pela thought back over the last couple of years, from her first calls into medical at the training facility on Tricticus. "No, not that I can recall. I'm sorry."

Doctor McKay glanced to Vanko, and he indicated for her to carry on. "Then, please, let's get the scans out of the way and hopefully see what is going on."

Pela followed, twisting her hands in front of her. She was sure from her frayed nerves that all they'd see on the scan was how fast her damned heart was beating.

***

The room was large, with glass windows and a silver ring inside it. There was a chair and screen for her to also change behind. The silver ring she knew she'd have to step on; no doubt the doctors would wait behind the glass.

So when they asked her to take off her outer clothes, she didn't hesitate and neatly put them on a chair behind her. Then pulled over her chilled body the garment they'd also left for her there. The cool material did nothing to keep her skin warm in this room. Stepping out, she pointed at the ring on the floor.

"Yes, please, step onto the ring. The scanning will take place and last a few minutes to observe everything about you. If you feel any discomfort or want it to stop, just raise your left hand, or speak out. We'll hear you."

Stepping onto the ring, Pela waited for something to happen. Then, when it did, she wasn't so shocked.

"Disabling the NIAI," a voice said. It seemed to come from inside the silver ring as it moved up her body. A thin beam of light caressed her. With Gondi gone, Pela suddenly felt alone. So very alone that she almost cried.

The few minutes inside the ring dragged on, and on. Pela's thoughts raced as it seemed to stop at certain points of her body. Her stomach and internal organs were either very interesting to the scanner or it needed to go in deeper to get through the layers of muscle. Pela knew she hadn't much body fat, but she had the right density of muscle for her size. That, of course, never helped her weight-wise: muscle burned more energy to maintain.

When the ring stopped and returned to the ground, Doctor McKay announced, "You can get dressed now, Pela, and walk back to the first room we were in. There will be coffee and something warm for you to eat."

That made Pela's stomach grumble.

The smell of coffee was lovely and the hot sandwich was even better. Pela sat, eating, and never even noticed her NIAI wasn't back online.

By the time Doctor McKay had returned, she'd no idea how much time had passed.

Vanko pulled a chair in front of her.

Pela glanced to Doctor McKay, but there were no reassurances from her. In fact, her face was pale, sweaty.

"Pela," he said. "The scans are visible here, and we know what's going on. Easy to miss, but an old miner's problem. We think it may have just been exacerbated by your clan heritage and your pregnancy."

"An easy fix though, right?" She completely blanked the word *pregnancy.*

Pela looked to them, hoping. But their faces didn't say that.

Chapter Twenty-Five

Emperor's Palace

Roma, Hellenic System

5/3560

Cassius felt like he could do no more, but this waiting was killing him. The Maraukians were coming for them, finally. It had been a testing time. Everyone in the senate had always bet on when or if it would ever happen. It seemed more appropriate now that the mergers had gone off with half the legion to find them. Almost as if it were supposed to be this way. Cassius was a great believer in fate.

It had taken him a good while to get used to the NIAI at his beck and call. The instant updates and the times people called were good and sometimes inappropriate, but now it was needed. He could leave his office and be anywhere he had to be when he got information, not glued to his desk or his AI that had been fitted around the palace. Now, the AI and his NIAI were working together for the good of everyone who lived there.

As large as the Hellenic system was, Cassius felt the worry of every person around him. As far as war and fighting this creature went, everyone had seen it all at some point. Service, to all of them, was a good thing. It prepared for the day like today.

Cassius stood in his office, proud of his people. They'd overcome the worst infection of politics and were now thriving once more. Now it was time for him to address everyone. They didn't know what the outcome of such a large attack would be, or what it meant. Word back from the mergers had been nonexistent. He needed to know what was going on out there. The thought that maybe they'd all been eliminated had crossed his mind, and the fear there terrified him.

Portia chimed in his ear. "*Everyone's waiting on your counsel.*"

"*Thank you. I'm ready. Broadcast.*"

"*Going live in three, two, one.*"

A tiny glowing light appeared in his vision. Even never having done this before, Cassius knew every citizen in Roma and her surrounding lands, planets, ships, and more could see him.

He remained as stoic as possible and then he began.

"Brave citizens and warriors of Roma, today sparks the battle of a lifetime. The Maraukians are here in our closest systems." He wanted to give them all hope, to keep them from panic, but he also had to be realistic. After what they'd just been through, they deserved that. "However, I wish to tell you about their strength. What we believed to be their usual tactics, they are ignoring. They are coming in much stronger numbers than any system has ever seen before." Cassius actually let himself smile now. "But let me tell you why they are doing this. They are scared—not the Maraukians, but the people who have been controlling them. They saw us coming and are scared. They may be higher in numbers; they may have that drive to kill. But do not fear. Our forces are stronger. Our forces are united, and though this way may be long and arduous for us, we will not be defeated. Today, I ask of you one thing. Today, there's no retirement. Today, there's no rivalry or jealousy. Look to your neighbors, your friends, even those you argued or fought with. Help each other. This is what makes us stronger than them: the ability to adapt and overcome. Today marks a time of war. I will keep you all informed. Keep tuned to emergency stations for updates."

When he cut the broadcast, Cassius felt a wave of messages coming in, but he wouldn't accept anything apart from the top tier in his military.

Damus was the first he turned to. "Report," he said.

"The Maraukians are far enough out to not be in range just yet."

"Their ETA?"

"A week before we can start to assault them from space, another before they are closest to any satellites. A month or more before they could hit Roma."

“Their numbers?” Cassius asked this, but in reality, he didn’t want to know. The space legion would be ready for anything, he knew that, but he also knew how many losses they were facing. In every battle there was death, but this was all-out war. It would be beyond anything he could think about.

“There are eight spotted, but we believe there might be more on their way.” Damus let this sink in for a moment and then asked, “Any changes to your orders?”

“No, we are solid there. Engage them as soon as you can. Do not hold back.”

Damus cut the line.

Waiting on Roma would be the hardest thing the emperor had ever done. Watching the war raging above him, knowing death followed. Cassius sat down and ran a hand through his hair. “Mark Victor, wherever you are, whatever your war looks like, I hope you’re getting somewhere. I hope you can defeat these bastards once and for all.”

Chapter Twenty-Six

Medical Center

Refinery, Emarl System

5/3560

Pela stared at the both of them as they obviously talked between themselves via their internal systems.

"There is one other thing you're ignoring. You have a partner, right?" Vanko reiterated.

Pela nodded, thinking of Lucus. "We've been together a few years, yes."

"Sit down. Let me tell you what's going on inside your body," McKay said.

Pela shook her head. "No, just show me."

McKay moved behind her desk and then, almost like she had those many years before, she pulled up an image of her body and internal layers.

Then she noticed something else and almost took a step back. "What..." She pointed to her stomach. "Is...that..."

Vanko moved to stand by her hologram. "That, Pela, is your baby."

Pela moved to sit back in her chair, blinking at the image before her. Her hands shook. "I'm pregnant?"

"Yes, about nine weeks. Didn't you suspect something was going on? Why didn't Gondi say something to you? He must have known."

"Is that why you've disabled him?" She tapped the side of her head, still missing his connection. "He's broken?"

Doctor McKay nodded. "It will need some work, but shouldn't take long to fix him."

Pela was wary of her smile, though. "I need to speak with Lucus."

"At the moment, we can't allow any outside connections. I'm very sorry."

Pela covered her eyes and sucked in a breath. *I can do this*. She thought back over the last few years. They'd shared a lot of laughs, some arguments, and then more recent, the distance growing between them hurt. Pela thought back to the conversation with Aileen. If all her recent issues were because she was pregnant and sick, it would all make sense and there'd be no need to argue anymore.

"Is the baby safe from the mining sickness?" She patted her stomach, hoping there were no complications. Then she froze. She actually wanted this baby, even though it had never come up in conversation between them. It didn't feel alien like she thought it might, but it did feel strange.

"We need to keep you in for a few days, work things out of your system, make sure the baby is fine. But you'll be able to go back to work after that."

Pela felt light-headed. As if something was affecting her mind, her eyes. When she looked around, the room spun. But McKay handed her a drink. "Don't worry. We'll take good care of you."

Chapter Twenty-Seven

ENS Detector

Emarl System

6/3560

Captain Kemp hadn't expected the Maraukians to be this big. Studying their barges and weaponry systems, deployment tactics, and anything he could get his hands on still hadn't prepared him for this.

The four barges headed his way were immense. Everyone on the bridge looked to him. He wanted nothing more than to hit them with everything they had, but he knew he had to wait somewhat while the outer defenses started to strike.

"Patching you in," his comms officer said.

Captain Kemp moved to his chair and took a seat before he linked up with Jerome.

"Seems they picked on your side of space," Jerome said. "Reports are coming in live. You should have everything you need at your disposal."

Captain Kemp agreed. He couldn't be better informed or ready to strike, although his stomach may be rumbling just a little. "Thank you."

Kemp looked across to his tactics stations. Part of their upgrades meant they'd been kitted out with controls that could link in with anything they had permission for. That now meant they were the ones about to pull the trigger on the Maraukians.

"Ready, Boyez?"

The red-headed officer at the station nodded.

"First round, make it count. Anti-matter-tipped missiles were threaded throughout the RSDs and in among the nuclear ones, just a couple. We need some dummies to strike out their defense and get in closer. Then the real ones can hit home."

Though Boyez looked a little green around the gills, the equipment he had was top-notch.

"Then let them have it. Launch in waves. As much as it pains me to keep the best till last, we need damage from afar for now. Whatever it takes to get those missiles in close, do it. Watch the reaction of the Maraukians, and counter it as you need to."

"Yes, sir." Boyez's fingers were fast. "Targeting is stable. They will sail right into the paths of the RSDs. Damage should be accumulating then."

Kemp nodded. The thousands of missiles lining up would only be the start.

Kemp felt the tiny prod of a connection waiting. "Captain Grild, you going to be joining us?"

"We are moving to engage, possibly flank them from taking another direction."

Kemp was surprised at this, but agreed. If the Maraukians decided on any other targets in the system, they might stand a better chance of hitting land. That was the kind of tactic he expected from them, though, so if they had to bottleneck them in and push them to a chosen location, it would be where they were heading now, a denser populated satellite. Although their first rounds were fired, the waiting time till they'd be in range for a strike was tough. Kemp sent down for a food delivery. The next few days were going to be the toughest in their lives; he needed to make sure the bridge crew had supplies on hand. They'd more than likely be swapping watches, but rest wasn't going to be easy now.

***

Julieus watched what was going on in the system above him with great clarity in his mind. He knew the Maraukians were coming down on them. There would be no escaping this. The ships above him were going to kill as much as they possibly could. That was evident as the carriers and the main battleship moved into position. They were corralling the Maraukians into a trap almost, a trap above his head, and that he didn't like.

However, standing with Sun, and Donny, they all watched.

"We are preparing all RSDs and more to take on any ships that begin to enter the atmosphere," Sun reported. "All eyes are on the skies, Legate."

Julieus turned to her, and he could almost see the thoughts racing through her head. "The space fleet have anti-matter weapons. The Maraukians haven't seen that before. It should mean less get through."

"Even one barge has over two million enemies on board," Sun said.

"Never had that amount facing you?" He watched her reactions closely.

"Almost that in our escape from Earth, but this enemy doesn't care about our people or the tactics we use. They just want us dead."

The door opened behind them and Phillips stepped inside with them. Julieus had met him twice now, though the man seemed to almost be a ghost around the W3C headquarters. But he'd been easy to relate to. The man had stature and wasn't afraid of anything, that much was obvious.

"Sir," Sun said. "The Emarl fleet has engaged with the enemy."

"I guess we should watch the fireworks together. New weapons?"

Sun looked to her screens.

"They've never encountered that before. It should be an interesting sight to see."

Sun pulled up the closest relay stations for movement and views. The Maraukian barges were now deploying their own missiles and retaliating against the missiles the RSDs launched. Some wouldn't make it in close enough to get a strike, but if the anti-matter ones got even close, the blast radius of those could be enough to damage their hull.

Julieus stared at the screens as it seemed inch by inch, their missiles were speeding to their targets. In reality, they all knew the vast distances these weapons traveled and how fast.

Julieus watched as that first wave was struck with defense, exploding in the blackness of space with tremendous force. The few anti-matter missiles that were seeded in with the others were spaced out enough that when they went off, they didn't blow their own. Instead, though, they did take out enough of the enemy defense that their next wave would be much closer to their enemy.

Julieus found himself pacing slightly as they watched. However, when he looked to Phillips, he noticed the man was preparing other orders, for those on the ground. With his eyes now on Phillips instead of the main battle in the skies, he missed their first blood. Sun almost exploded with a cheer and as he turned to see, there was nothing but space debris everywhere.

"What happened?" he asked.

Sun looked at him, her eyes sparkling. "The second wave hit home—more anti-matter rounds. They got through and the impact was like nothing I've ever witnessed before. Those weapons..." She looked to Phillips.

"You don't mess about with anti-matter," he replied for her.

***

"Captain, it seems the third barge is splintering off from their vector," Captain Grild's comms officer Dev said.

Captain Grild and his section of the fleet were coming up to flank the enemy. Their RSDs launched to strike the enemy barge almost at the same time as Kemp's second wave. They weren't holding anything back, but it wasn't looking as hopeful as he'd first thought.

Not wanting to appear behind them and catch stray rounds, this would always be the best plan of action for his ships. They were too late to see the first rounds fired from a distance, but they weren't too late to watch the engagement of the others.

"The Maraukians have counter strikes." The information coming through wasn't looking good.

"Captain Kemp?" he asked through his NIAI, linking in as quickly as possible.

"Strike while you can, Captain," came his reply. "I don't think we're coming out of this one."

"Drop-ships?"

"All ships are away. They'll meet with the ground forces and continue the fight. We're not going to."

There was nothing Grild could say or do that would really help. But it pained him. "An honor serving with you, Captain."

"Likewise, Captain." They shared a moment before Kemp added, "Make sure you kill all of them. Let this war be the last."

Grild hoped it was, but he wasn't sure about promising an almost dying man something he personally might not be able to deliver.

It was a few more hours before the ship would explode around him. Kemp would die knowing he'd taken out two of the barges. It might have felt good for him, but the sorrow was there.

Now it was Grild's time to strike. They were coming in fast for a swinging close assault. Accelerating upon them would give a shorter window to fire but it also meant the Maraukians couldn't strike back too. Captain Grild had only one shot at this and he needed to make sure it worked. Losing the other ships was not going to go down well.

"We're coming up on launch coordinates, Captain. But it does appear the third is indeed heading off with a vector possibly toward Tricticus."

"Right, let's make this pass count. Theo, we'll need you to recalculate us and get us back on their tail as soon as possible. They mustn't make it any farther into the system."

Theo was soon quick at work, and Grild knew he wouldn't let any of them down. New coordinates flashed before him in mere minutes. "We'll be able to follow but our speed won't match theirs after a turn."

This would be it; they'd be out of that fight. "To strike the fourth barge, stick near Tricticus?"

A minute passed. "Sir, all calculations agree—that's the better option."

Captain Grild was already linked in with Tracy. "Coordinates are incoming. We're to assist Tricticus as best we can."

"The other barge?"

"Will have to be dealt with in-system."

Aaron took a moment for her. "Tracy, your kids are safe."

"I know," she said. "Coordinates loaded. All systems on standby, ready to launch."

Grild turned his attention back to Theo and Dev.

"ETA till we pass, ten minutes," Dev said.

Grild sat down in his chair, his attention slipping in and out of melancholy. Space was a great place to be, but to fight in not so much. When you could predict everything that would happen and know there was no altering it, when your time was up, it was just a waiting game.

Grild watched as they came upon the massive barge which carried so many of their enemies. Of course, they'd opened fire on them as soon as they had been able to predict their trajectory and speed, but they hadn't been able to predict the fact they were gaining it. Those minutes passed by very slowly and their connecting missiles struck the third escaping Maraukian barge just as Kemp's last few exploded on the second one.

The ENS *Detector* with Captain Kemp standing proudly on the bridge, the EMFC *Sporadic*, and *Fearless*—all he could hear through comms were their whoops of joy at their success, not their true calling. Doomed. It was a bittersweet hit for him, because as their ships sped on past, they then witnessed all as the other three were struck down. Grild watched for those few painful moments as their lives and the lives of their crew ended. And even though he'd not promised anything, he would do his utmost best in this to end as many Maraukian lives as possible.

***

Julieus turned back to the mess of the Maraukian ship in time to see the second one take on anti-matter hits. The screen didn't flinch but he did. A thousand rounds hit home, and within what seemed like seconds, the light exploded within it.

"Begin ground preparations," Phillips said.

"Belay that order," Julieus said, spinning on Phillips. "They've destroyed two—what makes you think they're going to hit ground?" Julieus watched as the man's face before him paled.

"You failed to see their defense strike back."

Turning back to the screen, Julieus watched as the wave of destruction headed straight for their fleet. The sheer amount of missiles and rail gun rounds would be impossible for any deflective tactics. Julieus placed his hand on the table to steady himself. It would take its time to get to them, but he was about to watch the men and women up there defending Tricticus die. The small victories he'd witnessed were nothing compared to the loss of so many.

Sun's voice echoed behind him as she started to relay Phillips's orders through the comms channels, preparing their forces for the next wave of impending doom.

Julieus couldn't see it as anything else.

When the Maraukian missiles started to strike the ships and freighters, he swallowed. He'd already failed them and his father. He turned back to Phillips, whose eyes met his with something he'd not expected: compassion and clarity.

"Start moving your forces, Legate. Malazar Skill School needs your backup."

Julieus swallowed and within a moment, his NIAI was linking in with the men under him and then down the chain of command to the Bellona, Gorgon tankers and troopers on the ground.

Chapter Twenty-Eight

Emperor's Palace

Roma, Hellenic System

6/3560

Portia's voice came in and Cassius was awoken before he knew it. "Report," he said.

"All anti-matter missiles are strategically placed throughout the system," Damus said. "We're recalling all ships. They're to assist in the evac of some of the outer stations. Those that can't be moved."

"Do you think that's necessary?"

"If the Maraukians are doing anything out of their ordinary patterns, then yes, I believe anything in their way might be struck off first. If we pull them in, at least we have more numbers in other systems."

Cassius thought about this for a moment and then agreed. It need not be hasty to start an early pullback, but it might prove useful later on. "I want them moved to escorting the retired legionnaires out to prospective battlefields next then."

"Of course. Do you know how many are willing to join us?"

Cassius laughed. "We're talking about legionnaires, Damus. All of them, even the auxiliary, are signing up. I've got a few more freighters around that can help with their deployment, but those other ships can help for now. I want them deployed and ready as soon as possible. If we can't make a stand now with over a thousand years in preparation, then I don't know when we ever would be able to."

"I'll let you get some more rest. Sorry to disturb you."

Cassius pushed the cover off and moved to slip out of bed. *Rest what the hell is that?* His wife, well used to it by now, was still sleeping. "No need to worry. Sleep hasn't been coming so easy for any of us these last few months."

"No," Damus agreed. "I am ready for this fight. I just wish it would hurry up."

That was something Cassius readily agreed with. "It will be upon us soon enough and then we'll be wishing it was over. Keep the reports coming and if anything changes out there, let me know."

"Of course, sir."

When he'd signed off, Cassius eased out of his room and to his office, where he sat looking out onto Roma's vast city. The lights flickered in and out as tiny little beacons. For such a beautiful world, there was such pain in it. His thoughts moved to the woman whose bed he'd just left and, silently to himself, he prayed over their survival.

Chapter Twenty-Nine

VCF Fernix

Tricticus, Emarl System

6/3560

Captain Grild watched as the Maraukian barge started to split. No matter how quick they hoped they could be at this range, they wouldn't take out as many of their assault barges as he'd have liked.

"Fire," he said.

Dev hit the console's button with clarity on his face, relaying the order to all the other ships that had anything worth firing left. This had been one of the longest face-offs he'd done, but only because the Maraukians were so large and almost impossible to deal with in space. He also knew every other vessel was doing its utmost best to blast the third barge to pieces before it reached its destination. Its trajectory seemed to skirt more of their defenses than he thought possible, but if they could, they'd be all over Tricticus in a heartbeat.

The Maraukians weren't that clever, and it just drove home the fact someone was not only controlling them but the ships themselves. Were they getting feeds from them in almost real-time? These facts worried him. After knowing the mergers were about the only ones capable of this, even at such vast distances, Grild could see why this fight had come to this point. Inevitability.

"You have an incoming message from High King Desialias."

Grild linked in.

"Status?" Hael asked.

"Hitting them with everything we've got. They just deployed."

Hael's voice was cool. "Our forces on the ground?"

"Ready and waiting. I've been coordinating with Legate Desialias, and the mergers command."

It was almost as though he were distracted for a second. "Four more barges have been sighted."

He could almost hear the calculations going on the king's head. Captain Grild's stomach knotted. "Your orders?"

"Do your worst there, and prep to intercept. Meet with some of the other ships from the fleet at rally point seventeen."

"ETA?"

"As soon as I get it confirmed, you'll know."

He was gone. Grild looked at his bridge crew. This would be a difficult move for them, but they had no other choice. If they didn't try to stop this next assault, the cities down there would be in for more of a shock. "Prepare for one more assault on the barge, then input new coordinates for rally point seventeen."

"Captain?" Dev asked. "We're in dire need of supplies. We—"

"We'll pick them up on the way. Launch everything we have at those assault barges. Take out as many as we can."

Dev began to comply and Theo reported, "Beginning prep to leave orbit."

Grild linked in with Delmotte and relayed their orders. He had no hopes they could destroy the barge. They had no major artillery left to throw at them. But, watching as the enemy ships left orbit, headed to destroy everything they touched, they had to do as much damage here as they could.

Next, he linked in with Legate Desialias, Phillips, and Dodger. "Orbital support is withdrawing."

Legate Desialias was the one whose anger came through the most. "You can't do that. I've got men dying down here."

Phillips was the one who asked. "How many?"

"Four more incoming. We're to head them off."

"Don't worry about us down here!" Dodger said.

Grild could hear explosive rounds echoing through their connection. "We'll hold our own. Go get them fuckers. Will make my job a hell of a lot easier."

Grild had spoken to this merger a few times in the last week. His grisly sense of humor had a smile curl up the side of his face. "Show them who's boss, Dodger."

Phillips also replied with, "Thanks, and good luck."

Grild turned his attention to the rail gun and missile shots they'd just let loose, everything they could... They then started to move and his view changed. "Good luck to you too," he replied, but they were already gone.

Chapter Thirty

Medical Center

Refinery, Emarl System

7/3560

Pela woke in the hospital room, attached to monitors and pumps, and more, they were beeping and hissing at her. Whatever they'd been giving her had run out, that was obvious.

Pela pulled her knees to her chest. Her trips here had been few and far between, and although Aileen had managed to go with her once more, she'd a job to do. The miners and refineries were in overdrive. Pela hadn't told Lucus about the baby yet; she hadn't been able to bring it up. The sickness and her gaining weight was more important. Well, gaining weight she was, enough for the extra one she carried.

Gondi had been fixed and put back online, though he was also under strict orders not to pass on her condition. Pela made sure the doctors at the medical center also didn't tell him. This time when she stood, she wobbled on her feet, feeling sick. She rushed to the small bathroom and vomited. Everything spun, the world around her moving so fast. She also felt very different. Larger than she should be. Pela ran a hand down her belly, and noticed no difference, just the extra padding... Not padding, she remembered; inside there somewhere was a baby.

Lucus!

Finally steadying herself, she went back to the room, found some slip-on shoes and walked to the door. It was unlocked, and things looked as they seemed: just a secure hospital. But, the truth of the matter was every time she entered the facility, they disabled Gondi. He wasn't online now, and this pained her. For the last few years of her life, she'd never not been able to access everything she wanted, and now wasn't the time for her to be cut off either. She knew of the impending Maraukian attack; she knew of lots of things could affect her and she didn't want it to.

First off, she had to get Gondi back online. She knew nothing about NIAI physics, and how they worked.

Moving about the corridors of the hospital, Pela realized something was going on. Everywhere was too quiet. There was no way this place would have no personnel. She'd seen it earlier on, and it was busy. So what had happened? Why had she been left behind? For a moment, she wondered whether she'd woken in a dream. But the more she padded about, the more she thought it wasn't.

Making her way through to the room where she met Doctor McKay, she found the office desk, the drawers open and papers strewn about.

This really was a nightmare.

Pela saw the computer was open on her file and it had been downloading something, something about her onto a chip. Pela pushed Continue and waited. It slowly crept up in percentage. In her mind, although Pela felt nothing but panic, she knew she had to get Gondi back on. Moving to the back of McKay's office, she saw the silver ring. She was quick to move to its station behind the glass wall and she rushed through the procedures that it had done from the previous visits. Pela had been under observation now for over a week. There was a "revert" option and she knew it was her only chance. Stepping onto the ring a moment later, Pela felt it start up. The bright lighting around her seemed to penetrate the clothes she still wore. It took a few minutes but then Pela heard a familiar voice in her head. "Hello, I'm your NIAI. Would you give me a name?"

"Gondi?" she said. "Tell me you can re-boot or do something? I need your help. I need you to get me out of this hospital."

It took several minutes and Pela rushed back to the doctor's office as more rounds impacted the building around her. There was no stopping what was going on outside; she just knew she needed to get out and to get out as fast as she could.

The status bar was at 100% and the disc was loaded. Pela pulled it, tucked it in her bra, and she ran.

Gondi started to come around a few moments later and he began to fill her head with information. The Maraukians landed in Emarl three days ago. That meant so much to her: what and where everyone had gone. They'd been evac'd, that was for sure, but why hadn't they taken her? Was she that much of a secret she'd been left behind to die in the Maraukian invasion?

Gondi's voice confirmed a few suspicions. "*I can't get access to the net. I can talk to you, but there's a few things that aren't working.*"

Pela ran, following his bouncing ball as per usual, but it wasn't just leading her out of the hospital. It seemed to be leading her into more and more danger.

"*There's many incoming messages, I...can't compute.*" Gondi struggled and seemed to falter, and so did the ball.

Pela stopped and looked around the corridor and the halls. She could only make one decision for herself. She turned right and kept on running. Straight into the side of the biggest man she'd seen in her life.

The man looked down at her. "What the fuck are you still doing here?"

The man reached down, grabbed hold of her and swung her around as claxons sounded throughout the refinery.

Chapter Thirty-One

ENS Homeland

Oort Cloud, Gl 829 System

7/3560

Hall let out a heavy breath as they entered Gl 829.

"Transition complete!" Yeltsin said.

Rasalov was bent over his screen with the others in his section. All of them were looking to update the sensors as fast as possible.

They weren't able to send in scouts ahead so they knew nothing of this system. They were going in blind, other than the fact the signal came from this location.

The star system updated quickly as they all saw the situation of the system.

"We don't appear to have any ships on sensors in a three-minute range, three minutes ago," Rasalov said. "We're clear out to twenty light-seconds."

"Yeltsin, get us a plot to the planet. I want to get there as soon as possible," Hall said. "If nothing is found in ten light-minutes, move everyone off ready stations and back to their regular shifts."

"Sir," Guy said, sending out the commands to the fleet.

Some of the tension on the ship bled off but the fact was they were in an unknown system with a signal that commanded humanity's greatest enemy.

They didn't know what to expect.

Humans had never made it into this system before, only looked at it through telescopes.

"We have updated imagery of the planet," Rasalov said.

"Guy, forward it on to Charles and the ground forces."

"Yes, Admiral," Guy said.

Hall continued to focus on the situation in the system while the others worked their stations. It wasn't long until Guy told the shifts to step down and the fleet, still moving in formation, adjusted its flight plan as Yeltsin, Rasalov, and the other navigation and sensor operators updated the map and flight plan to avoid dangerous areas and to improve the flight time to the planet.

"General Nerva is calling for a meeting and requests your presence," Guy said.

"Understood. I'll take it in the conference room." Hall stood.

Chapter Thirty-Two

ENS Moby

Oort Cloud, Gl 829 System

7/3560

They had been inside the Gl 829 system for nearly an hour now.

They now had a complete image of the system and they could even see down to the planet where the signal was coming from.

Everyone looked to Nerv, who was deep in thought. He was in charge of ground operations.

All of the commanders of their respective groups were sitting there: Major McDougall, Admiral Hall, General Ortiz, Major Victor, and Lieutenant Colonel Yu.

Nerva didn't wait and launched into the briefing. "All right, we've located where the signal is coming from on the planet.

"It looks to be buried in a mountainous region on one of the secondary continents. The planet appears to be inhabited by Maraukians but they are moving in set patterns and not building ships. It is the science division's thoughts they are being controlled by the Sharventi directly. With the information we've gathered, we're able to see that the Sharventi were using the asteroid base as a kind of forward observation area to watch over and order the Maraukians from, leading the offensive against humanity.

"This looks like it is a research and improvement station were the Maraukians were made originally. As we've gained the information from the asteroid base at Hip 10 30 39, we know there are no non-combatants in the Sharventi. I propose the plan that we orbitally bombard the bastards into nothing. Once we've turned their base into a crater, we send down the Vanguard and the troopers to make sure there's nothing left down there. If another signal appears, then we go and hunt it down. We can change and adjust this plan as needed." Nerva looked to them all. "Admiral Hall, thoughts?"

"It shouldn't be hard to carry out. The mergers have some of the best processing power so we can figure out a firing solution and hit them farther out, hit them as soon as possible." Hall looked to Mark.

"We can do that," Mark agreed.

"What's the plan if it doesn't work?" Ortiz didn't look as if he wanted to be the one to ask the question but he needed to.

"If we can't destroy it, then we move to the second part of the plan. We're going to have to get into those mountains ourselves and push through, kill the Sharventi and the Maraukians, destroy their base," Nerva said.

Everyone's faces were grim.

"Fucking hate fighting in mountains." Ortiz spit into a bottle that he had brought with him.

The others who were part of the ground forces all agreed.

Chapter Thirty-Three

ENS Moby

Inner Gl 829 System

7/3560

The calculations had all been run. All of the fleet was ready as their time window approached.

They were still some three light-minutes out from the planet, but they had been able to figure out a firing solution that was supposed to land their rounds onto the mountain range on the planet that was being called Crater Mountain.

"Fire!" Admiral Hall ordered.

Travestki, as well as all the different gunnery officers, initiated the fire plan input into their weapon systems.

A stream of rail cannon rounds followed, one after another, carefully calculated to pass through the system and even make it past the planet that the inhabited moon orbited.

Chen looked from the target to the binary stars that circled one another. It was a rare sight and one that Chen had never seen in person before.

Here, among the beauty of the stars, he was once again waging war.

He shook his head and focused his thoughts.

"New flight plan received," Yeltsin reported.

"Execute," Chen said.

The *Moby* used its thrusters and, with the rest of the fleet, they continued on their path into the system, following behind their rounds.

"Hard to believe anything will be left behind," Carla said.

Chen nodded. The rail cannon rounds had already been fired out at hypervelocity speeds as it passed through the system. When it passed around the planets, they would increase in speed; then, entering the atmosphere, would increase the speed once more.

Even a pin traveling fast enough could crack an asteroid.

"We can only hope," Chen said.

***

It took three days for the rounds to reach the moon. They carved through the planet's atmosphere. A few of the rounds didn't make it through, turning into bursts of light as they burned up in the ether.

The rounds peppered the mountain range. Hits landed around the mountain range, ripping the natural landscape up and sending pillars of destruction into the atmosphere.

"The fuck?" Rasalov said as something strange appeared.

Rasalov zoomed in, able to see that rounds were striking an invisible wall. Rasalov checked through different filters until a yellow sphere covered the mountain range.

"What are we looking at?" Chen asked, an uneasy feeling turning his guts.

"I'm not sure. Sending it to the engineering and science teams." Rasalov sounded as confused as Chen.

Charles directly contacted the bridge, Guy allowing him to speak through the bridge's speakers.

"It looks like some kind of energy-based defense. I would say it's some kind of shield," Charles said.

"A shield? Wasn't that ruled out as theoretically impossible?" Carla asked.

"Theoretically, yes, due to the power requirements, but we know that the Sharventi were using anti-matter power sources for the laser cannons on their asteroid base. It looks like they must have anti-matter here, or a power source of similar power to stop these rounds," Charles said as round after round rained down on this shield.

The air across the planet was stirred up, but there was no sign of the shield failing.

Around the shield, the landscape was turned into a wasteland but the area inside the shield was untouched.

"Send Admiral Hall a message with the information we have, Liang." Chen sighed.

"Charles, do you think we will be able to break down the shield with our shipboard weapons?" Chen asked directly.

"I'm not sure. I will need to do some testing and I don't know what kind of power sources the Sharventi are using down there," Charles said helplessly.

"Do your best." Chen sighed as he checked. Indeed, Mark and the other members of the Vanguard were listening and hearing everything.

Mark sensed that Chen was looking for them.

"I'll inform General Nerva," Mark said.

Chen frowned and pressed his lips together. It looked as though the ground forces wouldn't be spared.

Twenty minutes later, Charles sent out a report on the shield technology that was covering the mountain range.

***

Once again Mark found himself in a conference room talking to the leaders of the fleet, now joined by Charles.

"The shield is an energy construct that isn't technically a sphere. It's a number of projectors that are placed in key positions and they work together to fight off incoming strikes with blasts of charged particles, shred them into nothing and it's like they hit a wall. This allows them to conserve energy and give them a multi-layered defense so that even more powerful rounds can be resolved with the projectors working together to deplete the attack force. Based on tests and what I've got from scans, I have no idea how much energy these projectors have stored or how fast they can recharge. Based off this, I have no idea how long they can last for or what damage they can take. I can tell you one thing. The rounds that we sent at them barely even affected the projectors," Charles said to those in the conference room.

"What about anti-matter missiles?" Hall asked.

"I say it would be worth a try with a concentrated amount. The problem then becomes, with all of this destructive force, the planet is going to be turned into a frenzy if repeated bombardments don't work. That means trying to land anything on the planet is going to get much more difficult. If we don't wipe out the shield, and we need to send people down there to clear the rest..." Charles's words trailed off, letting the others figure out the rest.

"Let me know how many missiles you'll need for your test and I'll okay it. If it doesn't..." Hall looked apologetically at the ground force commanders.

"Then we're going to have to put boots on the ground and clear out the mountains," Nerva said.

"If we have people on the ground, then they can move forward and take out the shield projector strongholds. Once these strongholds fall, it will be harder for the shields to recharge. Also, as these projectors are taken out, then gaps can appear in the defenses. The fewer they are, the harder it will be for them to fire on ordinance at higher altitudes," Charles revealed.

"So, what is our plan if this goes to a ground offensive?" Hall asked. It wasn't long ago they were talking about the slim possibility of needing to send their forces down to make sure they had destroyed the base. Now they were looking to assault the planet.

"The enemy is embedded into the mountains of this region." Nerva pointed at a hologram showing the shielded region in detail. "We're going to have to drop outside of this shield's range, bringing our full weight to bear. It's going to be a pain in the ass but we're going to have the Vanguard in the lead. We've got Maraukians and Sharventi here. We don't know what their combat capability will be like with the two combined forces.

"We will need to react based on the situation on the ground, either moving forward or moving into a defensive posture if needed.

"We don't know at this time if we can rely on artillery or the RS-Ds. We will need to run trials for that. At the basic level, we will advance through this valley and on the mountains on either side. The target will be to destroy the different strong points which hold the shield projectors. As we do that, we will weaken the overall shield and be able to carve a path forward that we can call support down on. If we retreat, we know that we'll be in range of our own guns," Nerva said.

"Just one valley, though?" Hall asked.

"Mountains are a pain in the ass to fight in. You're working on an angle, you don't know if your enemy is above or below you, on the other side of the pass. Assuming this place is covered in sensors, which is what I would do if I was the enemy.

"Then they can see us days out, plan an ambush and hit us. Sniper fire is going to be the worst to deal with. We've got little cover other than what's naturally around us. If we need support from the drop-ships or the RSDs, it's going to be a pain in the fucking ass to deal with if we've got bobbleheads and Maraukians shooting at us. We're going to have to pull back wounded ourselves if needed before we can move into a covered area and evacuate them via shuttle." Ortiz shook his head, his expression gloomy.

Mark's eyes rested on those mountains and valleys, specifically the one that Nerva had picked. There were dozens of positions marked out, the different strongholds held by the Sharventi and Maraukians.

Thankfully, it didn't look as though there were strong points and dug-in matrixes of fallback positions. Trying to assault through that, he wouldn't have taken his people into that. There was no way to win.

Mark held his chin and looked at the map with dead eyes. "If we don't get support in there..." His words left the conference room in silence.

"Hope for the best," Nerva started.

"Prepare for the worst," Mark and Ortiz finished off Nerva's saying, though none of them looked happy.

Chapter Thirty-Four

Medical Center

Refinery, Emarl System

7/3560

"What do you mean? Why am I still here?"

"Everyone who is non-essential is being evacuated."

Pela knew she was small, but the guy in front started to push her forward. She still, however, wanted to run away. Run as fast as she could in the opposite direction.

However, she was joined by a plethora of other people, all moving in one direction. It didn't seem as though she had much choice.

"What's going on?" she asked the woman next to her as they were shuffled onward.

"They're just keeping as many of us as safe as they possibly can."

"It's serious out there then?"

The woman nodded. "Yes, very."

They were all retaliating, fighting off their enemy. Pela's heart sank, knowing the Maraukians were really here, laying waste to anything that crossed them. She thought more of Lucus, and her friends. Where were Aileen, Remy, or Ashaeed? So she looked inside, and tried talking with Gondi.

"*Did you re-boot?*" she asked.

"*Files missing. Re-boot, no.*"

"*Okay, what can you tell me?*"

"*You're pregnant.*"

Pela shook her head and tears ran down her cheek. This was all insane, all of it. "*Tell me something I don't know and that every human out there can't tell by the size of me.*"

"*You'll be getting on the 371B Freighter for the Ark.*"

Pela almost laughed. *For their safety? Seriously, they were heading to the Ark? Wasn't that some kind of old text from Earth?* She remembered reading about their history and stories and one night recounting it to Lucus.

The fact that Gondi confirmed everything the woman had told her gave her some hope he could be fixed properly, by someone else, probably at the Ark. Finally, the moving stopped, and so did the assault on her eardrums from all the people around her.

Someone approached her with a flask of something. "Just water, ma'am," the woman's voice said.

"Thank you." Pela took the water and drank. *So damned thirsty.*

The woman held out another for her.

Chapter Thirty-Five

Malazar Skill School

Tricticus, Emarl System

7/3560

Dodger took his order to defend the Skill School from Damus as soon as he'd landed with those left in-system of the Vanguard, and any trained and recently merged trainees. Some were a little on the green side, but they were fully functioning and capable Maraukian killers.

Malazar Skill School was one of their best, the best students and teachers, so to Hael and the others, an important asset to protect.

Watching now as the Maraukian assault barges started to come in, the sky lit up with protest and the noise levels grew.

As he turned back to watch the Skill School and its surrounding weaponry open fire, his memories returned of those he'd lost years before, and he fought them back. There was no time for this right now. As much as he'd wanted to retire and only train, he knew that there was one more battle in him. One more war to win. This time he really hoped it would be the last.

Sergeant Shawna Atkins approached from behind. "All the students and teachers are inside. Locked up tight."

"Good," he said. "There's more insertion barges coming in. There's never been a wave like this before. One after another. We just lost orbital support in the hope they can head them off."

Shawna didn't flinch, though. That made him proud. His students, his work at the Ark, had been worth it. For every merger who passed, as much as it pained him to know they'd altered their lives forever, just as he had—he knew it was for a greater good.

"They're waiting on you," she said.

Dodger looked back to the main building. "Always meetings." He sighed. But at least this time it would be over quick. He followed her inside, to find the others checking and making sure their positions were going to be the best places for them. They looked over a 3D holo of the Skill School and the surrounding areas. With them, linked in were the commander leaders over the other major cities: Legate Desialias, Primus Damus, and High King Hael.

The four men moved aside and waited while he glanced over the map. He was assessing their competence as much as the plan itself.

"Once they hit land, they'll come in fast. We will bleed them here, here, and here." Shawna pointed to the key spots around the outer spiral of the school.

Dodger knew most of the Maraukians would head for Crisidium, the planet's main city, but with dense populations at several main spots, his Vanguard were now spread out thin. Legionnaires and troopers, all kinds of military trained personnel were spread with them. Dodger's confidence was high the Maraukians would never get through their defense. But being back out there, in the midst of real fighting, had his nerves frayed before they'd met land.

Shawna dismissed the men and, walking with him, asked cautiously, "Are you all right, sir?"

"Hear that?" he asked.

Shawna listened. "The sound of war?"

He didn't need to answer her question.

Chapter Thirty-Six

Legion Headquarters

Roma, Hellenic System

7/3560

Admiral Nessa observed all the information coming in from the ships around her. Eighty in total. They were the standing defense, ready and waiting to protect the outer planets and its surrounding colonies of people.

Across the system, she knew everyone was fighting for their lives. Each soul in the way of one of those creatures was hurting. This war raged on, not seeming as though it was going to give up.

"Admiral, they are waiting on you."

Nessa didn't wait to answer the comms officer. She left the bridge for her office and linked into the other captains around her. "What's the situation?"

Damus was the one who brought them up to speed. "Emarl have lost the VCF *Detector, Sporadic,* and *Fearless*."

The admiral didn't allow herself any show of emotion, but over the years her losses had added up more than most. No matter whether she knew them personally or not, the loss was great.

"And the ENS *Fernix* and *Avenger*?"

"They are currently still engaged with the fourth barge over Tricticus. The assault barges have already splintered off, though. Seems the only rounds that had a shot were the anti-matter. The Maraukian defenses otherwise pick off any other RSDs or missiles too easy."

Nessa looked around the room to Legate Kaeso and Fidelis, who were already occupied in a different system than the eighty captains.

"We're ready to engage," she said. "We'll hit them as much as we can from a distance. Those outer launch defense rings were the best idea we had."

Damus nodded. The legion had a thousand and more years to prepare for this. Nothing rusts in space. All weapons were online no matter how old they were, and they were ready to come into contact.

"Let's hope that we nail a few before they reach you," Damus said. "Fire when ready."

From the distance, they were just blobs that were the enemy; they seemed to just sit still. Nessa knew they were indeed moving through and moving at a pace that would scare most on Roma. From around the system, there were sparks of light as older ignition reactors flared.

"All missiles away, Admiral."

"Time to targets?"

"Too long," her helmsman whispered to himself while he was calling up calculations.

"Well played." Admiral Nessa found she actually let out a chuckle.

Chapter Thirty-Seven

Freighter 371B

In Transit to the Ark, Emarl System

7/3560

Pela had learned the woman's name with whom she sat with. Kami. To Pela, she had seemed so nice, but the moment Pela had wanted to do something other than sit still, she was on her like a terrier.

"Sit your pregnant ass back down. You need anything, I'll go get it."

Pela sighed and did as she was told. "If I can get to a console, maybe I can figure out what's wrong with my NIAI."

"What do you think is wrong?"

"I don't know—some corrupt code, anything. I didn't even know that you could shut one off like that?"

Pela watched as Kami went quiet for a few moments, then she smiled. "I think there's some terminals in the back. If I can persuade one of the crew to let us in, do you think you can fix it?"

Pela smiled. "I think I can, yes."

Kami stood and made her way past all the refugees.

Pela hadn't thought of them as this, but looking around the area they sat in, slept in, there was no other way to say it. She was on a freighter, headed across the system to be placed somewhere safe, somewhere the Maraukians wouldn't assault. "Oh, Lucus." Her hand trailed to her unborn baby.

Kami returned a few moments later. "We can go through to engineering. Once you're there, the techs will take a look over you and the NIAI."

Pela pushed herself up, feeling a little conscious of the clothes—well, lack of clothes—she had on. But she made her way toward the crew member watching over them and looked back.

Kami smiled. "You'll be fine." She sat back down.

As she followed the man through a couple of corridors, he asked, "How long till the baby's due?"

Pela glanced down. Despite her being so small, she had a growing belly; she couldn't hide it anymore. "Seven months to go still," she said. "I'm just not carrying it well."

The man looked at her and smiled. "You're carrying it very well; your fella must be ecstatic."

Pela just remembered their last argument, and let out a sigh. Her stomach felt heavy, her mind almost as much.

Walking into the engineering section, Pela breathed in. It felt like coming home.

Her escort glanced at her. "I'll see if I can dig you out some better clothes, miss." He left her to stare at a much older lady at the station head.

"NIAI problem, I believe." She held out a hand and Pela shook it.

"Yes, I just need a console. I'm sure I can sort it myself."

"Engineer?"

Pela grinned at this. "One of the best out of Malazar Skill School, ma'am."

"Good to know. I won't need to supervise you much then. Please..." She indicated toward a small unused space. "Go ahead. If you need anything specific, just ask and someone will help you."

Pela thanked her and moved to the workspace. It was something older than she was used to, but she soon found her way around. Then started some diagnostics on Gondi.

Chapter Thirty-Eight

ENS Doomsday

Inner Gl 829 System

7/3560

Quina looked to her troopers as she finished going over the plans and the roles that her company would be playing.

None of them looked pleased as they looked at the 3D hologram map on the ground with different locations marked out as well as their route into the mountain ranges.

Even Quina felt the information she'd been given from Mark and his tactical teams was lacking somewhat. But she digested it, and made some good assumptions of her own. *Don't know what the forces are going to look like on the ground, what kind of positions they have, or the kind of support we can expect. But, I can predict.*

The artillery, RSDs and drop-ships, if they could enter the shield or not—they were all unknown.

"We've got to remember these Sharventi don't have emotions. They care about one thing and that is eradicating their enemies. They turned the others who were in an alliance with them into the Maraukians so they could wage war against others better, for nothing more than their purpose." Quina looked at the men and women in front of her, gauging their reactions. She hoped that she would have been able to give them some better news but this was all she had. They would all have to work with it, and get the job done.

She witnessed the cold and hard looks on their faces, the crossed arms and the glares at the map as they tried to imprint on their minds what those mountains and valleys would be like. She allowed them the time to understand what the damn place would look like inside and out.

There was no way to know truly what they were walking into.

"Brief your people and get your armor and weapons checked out. We're going to be running simulations with the rest of the force tomorrow so we can get some kind of experience in." Quina saw a few people relax a bit more. Still, they all knew this wouldn't be an easy fight. If the Sharventi wanted to hold their position, then the Emarl forces were in for one hell of a fight.

Chapter Thirty-Nine

ENS Moby

Inner Gl 829 System

7/3560

Jess, Gomez, Maxine, and Charles as well as their teams had been working nonstop since they had entered the system, from figuring out a firing solution to hit the planet base, to now unraveling the secrets of the shield.

"Over the continuing bombardment, we've been able to get a few clues as to what is going on with other projectors," Jess said with Gomez beside her. Their teams were the best suited to deal with the shield, but all of the teams had been brought in on it.

"As we know, they're shooting out charged particles, disrupting the structure of the incoming ordinance.

"The faster the rounds travel, the faster it will be destroyed and the less energy it will take for the projector. This is due to the particles being fired at a high fraction of the speed of light, meaning they nearly instantly hit the incoming rounds like a wall, with the kinetic energy of both being so high they mutually destroy one another.

"Also, with the charged particles, it creates instability in the atoms of whatever it strikes. In the case of the rounds, it tears them apart. We need further testing and a trial, but we think that the dropships and the RSDs will be fine in the mountains as long as they don't get too close to the projectors.

"The projectors are meant to defend the sky, not the ground. They're buried in different strongholds. This means that hitting something that is around them is going to be difficult. If we were to fire, say, missiles at the base from in close, then we would still need to use an incredible amount of them to overwhelm the projector and then destroy it." Jess shook her head.

"So the RSDs and drop-ships should be able to enter the mountains if they're moving low and under the projectors, though they can't directly engage the strongholds."

"Yes, and the LBMs won't be usable," Gomez said.

"Artillery Gorgons?" Maxine asked.

"Yes, but limited. Their angle can't bring them into range of the projectors. The first target should be to remove the projectors. Once they're knocked out along the path of advance, then the forces can move up in strength, with support from the tanks and artillery as well as drop-ships and RSDs," Jess said.

"We don't know the power of the projectors, but once we take one, they should be linked by hardline. If we can crack the Sharventi coding, then we can attack their main systems and start taking down their network," Gomez said.

Charles's eyes shone. "If we take just one of these strongholds, then it's possible we can use their landline network, send nanites throughout the Sharventi base and take them down from the inside?"

"I don't see why not." Gomez shrugged. "They are also using antimatter power sources. Even if we're not able to control their systems, we can use nanites to open up the containment tanks for their antimatter power sources."

"The fact of the matter is that there is eight kilometers from the planned drop point and the nearest stronghold, with mountain ranges and no ability to support in between," Maxine said.

The growing excitement in the room chilled.

Gomez and Jess had both been legionnaires in the past. They knew how hard it would be. Maxine and Charles, after becoming mergers, had come to understand how just a mere eight kilometers was no small distance and that everything and anything could go wrong between the two points.

"It at least gives them options," Charles said.

***

"Well, this changes things." Nerva looked over the information that Charles had brought him personally. Maxine, Jess, and Gomez were there as well.

He put down the report. "So, if this place has a hardline connected to all of them, then we can send out nanites and start taking out the surrounding projectors. Even if not, we can use them to destroy the anti-matter containment systems or power systems. With that, we can start getting support from the artillery. We will just need to hold position, with the nanites moving from base to base, destroying the projectors, making the network unstable before reaching the central area and the headquarters of the planetary base." Nerva sat back in his chair. It was a much better plan; if he could rip out the defensive infrastructure out from under the feet of the Sharventi, it would turn from an assault into holding the stronghold.

Ideas and plans rushed through Nerva's mind.

"Looks like we're going to need earth-moving equipment."

Chapter Forty

Malazar Skill School

Tricticus, Emarl System

7/3560

The front line had been getting battered. Everyone around him had been fighting for days now, but it had gotten quiet out there. Dodger worried the Maraukians were up to no good. They'd almost halted their advance and were digging in again. That meant usually one of two things: they'd come back with a vengeance or they were waiting for their reinforcements.

It hadn't been long at the line when the comms call came in from their orbital support. Captain Grild had to deploy elsewhere. There were more Maraukians heading in.

Dodger had very few options, and if they tried to hold the hospital as it was, it could mean they would lose lives. He looked around at the mergers he commanded. They were fresh out of the vats, but they were not green. Each of them had proved themselves in his school and they were proving themselves more and more out in the field.

"They're making a move!"

As his M20s formed and churned out rounds, his thoughts of the first mergers and all their memories and loss hit him like a brick. He'd been trying harder to not let them surface, but it was nigh impossible with this war raging about him.

That's when he felt the familiar feeling of the others, so far out, and this was the first time he'd felt them.

"Cover!" he shouted, to the merger on his right, Brandi Folks. "Emergency meeting. Don't let them in. Relay to the Bellona with us for support."

She confirmed with a nod, and he pulled back from the front line once more. "Mark?" he questioned.

"Sitrep?"

"Surrounded, bleeding them in four locations. Holding out. So is the rest of Tricticus."

"Losses?"

Dodger froze, but shaking it off, answered quickly. "No mergers," he knew Mark would know that, "but there's been a lot of life lost both here and in space."

Dodger knew that would pain Mark as much as it had everyone in Emarl. "How are you doing out there?"

"The Maraukian leaders are cold, calculating, and fucking smart," he said. "We're not faring so well either, but there's a solid plan." Mark seemed to flicker in and out of Dodger's mind.

"Passing you the information we have so far. Make sure Hael and the others see it," he said.

"Breech!" someone yelled, and Dodger's swearing became verbal diarrhea.

"Go," Mark said. "Am right there with you."

Those few words gave Dodger the strength of mind he needed. "Back at you." He rushed for where the Maraukians were making their move once more.

Chapter Forty-One

Freighter 371B

In Transit to the Ark, Emarl System

7/3560

It hadn't taken Pela long to find the program she needed to look at the functionality of her NIAI. There had been very few recorded malfunctions over the entire usage of their existence, and it looked as though there were some ways to easily fix them. All she needed to do was get inside a large tin box. Not quite like the scanning ring that she'd previously used.

Pela stared at it and swallowed. She'd not been bothered about being thousands of feet underground in a mining pod with machinery, but the idea of getting in a little box scared the hell out of her.

Kami had found her and just seemed to stand, watching everything around her, while Pela worked and when she'd paused, the woman walked over. "Everything okay?"

"I've gotta get in there." Pela pointed at the box.

"Don't like small places?"

"No, I don't, actually."

Kami moved to it, and with a hiss, slid the side out of the small tin-looking box. From the inside, it looked lovely—white, plush, soft cushioning. "Be great to get in there," she said. "You'd find that you'll probably be asleep in minutes." Kami watched her carefully. "Ahh, that's what you're worried about. Think we're going to leave you?"

Pela nodded. That was exactly what she was thinking. "You won't leave me, will you?"

Kami seemed distracted a little as she looked around. "No, I'm not gonna leave you. Now, come on, jump in and we'll see what it can do for you."

Pela heard the urgency in her voice and presumed that there were things going on outside she wasn't aware of. She pushed the initiate buttons and then tentatively got inside the unit.

"See you in a few." Kami closed the hatch properly and then waited, eyes fixed on her.

Pela fell asleep and she knew Gondi began to repair.

Chapter Forty-Two

Malazar Skill School

Tricticus, Emarl System

7/3560

Shawna's M20s were formed and ready before Dodger blasted forward with some of the others in tow. They were all locked and loaded and ready to fight. Accessing her HUD, it looked like that was going to be the case. There were fast-approaching images in their direction.

"Breech on the far walls. They're flooding in fast. We gotta move," Dodger said.

Shawna complied, making sure she was hot on his tail.

Dodger was fast, and within a breath, he was ordering the others into positions at the opposite sides of a collapsed wall. Three moved out and took full stances, firing rapidly into the hole.

"We're not going to be able to hold here long. Once they're in, they'll flood through fast."

"We'll hold long enough," Dodger said. "Seal it then we'll get the fuck out."

Dodger moved to the other side, following any Maraukian movement with orders. Weapons fire began to erupt ahead and Shawna focused.

Dodger yelled out as large rounds from the Maraukian hoard outside battered the wall. "This place isn't going to last." He was through comms channels in moments, finding out where he could shift reinforcements from.

Legate Desialias's voice came through. "RSDs are incoming," he informed them. "Hold that line and on my mark, fall back."

Shawna watched as, within a second, his M20s had slung behind him. The Maraukians weren't taking their fire as an answer. And it looked as if it were getting a bit too real. Close up combat with them was not ideal, but it looked as though Dodger was going in close.

"Thirty seconds!" He drew his blade. "Keep firing."

Those thirty seconds would be the longest of her life as the few who had come with Dodger managed to slay as many of their enemy as possible. They were advancing fast. What the hell had gotten into them?

"Fallback positions, ready," he shouted, looking directly at her. His blades cut down enemy after enemy as they tried to force their way in and through toward the school. Shawna nodded at him, her guns still blazing.

Ten.

Nine.

The wall beside her was blasted apart; debris and shrapnel hit her helmet. It could withstand a lot, but the shock still stung.

Eight.

A cry came from one of her team. She felt the searing pain through the merge as a round penetrated the armor and tore the leg apart.

Seven.

The area behind Dodger became a blur of Maraukians as two of her other mergers went from using M20s to melee. This close wasn't good, especially with incoming RSDs.

Five.

There wasn't any time.

"Ready!" Dodger said.

The sound of the incoming artillery assaulted her ears.

"Move!" Dodger yelled. "Fall back. NOW!"

The others started to pull back, weapons cutting down Maraukian after Maraukian. But they were fast enough to get out quick.

Shawna heard the "Strike now!" from him as they raced for their defense line only three hundred yards away. Screaming missiles from their RSDs flew overhead and slammed into the ground and the wall. Within a moment, they'd brought it all down on top of the Maraukians' heads.

The wall was secure once more, at least for now. She looked to Dodger, whose face she couldn't see. But from his thoughts and feelings, she knew he was injured. She ran to him, noting a gash deep in his side. Grabbing for her med pack, she worked quickly to seal it.

"Thanks," he said.

Chapter Forty-Three

The Ark

Emarl

7/3560

Esamai watched on as freighter and shuttle after shuttle came in with more refugees and people from Emarl. She knew they had space enough, but it worried her in keeping them supported and happy while they waited on the Maraukians being defeated. She was positive no matter what they would be.

She also hadn't seen Jerome like this for a long time. His need to be awake and to constantly be at Emarl's beck and call was not only getting her down, but Tyler was starting to act up. This just made her jobs around the Yard all the more tedious.

Overlooking everything that was going on around them was mind-blowing. The sheer size of this operation, this whole thing frightening.

Their battleship was engaged with the others in a full-on space war with the Maraukians. The initial wave of ships defeated, now there were more. Esamai had underneath her the smartest and most efficient working men and women, but even she felt their time and efforts were strained.

Felicity and Johnny were in the midst of this war, mining, refining and pumping out as much as they possibly could. No matter the thoughts and feelings going on inside everyone in Emarl, they were working together.

The losses they'd suffered already were huge, and messages came in daily from one or another station where someone hadn't turned in, but for the most part, the newly formed stations and populations were as one. She couldn't have been any prouder of humanity. Facing their biggest hurdle, instead of falling apart, they worked at it; they would never give up.

Esamai dealt with the most important facts around the yard and the system that she had to, and she watched on her main 3D holo the movements of all the ships, freighters, and transports.

Jerome walked through the door, his face pale.

"What is it?"

Then the flash of news popped up on one of her screens. "Oh no..." Esamai got up and went to him, wrapping her arms around him to offer what comfort she could. "What's the plan?"

"They wiped out half our fleet in less than a week. All those lives..." Jerome pushed her away, his face red, his eyes large and on the verge of tears.

Esamai hadn't seen him like this before, but she knew the toll of war would get to anyone, even with his experience. There were people on those ships who she'd not only spoke to, but met in person, shared dinner with. They'd laughed, and told jokes. It all seemed too real, too finite.

"We brought them here, Esamai," he said. "We did this. We moved these people more than halfway across the galaxy in the hope they'd have better lives, they could be whoever and do whatever they wanted."

Esamai let him get it out. He needed to vent, to throw things, to hurt. If she couldn't allow him that, then what kind of wife would she be? When he collapsed in her chair, she moved to again encase him in the love she had. The pain of everything had never come between them, and it never would.

"I should be with them, fighting the real enemy."

"You are fighting the real enemy. You're protecting billions of lives."

"It's not enough!"

Esamai spun the chair around and kneeled before him. "It is enough. You've put your life on the line so many times, I've lost count over the years. You've put everyone and everything before yourself. Do you not see what you have done here?" She waved a hand at the 3D holo.

Jerome took a glance at it, seeing the thousands of dots around the system as they moved.

"What you've done is not only bring everyone together, you've managed to keep them there. This system, everything is run by the VC but it's run by those who started it, who believed they could make a difference. If you, Mark, and Tyler hadn't started this company, there would be nothing. The Maraukians would have won, all of it. Humanity would have fallen a long, long time ago."

"But..."

"No, no buts. That system out there is here because of you, yes. But also because of you, they have a fighting chance."

Jerome swallowed and pulled her to him in a tight embrace. When his lips met hers, there was passion, pain, and hope.

When he pulled back, she was breathless, but his eyes and breathing were calmer. "I love you."

Esamai smiled and moved to sit better in his lap. "I love you too. Now, let's speak with Hael and the others." She ran a finger across where his tears had fallen. "Wash up. Five minutes, yes?"

Jerome eased her off him and, with a squeeze, left the room. "Five minutes."

When he'd gone, Esamai crumpled in her chair, and her tears fell. She would never change any part of their lives together, but for the wars. They nor the people around her deserved any of this, and despite what everyone said—that behind every warrior was a strong woman—at this moment in time she didn't feel very strong.

Chapter Forty-Four

Emperor's Residence

Roma, Hellenic System

7/3560

Cassius received the information coming in from Emarl over their efforts and he knew they were facing similar circumstances. The Maraukians were not letting up. Instead of the usual wave of four, they'd sent eight, and then even more showed up to arrive in the not so distant future. What they defeated in space with RSDs and other methods was being replaced quicker than they were going to be able to rearm.

Now as he watched the assault on the Helis system and Velia Prime, he could see nothing but their fleet being absolutely bombarded. There was no other way to say it but in front of him was the worst thing he'd witnessed in his life.

He tried to tune out the information coming through Portia, but he couldn't. Thousands of his men and women were dying. They were being mass slaughtered. When the four new barges had appeared, he'd hoped and prayed that something in the other star system that Mark and his EN were doing would help. At first, the battleship and the fleet did well, taking out two of the enemy within a day. But, when the first of his ships started to fall, and then another, and another, so did his hopes.

Lollia opened the door to his office, and he glanced her way. "Did I disturb you?" he asked, watching as his wife slipped over to his side, still dressed in her night slip.

"No, I'm just worried."

Cassius pulled her to him. Her warmth embraced the deep cold that had settled into his soul.

"We're losing, aren't we?" she asked.

When he met her eyes, he saw her pain, and no matter what he wanted to tell her, he also knew that she'd see the truth.

"Lollia, you're a woman of Roma, a blessing and a curse to me." He kissed the side of her face, then wiped away her tears. "We're losing some of the battles, but the war itself is not lost."

"How many lives?" she questioned.

Cassius knew that she valued lives as much as he did. The most recent losses through the cleansing hit their society hard. Not just the lives lost in battle within their own ranks, but for the sheer amount of people who chose to leave Roma to move to Emarl. Cassius had not denied anyone their right to choose where to live, nor would he ever.

"The figure is more than I should be telling you, my dearest."

"*Damus wishes to link with you*," Portia said inside his mind.

Cassius didn't want to move his wife on, but things out there were really pressing. "I'll come see you, as soon as I can," he said. "But, I must marshal this war."

Lollia lowered her head and leaned in for one more squeeze. "I'll bring you some food in a few hours."

"Thank you." When she only moved slightly, he pulled her tight once more. "And of course I love you. Go settle our family. I'll make a broadcast for Roma before the day is over."

Lollia moved away and a moment later, the door clicked shut. Cassius locked it and then allowed Damus and Admiral Nessa to link in with him. There were no shared words as they watched the events unfold before them.

Their eighth naval vessel flailed above Velia Prime, and then they watched on as it was ripped apart.

"Felix," Damus said, not wanting a sharp or urgent tone to bring the emperor out too quickly to the devastation he was witnessing.

"Pull them back, Admiral," Cassius said. "Pull them back now!"

Admiral Nessa's link was gone for but a moment. When she returned, Cassius spoke clearly. "Regroup. Looks like the Maraukians are coming in for us after all."

"If they make it to Roma, they will be in for a shock," Damus said.

Cassius knew this. The people of Roma knew about the threats. Most of them had fought at some point in the long years of wars with the Maraukians, but they always felt protected, secured this far out. No way the Maraukians would ever come here...they said. Now Cassius knew different. They were here and they were coming for them. Their end goal nothing but devastation.

"I don't think they'll get that close, but we need our nearest planet systems to feel they have our full backing, because they do."

"And our citizens?"

"I'll address them shortly. Report back to me once all our ships and personnel are moving once more. I'll be in the command center."

Chapter Forty-Five

Legion Headquarters

Roma, Hellenic System

7/3560

Admiral Nessa looked over the incoming information. She had also just witnessed the downfall of the navy fleet in the Helis system before Cassius ordered her to pull them out.

"Well, it seems like the Maraukians put down the capital." She stared at the eleven insertion barges that were charging into their system.

"It looks like they're heading directly for Roma," a sensor operator said in the command center.

Admiral Nessa had initially wanted to be mobile but Cassius had shot that down, instead placing her in the command center located in the heart of the legion compound. From there, she not only commanded the forces of the Hellenic system, but the navy forces in the other systems.

The Maraukians were coming out of the woodwork and their multiple fleets moved to engage those Maraukian insertion barges that had showed up.

The more of them they could destroy in space, the less they had to face on the ground.

This was an overall win, no matter how you looked at it.

"Hail the patrolling forces. I want them to move to rally point fifty-three. From there, they are to organize into a fleet under Rear Admiral Scaloz and move in to hit the Maraukians in the ass."

She looked over the feed that showed the Maraukians as they were coming in.

Her defensive situation was a mix of stationary and fluid: Stationary with the three habitable planets and one moon getting their own grouping of warships. Fluid with the patrolling forces around the elliptical of the system.

Other than the main inhabitable planets and moon, there were hundreds of stations and ships that littered the Hellenic system.

"Give orders to all of the stations to begin moving. Have tugs move to assist along the Maraukian line of advance. I want all civilian traffic cleared from the system, either docked somewhere or orbiting any planet that isn't Roma. We'll start evacuating the planet as well."

Her eyes moved over the information and checked the plots. "Squadron Four over Mars—I want them moved to readiness. They're close enough to the Maraukian advance, they should be able to shoot right down their throats and then get out of the way before the Maraukians can bring down big casualties on them."

"Yes, ma'am," a communications officer said, sending the orders.

She needed to bleed the Maraukians. They were slower than her ships, so she could bring them under fire with the fleet she was moving into position—though, seeing the squadron, it was an opportunity she couldn't give up.

This was the role of the space legion: get people where they needed to be and try to weaken the Maraukians before they landed.

Chapter Forty-Six

Command Center

Roma, Hellenic System

7/3560

Cassius watched in the command center as Squadron Four, formerly protecting Mars, fired salvo after salvo of missiles and rail cannons into the face of the Maraukians. It was a long-range bombardment and it would still take five minutes for the salvos to reach the Maraukian barges, but he was hopeful.

Everyone in the command center was watching the main plot as the timer counted down.

The Maraukian ships didn't alter their course but they started to fire their own weapons at those that were coming for them.

There was only the front of the barge showing; the broadsides of the ships hadn't been deployed. Already the wealth of firepower was enough to make the emperor's blood run cold.

The space legion ships were already quickly leaving the area of operations, far outside of the Maraukian line of fire and the area they could engage other ships.

Missiles exploded and rail rounds simply disappeared. Still, the wave of firepower that the space legion squadron had unleashed landed on their target.

The rail cannon rounds tore into the armor, crumpling it under multiple attacks before the lead barge started to break down.

The missiles came in waves, exploding and tearing the forward barges apart. The destruction continued as the first ten layers of the insertion barge were destroyed.

These broken assault barges were released and tossed aside, nothing more than scrap.

The Maraukian fleet continued forward.

Thirty assault barges had been destroyed like that: half of the insertion barges' total payload, five million Maraukians, gone in a few seconds of fire.

It was a big blow, but compared to the rest of the ships and the Maraukians that were aboard, it was but a drop in the ocean.

The fleet under Admiral Scaloz's command was quickly catching up on an intercept course with the Maraukians. Stand-up engagements were a quick way to get the legion ships destroyed; quick hit-and-runs, breaking down the Maraukian strength, was the best way to go without losing too much of their battle strength.

"Tell Squadron Four good job and tell them to return to their station and await further commands," Admiral Nessa said, seemingly unaffected by the results of their first engagement.

Cassius couldn't do anything but continue to watch as the plight of the Hellenic system unfolded before him.

Chapter Forty-Seven

Legion Headquarters
Roma, Hellenic System
7/3560

"We have an additional transfer into the system," the sensors officer said to Admiral Nessa as information was being resolved on the main hologram that displayed the system.

A further twenty-four Maraukian insertion barges appeared on their sensors as they entered real-space.

Nessa knew this was more insertion barges than ever sent to a single system.

Still, she didn't let the shock overtake her as she started breaking down what actions she could take against the new threat.

"Plot a course for them. I want to know where they're going," Nessa said, her voice deep.

She had moved all of her assets to deal with the current Maraukian fleet. With another appearing—and so large—she couldn't process it. It wasn't according to the Maraukians' previous fighting strategy.

She couldn't pull another fleet together.

"It looks like it is heading for Roma as well," the sensors officer said. The plot changed with the current Maraukian course as they drew closer.

They were coming in on a different angle so she couldn't use Squadron Four around Mars or Admiral Scaloz's fleet.

"Launch RSDs in their direction on no power. Have pilots ready to go active when the RSDs are coming in range of the Maraukians," Nessa said.

The RSDs were a massive support and their power and usability wasn't small. They had bought plans and they were making as many RSDs as possible, recompensing the Victor Corporation. Still, even with the three thousand she could scrounge up, they wouldn't be enough. Not against twenty-four barges.

"Once we defeat the first Maraukian fleet, then we'll focus on the second," Nessa said aloud, making sure their priorities were clear.

***

Nessa nodded as she watched Scaloz's fleet passing the Maraukian fleet. They were far away. Just like the squadron, their cannons unleashed hell as they dropped off seeders and RSDs from the Emarl system.

Missiles moved in swarms.

It was an incredible display of firepower once again. The Maraukians engaged the weapons fire as the legion fleet was turning around, trying to cut their forward momentum. Their new course looked to intersect the Maraukian line of advance again and bleed them once more.

The supply ships in the fleet were resupplying those that had blown all of their missile and rail cannon magazines.

The avalanche of fire poured in and the Maraukians had been able to defend rather well against Squadron Four's fire as it was a smaller barrage. This had a fleet of some one hundred and thirty vessels; it was much harder to stop it all.

The Maraukian ships were specifically targeted as explosions started to meet the barges; rounds started to crumple armor and pierce habitats. A cloud of debris appeared around the targeted insertion barges.

The previously wounded insertion barge was torn apart by kinetic and nuclear forces. Three more joined its fate, turning into a cloud of escaping gases, parts of Maraukians, armor, and other parts.

Four more were heavily damaged. Their pace was slower than the others as they lost thrust from the attached assault barges.

Two had light damage, losing ten or less assault barges.

They forged onward as the fleet fought to change their trajectory.

Then the RSDs appeared. The Maraukian barges started to fire; the RSDs dodged and dived but still tens of them were destroyed in fiery explosions.

The RSDs opened fire, but they were headed right at the wounded insertion barges.

It was clear they weren't looking to just strafe the insertion barges as the first one pile drove into the ship. Its acceleration and the antimatter weaponry inside ignited, taking out a full fifth of the insertion barge.

More of the RSDs struck. Hundreds had been fired but there were less than twenty that made it into range as they detonated.

Two more insertion barges were knocked out.

It was a costly endeavor, but so far, they hadn't taken one loss of life.

If it was credits against lives, Nessa would spend the credits every day.

***

The squadron that had been stationed at Roma had their turn as they fired their weaponry until they ran dry.

Scaloz's fleet had already hit the enemy twice and they were now heading out to the second wave of barges that had entered the system.

They had left three complete insertion barges and two damaged barges, half of their strength when they had entered the system.

The Hellenic system's preparations were simply fierce.

The Maraukians ran into Squadron One and Two's bombardment, sustaining further losses as they lost a damaged ship and a complete insertion barge, taking their total of insertion barges down to three ships, with one severely damaged.

"Weapons network is online and ready. Squadron One and Two are reloading and rearming," a communications officer said.

"As soon as they're in range of our defensive weapons, I want to overwhelm them. I want no less than ten percent of the weapons cleared for the first salvo," Nessa said from her command chair—the queen of her domain, a tyrant with immeasurable power at her fingertips.

Her eyes weren't focused on the fleet that was closest to Roma. Instead, she looked over to the second fleet that was carving its way through the Hellenic system, missing the different parts of the system that were patrolled or where the inhabited planets and moon were located.

To her, the fate of this first enemy fleet had already been decided. The second, however, was a wild card and she would only get to hit it once before it entered the range of Roma's defensive networks.

The Hellenic system had been occupied for hundreds of years, with thousands of weapon systems added up for security of the planets against the Maraukians.

These systems didn't age as they were held in vacuum. Only the fire controls changed for the operators as more and more defenses were added, creating a sea of weaponry.

Roma's nickname was the Planetary Fortress: everything on the planet had been made with war in mind.

Just two hours later, Nessa got a report back.

"Weaponry ready to fire." A weapons officer forwarded the different weapons that were online and had a clear line of sight on the incoming Maraukian fleet.

"Fire and don't let up," Nessa said.

"All weapons, fire as you have targeting solutions."

With the weapons officer's orders, the weaponry that had been amassed over hundreds of years unleashed a sea of fire. Missiles, rail cannons—all of it was hurled out.

The Maraukians waded through the fire. Their own weapons came online as they took out the remote weapon systems. But they were fighting an uphill battle. The assault barges that made up their insertion barges were being eroded away as they were taking out tens of weapon emplacements in a sea of *thousands*.

They were like a fighter who didn't know how to give up, hit with hammering blow after hammering blow. It went on for three minutes of sustained fire before the weapon systems stopped.

"Maraukian fleet destroyed," the weapons officer said with a large smile.

"We've got another fleet coming in. Let's not celebrate yet," Nessa said, seeing the overjoyed and stunned expressions of everyone in the room.

Chapter Forty-Eight

Holding Bay 23

The Ark, Emarl

8/3560

Lucus had tried to find her, to get updates, to learn anything, but there was nothing—as if something had shut her off. *Death?* No, he wouldn't believe that; she was being treated well and recovering from her sickness.

After that, he'd searched any other way possible. But nothing had shown up. Aileen and Remy had comforted him as best they could, but his depression was absolute. If he didn't have her with him, he was lost.

Every moment he was in the Ark, with nothing to do, he had nothing but memories to occupy his mind: their last moments together, the arguing over her weight, her working too hard. Everything seemed more prominent. He hated the facts. They'd been struggling as a couple.

Aileen had been the one to tell him Pela was pregnant. It had all made sense then, once her friend had spilled the truth about her visits for treatment and her moods. He'd cursed Pela and Aileen for not telling him, then they'd cried together, hoping Pela was all right.

The baby clarified all for him now, made him realize life was everything. But, back then both their emotions were all over the place. He tried daily to work it out, but they argued over something simple and the last week he'd not even tried to talk to her, he'd focused on work. On doing more and more. Now, of course, he regretted it. All he wanted to do was hold her again, smell her scent.

The days had passed by so slowly. It hurt. Everything hurt.

Now, Lucus was cramped with Aileen, Remy, and Ashaeed in some small temporary quarters when there was a ping on his NIAI.

The voice that came through was terrified. "Lucus!"

"Pela," he cried out.

"I'm sorry, I'm so sorry." Information flooded through to him, and he couldn't take it all in, then she admitted. "I'm pregnant!"

He couldn't help but let out a cry, "I know, it's okay. Aileen told me everything."

Pela's sobs filled his mind. "Shhh," he whispered, then. "Tell me everything."

Aileen grabbed hold of his arm, eyes wide, and within a moment, they were all linked in and talking.

Pela then explained some of what happened to her, and that she was heading into the Ark.

Lucus sank to the floor. Finally, the news he wanted. After all they'd been through this last couple of weeks. She was well, and so was their baby. *Their baby.* The reality they were expecting also started to sink in. He wanted to be a dad, the best dad he could.

Her voice, though—it was almost as if she were a ghost, not the Pela he'd heard so many times through his NIAI.

Pela talked more about what it was like on the freighter than anything. She wasn't getting the medical care she should have been, but the crew there were helping her as best they could. Aileen, Remy, and Ashaeed eventually disconnected and left them to talk alone. Lucus felt his heart sink. "Tell me *all* the details, please."

While he listened, Lucus pulled a loose strand on his shirt, and it started to unravel. Rather fitting considering his life had unwound the day the Maraukians came in and evacuation orders were given out. Lucus's heart soared. It wouldn't be long now before she arrived there, and everything would change. He'd change. No more arguing, that he promised himself.

But, he didn't really care. Pela was all that mattered.

Chapter Forty-Nine

ENS Moby

Moon Base Orbit, Gl 829 System

8/3560

Mark stepped back into the drop pod. The pod locked onto his armor before the panel door came down and secured him in place. Mark shook with the pod as he was picked up and put into a drop rack with other members of the Vanguard.

They had been looking over the moon for days now and there was little that was able to escape their eyes.

The Maraukians were moving in roving bands across the mountain range underneath the cover of the shield. The Sharventi could be seen moving with them, carrying weapons of their own and controlling the Maraukians.

They'd picked out their target: one of the projector locations farthest out from the main base.

It sat on the top of a rise. The area had been clear cut, leaving it flat and giving it a dominating view of the surrounding area.

It would be a pain in the ass to take, but all of the strongholds would be hard to attack. But, thankfully, if the two closest strongholds wanted to assist, they would need to go through valleys that the Emarl forces could keep them pinned in.

The Maraukians might be hell to fight, but they couldn't go up cliffs or across water.

"Drop in ten seconds." Liang's voice carried through the ship.

Mark was locked into a drop rack now, with the belly of the *Moby* open to space and the moon below.

"Launch!" Liang said. The forward pods of the different racks dropped away, those behind falling once those before had cleared the ship.

They looked like old-fashioned bombs coming out from a bomb bay.

Mark grunted as the acceleration hit him and he shot out of the *Moby*.

Across the fleet, the troop transports were opening their doors as the drop-ships started lighting off their engines and heading for the moon below, carrying troops, tanks, supplies, and artillery parks.

Mark was thrown around in his pod as he reached atmosphere. *Fuck me. Feel like a fucking martini shaken into oblivion.*

Mark grit his teeth as he looked for incoming fire, but there wasn't any.

The Hell Hammers plowed through the skies, black missiles moving toward their target.

Mark could now see the mountain range as it got bigger and bigger in his view.

Tracers started to appear in the sky as the pods' limited engines moved them erratically, making it harder for the shooters to get a good bead on the Vanguard.

Pods were hit and turned to streaking debris. The forces tore apart most of the mergers inside.

The coil guns kept on firing, but their accuracy wasn't high and the drop pods were coming down as fast as possible.

Mark was crushed as his downward momentum reversed and his head tried to press into his chest. He grunted and groaned, and then slammed into a mountain side.

The front of the pod blew out with Mark's harness. He pushed forward, his sensors cranked all the way up as he looked around for threats.

With the weapons fire, his people were spread all over the place, with more of them coming down across the valley they would advance down.

Mark set out rally points for the different groups.

"Phantom Lords on the left incline; Devils on the right. I want everyone to push forward. I don't doubt that we're going to have friends showing up in the future. Keep your sensors running and mark any targets you see. We will advance forward. If we come into contact, we will destroy them. Miles, Desialias—I want you to leave a platoon behind to secure this LZ for the incoming drop-ships. Let's get moving!"

Mark was already jogging across the rocky terrain. There was some kind of trees or shrubs on the planet but Mark didn't have time to deal with that as he looked over atmospheric checks.

The planet's air was too saturated in nitrogen for humans to survive in. The Vanguard would be okay, but it added another layer of difficulty for the forces under Nerva's command.

Mark took off, flying as he advanced through the valley. The mergers regrouped and moved forward up the valley as fast as possible.

The farther they got, the better.

"Mark, on sensors, we've got Maraukians and Sharventi headed for your location. They should be there shortly," Nerva said.

"Looks like the fun is coming sooner than we expected," Mark said.

"Landing in seven. Should have support up and running five minutes afterward," Nerva said.

"Gotcha. We're on our own for twelve to fifteen." Mark looked up into the sky, where the drop-ships were starting to break atmosphere.

He picked up speed and continued the advance as his two regiments reorganized on the fly, replacing the people who had been lost and getting ready for the fight.

"Pretty much," Nerva said. "I'll leave you to it."

"See you on the ground soon," Mark said. The channel was cut as Mark flitted forward between the shrubs and rocks of the valley.

It was covered in weird plants of purples, pinks, and grays. A body of water, too small to be called a stream, moved through the center.

The higher one went up the sides of the valley, the sparser the vegetation was.

Ava and Evan had pushed out their best long-range snipers into the higher regions so they'd be able to see the Maraukians and Sharventi coming and ambush them or bring them under fire at greater distances.

"How we looking, Dominguez?" Mark asked.

"We lost forty-seven people. We've got enemy forces coming at us from every damn direction and grouping together as they come through the valleys. We're going to be trying to take a hardened and dug-in position and our support is fifteen minutes out at least. Same shit, different day," Dominguez replied.

"Always looking at the bright side," Mark said.

"Ain't that a warrant's job?"

"That is true," Mark acknowledged. "You got any modifications you want to make?"

Mark was a good leader. As such, he knew that he couldn't catch everything and others, like Dominguez, might solve these shortcomings.

***

Kovyas was advancing with his people. He had pushed out his flank security but they were pushing forward as fast as possible. The farther they got before coming into contact, the closer they would be to their objective and the less distance they would need to fight to it.

"Contact!" Malay yelled out as they marked Maraukians under the command of several bobbleheads rushing into the valley up ahead.

The Sharventi opened up with their coil guns as the Maraukians raised their torsos and pulled out their weapons, firing at the Vanguard.

Kovyas's platoon started reacting to the enemy fire without needing to be told anything. They dropped into cover and fired back at the enemy.

Using fire and movement, they were able to suppress them. Kovyas moved with his people as they continued to advance in groups.

The Sharventi and Maraukians numbered in the hundreds but the Vanguard were all moving in support of Kovyas's section and were able to overwhelm them with firepower.

"I think we can safely say that the bastards have the valleys rigged with sensors!" Second Lieutenant Arcega complained as another patrol was taking potshots at them as they moved.

"Fuck," Kovyas said as the rounds flew over his head and he fired back.

It wasn't that he was some kind of hero, but the fact that being under fire for a long time, you became numb to it. Working to take your time and kill or suppress the enemy instead of jumping around like a rabbit, scared of the whizz and eventual crack of the rounds around you.

They might fucking get me, but I'll get ten of the bastards before then.

"Four Section, press out toward the rise more and establish a fire support base there! The Maraukians don't care about dying, but the bobbleheads seem to at least grasp tactics." Kovyas saw bobbleheads using cover and getting their Maraukians to spread out so they weren't all killed in one burst of automatic weapons fire.

Just what we need, a smart enemy.

Chapter Fifty

Front Line

Roma, Hellenic System

8/3560

Damus watched as the second Maraukian fleet in the Hellenic system was met by Scaloz's fleet. The supply ships only had a limited amount of munitions, so they weren't able to fully restock the fleet.

They put down everything they had and it had taken out two insertion barges and damaged another.

Now they watched as the RSDs that had been launched days ago reached their targets. All of them started coming alive as their pilots remotely connected.

Their orders were simple: pierce or get close to the Maraukian insertion barges and detonate. With no one aboard the RSDs, there was no loss but credits.

The RSD pilots did everything they could but they couldn't stop the insertion barges' forward charge. Three were damaged and another two were knocked out of the fight.

Damus let out a heavy sigh and looked to the reports in his hand on the readiness of his forces on the ground. Not many of the Maraukian insertion barges would be able to deploy on Roma, but inside of each of the insertion barges there was over eleven million Maraukians. Even one of them would be a calamity.

Damus was ready with his defenses. Roma had been built to fight a war.

His predecessors had fought battles across the Roma Union, all the way back to the first battle against the Maraukians. Now he would be the next legate of the Ninth to fight the Maraukians on Roma.

Chapter Fifty-One

Legion Headquarters

Roma, Hellenic System

8/3560

The second Maraukian fleet just kept on coming, weathering everything that Nessa had thrown in their path.

The squadrons protecting Roma had unloaded on the fleet and they were now turning around to return to Roma as the second fleet reached the orbital defenses of Roma.

The battles before seemed like prelude as Nessa watched the Maraukian insertion barges rushing forward, rocking with hits as their own weapons reached out and destroyed the weapons system around them.

The net of weapons that had been set up over hundreds of years had a growing tunnel through them.

Assault barges were broken apart under the weight of fire, the insertion barges themselves showing broken assault barges all across its frame.

Another insertion barge was torn apart, but it wasn't enough.

"Assault barges are releasing!" Sensors called out as the insertion barges seemed to explode outward. The insertion barges disengaged from the main structure and shot toward the planet, looking like canister shot.

The defense systems destroyed hundreds of them, but it was too little in the face of the six hundred of the Maraukian assault barges.

They started entering atmosphere, trying to land on Roma below.

"Activate ground-based cannons. Bellonas are free to fire," Nessa said.

"Ground cannons active!" Weapons reported as massive planetary cannons, built into remote defenses, opened up. The Gorgons, which were spread out in defensive lines, fired. Dust and dirt flew as both fired. Their rounds arced up into the sky as auto loaders whirred and reloaded the cannons.

The Maraukian assault barges couldn't do anything but follow their flight plan. A few tried to dodge but the forces of Roma's atmosphere and physics instated their laws, tearing at the assault barges and throwing them into chaos if they didn't correct quickly.

Explosions bloomed in the upper atmosphere of Roma. The skies filled with destruction as insertion barge after insertion barge released their payloads.

Thousands of Maraukian assault barges filled the skies. Weapons fire reached up to smack them as missile batteries were covered in waves of exhaust. One after another, they fired repeatedly, coming out nose to tail.

The explosions and rumblings could be heard from the ground as legionnaires gripped their weapons tighter and checked their gear.

War had returned to Roma.

Chapter Fifty-Two

The Ark, Emarl

Processing

8/3560

Pela had fixed Gondi. She'd been in constant talks with her friends now, and was finally glad to be able to dock, and unload at the Ark.

Her first conversation with Lucus had gone differently than she'd thought. There were no arguments, no harsh words; he cried and said nothing but nice things about her and their baby. Now she wanted to hear them in person.

Stretching her legs, she and her growing belly went out and toward the registration process. She was given food and water, and more food and water as soon as they realized she was carrying. Pela looked to the others around her and frowned. Preferential treatment was good because she was starving, but there were a lot of people who were hungry.

No sooner was she registered than the link from Lucus came through, Gondi alerted her.

"Hi," she said.

"I'm waiting by the shop as you leave processing. Come quickly, Pela." His voice was fraught with emotion and she found herself tearing up.

The line was long; the wait to get out and to move to designated areas was thorough, but painstaking. The longer the process seemed to take, the more she felt sick. Sweat dripped off her and soaked the clothes she'd had to borrow.

Finally, she made it through, but the line of people leaving the area was still hard to get through. Pela moved slowly and carefully, trying not to get pushed about by those eager to also get out of there.

Then she spotted Lucus. Greasy hair clung to his face, and she could see his puffy red eyes from her spot. She wanted to run to him, but couldn't.

When he saw her, though, her heart leaped and it was Lucus who ran for her. Wrapping her up in his arms, he held her tight. "Oh Pela, my love."

Pela found herself sobbing, breaths coming in quick gasps as her emotions overwhelmed her.

"I'm so sorry," he said. "All the arguments. I don't ever want to be separated from you again. I don't care where you go, I'm gonna be right by your side."

Pela looked up into his eyes and he wiped her tears away. "You really promise me?"

"I promise." He rubbed her back, moved her away from the crowds passing and into the parted doorway. "The baby?"

"She's fine," Pela said.

Lucus's eyes lit up. "We're having a girl?"

Pela nodded. "I found out the other day. Yes, a girl."

Lucus dropped to his knees and Pela laughed as passersby stared at him as he nuzzled into her belly. She, however, didn't care. To feel him here, to touch his hair—nothing could make her happier. When he moved to stand up once more, he paused. Pela looked down at him and then noticed he was holding something. No, not just something. He had a ring.

Pela choked up once more. "Lucus?"

"I'm not waiting any longer." His voice cracked. "Pela Nault, will you marry me?"

All of the pain, the worry, the hurt of the last few months seemed to melt away as she nodded. No words formed on the tip of her tongue. Lucus swept her up into an even bigger hug. His lips met hers with emotion and passion, and around them erupted rounds of applause and whoops of joy. Pela peeked out from his grip to the crowds that had stopped moving to see their reunion and witness his proposal.

"Say it," he said. "I need to hear you say you'll be mine forever."

Pela looked back up at him. "Yes," she said and she meant it. "I want to be yours forever."

Chapter Fifty-Three

ENS Homeland

Gl 829 System

8/3560

"Shit, it's going to be one hell of a fight to that base." Hall was looking over real-time maps of what was happening down on the moon.

The drop-ships were just starting to land as the Vanguard positioned at the LZ had cleared away vegetation for the drop-ships.

The forward elements of the Vanguard had come into contact with the Maraukians and their Sharventi commanders.

They had rushed into battle, but it was clear they knew where the Vanguard was. They were fighting over a range measured in kilometers. The Vanguard were able to reach out that far easily with their weapons and abilities. The problem was that the Sharventi had good aim and the Maraukians might not be accurate, but they coated the sides of the valley in rounds. Even if it was a waste of ammunition, it only took one round to kill a merger.

Hall checked on a priority report that had come from Moretti.

Maraukians seemed to have been woken up and they were gathering their strength and heading for the populated systems.

Looks like we know what that signal did for sure now. If we can control the signal, or destroy it, then the Maraukians should fall apart with no masters or orders to tell them what to do.

Through the engineering and sciences groups' findings, they determined the Maraukians were basically brain dead other than their herd-like instincts.

"Admiral," Guy said, interrupting Hall's thoughts.

"What is it?" Hall asked.

"The RSDs are testing whether they will be able to support the forces as they move forward."

"Understood." Hall pulled up the information from the command table as he watched the tester RSD being piloted forward of the landing drop-ships.

It swerved through the valley and fired on the Maraukian and Sharventi formations.

Their anti-matter missiles left a streak across the sky before landing among the enemy.

The mountain range shook as waves of pressure flattened or tore plants away.

The Maraukians that had been located by the Vanguard were torn apart.

The RSD banked away, moving into a holding position, ready to be called again if needed.

Hall pumped his fist in victory.

There were RSDs loaded and ready to move, as well as more inside the planet's atmosphere. No matter what, the troopers and Vanguard on the ground would have the support they needed.

Chapter Fifty-Four

Death Pass

Moon Base, Gl 829 System

8/3560

Mark fired on the group of Maraukians that had come through a mountain pass, hitting the Vanguard from the side.

"Hell Dog One, this is Vanguard Actual. Pinged target. Awaiting rounds." Mark radioed a Gorgon tank that was rolling through the valley. All of the trooper forces were on the ground and they had some artillery support online.

Ortiz was leading the forward element, while Nerva was getting the camp sorted out so they would have an operations command center outside of the shield, allowing them to receive support from the fleet in orbit.

"Understood. Target acknowledged." McDougall's voice came back.

Hell Dog turned its main gun and elevated it at the same time as acceleration rails behind its main turret were revealed and fired off high explosive mortars.

The Gorgons were smaller than Bellonas but their firepower was impressive.

Instead of the tri-barrel system of the Bellona, it had one barrel that could change according to the round loaded in it. There were still two forward support weapon perches that could see everything in front of the tank.

The tank's main gun fired. All around it, dust was thrown up as the tank shook with the power from the outgoing round.

The closer artillery got to the shield, the less made it through. The tank's main gun wasn't arcing the rounds into the visible range of the projectors, so it was much more reliable.

The round hit the target; a fireball appeared, followed by gray dust before the noise rushed to slap the Vanguard.

"Move it!" Mark yelled. They had to keep stopping to clear out these Maraukian and Sharventi ambushes as they gained access to Death Pass.

"Report," Nerva asked in Mark's ear.

"We've cleared out the fuckers on the hill. Moving forward. We just don't have enough sensors to see them all. Those Sharventi have damn good aim. We might be good troops, but having them pop out of fucking nowhere and kill some of our people before we can hammer them into oblivion, it's not doing good things for morale." Mark kept everything businesslike. He couldn't think about the losses or people yet; he hadn't completed his mission. After, it would be time to say good-bye and remember them.

"Understood. Nothing to do but move forward," Nerva said.

Mark simply grunted as he pushed his ass out of the small depression he had crawled into and continued to march forward. Dropships moved in to assist the wounded and drop off supplies. Behind the Vanguard, troopers followed behind, ready to assist if needed.

In the valley, it was hard for the Maraukians or the Sharventi to get numerical superiority. Though the troopers mostly hung back, to make sure they didn't cause a friendly fire with all of the movement and weapons fire going on.

Mark could zoom in and see the projector that sat on a nearby ridge. The air around it would shudder slightly when it fired, taking out incoming ordinance that got too close. Right now, it was all quiet, giving one an eerie feeling.

Mark heard the crack of rounds. Seeing as they weren't near him, he got low and flew forward, scanning for where the weapons fire came from. He checked the sensor feeds.

"Shit, Mark, looks like they massed their forces together in the other valleys and they're pressing in toward us," Dominguez said as Mark saw what she was seeing.

"Shit." Mark pulled Evan and Ava into the chat.

"Use the charges. Get in cover and hold the line," he said as he linked Nerva in as well.

"We've got a large Maraukian and Sharventi force advancing right for us. It looks like they built up their forces in the surrounding valleys or even at their projector location. Evan, Ava—I need you to get dug in now. They're coming fast and hard. You're going to get hit soon. Nerva, I'm going to need your troopers to move up in support of the line." Mark saw Vanguard members throwing out cratering charges as they picked different areas to get stuck in with interlocking arcs of fire.

They couldn't make a complete line across the valley; it was just too wide of an area to cover it all without the support of the troopers.

Green lights popped up on Mark's HUD as he neared the line. He threw out his own cratering charges and jumped into the small hole. He started to pick out targets.

The Gorgon tank's engines revved as they moved off the road they'd carved into the valley.

The Hell Dog fired. Its round screamed overhead before it landed deeper in the valley, exploding among the ranks of the Maraukians that were emerging out of the valley's underbrush.

Mark looked over the fight as the Vanguard merged together. Their reaction times increased as artillery fire orders were called in, forces organized, and M20s started laying fire down into the coming Maraukians. Sharpshooters picked off the Sharventi as they moved among their brainwashed slaves.

Mark ducked as rounds pinged around him. He raised both of his arms. Sarah picked out targets; she used one hand, targeting the

Sharventi, as he used the other arm, raining down fire on the Maraukian lines.

Fire shifted as the Vanguard worked to their strengths and found the best angles of fire on to the enemy that was being ground down as they advanced.

Silver lines of tracers burned through the valley as explosions dotted the Maraukian charge.

Rounds whizzed, cracked, and buzzed around the Vanguard as they stood there, a wall in the face of thousands of Maraukians pouring in.

Troopers who had been in the rear moved up in platoons, rushing through the fire to support the Vanguard.

Mark couldn't help but be proud to be with these people as they threw caution to the wall, and ran into fire to stand beside their fellow soldiers.

Artillery rained down from above. The successive hits tore the landscape apart. The Maraukians got in range of some of the Gorgons' forward weapon systems as they opened up with their machine guns. High-velocity rockets exploded as they were taken down by close-in defense systems.

Sections of the line were torn apart by the Maraukians' withering fire, from coil guns, plasma blasters, and hypervelocity missiles.

All of them were much stronger than the versions that the Maraukians had used when attacking humanity.

Even as their herd commanders were killed, it was hard to tell how much crazier the Maraukians got as they were charging forward under the Sharventi orders as they looked to stay back and pick off the Vanguard from range.

Mark ducked back into cover and reloaded. He rocked himself before turning and firing on the Maraukian charge.

"Shit." Mark could see the flow of battle, and he could see the concentration of Maraukians that were hammering a strong point farther down in the valley as they pulled out their vibro-blades to clash with the mergers there.

"You five with me," Mark said. Sarah translated his thoughts into orders for the five others as they moved from their positions that weren't under heavy fire, bounding behind Mark.

When he asked them to go, there was no need to tell them what he needed them for or why.

They ran right at where the rounds were coming from, running, falling, and stumbling down the hill. They used anti-grav here and there as they moved closer to the strong point under siege.

Mark slammed into a boulder and the other five joined him.

"All right, we're going to go over this boulder and hose those fuckers back. If it comes to it, then move to use your melee weapons but we need to hold this point." Mark could feel their fear, their nervousness; he could also feel that part of them that came out, gripped them and pushed them forward. It was their training; it was their sense of they weren't going to leave another person behind.

"Three, two, one—jump." Mark and the others jumped up and landed on the outcropping of boulders. As they opened fire, Maraukians were churned up as Vanguard were fighting ahead of them. Somehow, even with the bullets, they were able to move through the Maraukians and not get hit once by friendly fire. Only through merging this special blend of insanity could be pulled off.

The sudden weapons fire and the Maraukians that were all bunched up with their melee weapons allowed the original defenders to disengage and pull back, deploying their own M20s and taking the Maraukians under fire and pushing them back.

"Firing!"

"Moving!" Without prompting, the Vanguard started to move. People got their shit together as they worked in groups to push onward.

Then he was back in the stronghold point, with the Maraukian press calmed down. Mark surveyed the battlefield. Others were getting pushed back as well.

The troopers were now moving onto the battlefield and reinforcing, but there were troubled pockets.

"Dominguez."

"Sir?"

"Get together a group of people. We're going to be running command and control over quick reaction forces. Anywhere there's more pressure from the Maraukians, we're there to even things out," Mark said.

"Got it." Dominguez cut the channel.

Mark trusted that she would know where to use the forces at her disposal.

"All right, Lindskoy, Faulkner, Richter, Koi, and Lee—seems that today is your lucky day. We're taking a tour of the line's hottest locations. We're QRF until the troopers can get their positions set up," Mark said in a mock happy manner.

The Maraukians were fast, too fast for the line to be set up all the way across and not be broken. They were starting to intermix with the Vanguard, who drew their melee weapons, ready to engage in close combat.

They had strong points up, but they just didn't have the firepower. There was cover they couldn't see through and the Maraukians seemed to pop out of nowhere, right into the Vanguard. He was throwing them into hell, and they knew it.

"We're with you, Major," Lee said.

"Good shit," Mark said. Then he didn't have time for more words as he sent them the next location he'd been monitoring on the tactical map.

***

This wasn't a battle; it was a fucking slaughter.

The troopers finally got into position. With their weaponry and numbers, they were able to hold the Maraukians back, though that wasn't their task. If they just held here, then more Maraukians and their Sharventi leaders might show up. These bastards were smart; they were holding forces as high in the valley as possible so they could bring more weapons to bear on Nerva's forces. They were spread out and sending their Maraukians in different groups, testing the defenses. Where they found a weakness, they then had their Maraukians move in from other locations, only massing right before the weak point.

Mark had formed a quick reaction force and it had ballooned from a half section to a full section. The other was commanded by Dominguez as they tried to react to these weaknesses, stall the attacks, and push forward.

Nerva opened up a channel to Ortiz, who was on the front, and Mark. "Mark, if we want to make it to that projector, we're going to have to start pushing back. We can't just hold," Nerva said.

If it was someone else, Mark might have raised an argument. But he knew that Nerva could see everything that was happening on the ground. He also understood that Nerva *knew* what was happening on the ground; he had too much combat experience not to.

"What's the plan?" Ortiz asked.

"We carpet the area ahead with RSD fire and missiles. Vanguard lead—direct support from the tanks and troopers. Advance by platoon. If momentum stalls to the point where we might lose it, we're going to need to call down all of the artillery on top of the Maraukians, have the Vanguard move forward through it and the troopers remain behind, slowly advancing behind the curtain of raining metal, making sure that no Sharventi or Maraukians make it out alive."

"Was too calm here anyway," Mark said.

Ortiz snorted and then spat. "You're telling me."

***

RSDs shot overhead, so low that Quina felt the air pull on her as her suit cut off the noise coming from outside.

"Heads down!" Nerva barked.

They all dropped. Quina saw through underbrush as the Vanguard were still fighting, their buzz saw M20s laying waste to the trees and obstacles in their way as they cut down Maraukians with terrifying precision.

The RSDs let rip. Thirty thousand rounds per minute was a sure way to clear anything out of one's path. Quina's eyes went wide as she saw the RSD missile bays open and fire.

Waves of explosions ripped through the valley. Quina was pushed back by the forces of the faraway blasts.

She'd been told the plan by higher, but hearing it and then seeing the damn crazy bastards carry it out was another thing.

"Don't waste the cover! Move by regiment!" Ortiz yelled.

She started to move forward with a company.

"Move!" Quina yelled. Her regiment rose from their positions. The other Vanguard regiments were suppressing the Maraukians in their area. As they rushed forward using their anti-grav, the stunned and confused Maraukians were torn apart, coloring the plant life blue as Quina's regiment dropped to the ground again, lying in what cover they could find and the best position they'd been able to mark out as they continued firing.

"Moving!" Another regiment started its forward bound as well.

Quina had to grit her teeth when she looked ahead. Hell faced them.

She raised her rifle up as she saw a Sharventi's limbs flopping around. She steadied her aim and fired at it, blasting bits from its main body until it stopped moving.

Three Maraukians came out of the blasted to shit landscape. Quina flipped her weapon to auto, sending bursts through the Maraukians' faces.

Repulsors opened up at the sides.

"Covering!" The regiment commanders on either side said as one, their regiments laying down tracers into their frontage.

"Moving!" Quina yelled to her people and the other regiment commanders.

The regiment got up and ran forward.

"Take a double bound," Ortiz ordered. "We can't let this advantage get by. We're almost there."

Another RSD buzzed overhead, shooting through the dust ahead that was lit up with the silver light of the Vanguard leading the charge.

The RSD's cannons fired, clearing out more Maraukians.

Quina saw the dust move enough to see their objective.

Like an island in the middle of the mountain range, a tall hill jutted out from the ground with the valley curving around it on both sides. It looked as if it had been part of the mountain range but it had eroded with time, leaving just one section jutting up.

The top of the rise had been cleared off, now hosting Sharventi equipment and the projector that stood tall and proud, watching the oncoming forces.

Gorgon engines revved as they cruised out of their positions, rolling over the landscape and dominating it as their forward weapon systems spat out rounds.

Several high-velocity missiles that had to have been coordinated shot toward a nearby tank, overwhelming its defense systems.

The tank took several hits before its armor couldn't take anymore. A missile went off inside the tank, blowing hatches off and burning the tank from the inside.

Quina dropped down into cover. The flames burning inside the tank made her gut turn. She looked for targets moving in the clearing valley. They were neck-and-neck with the Vanguard, mutually supporting one another.

"Covering!" she yelled, her voice hoarse.

"Moving!" The two other regiments of the company pushed forward to meet them.

The Gorgons couldn't be taken out with one high-velocity missile, but a collection of them was enough to knock them out. The Sharventi seemed to be putting it into practice.

As they advanced, the Maraukians and Sharventi weren't stopping. They actually increased their pace so they could bring the enemy into contact.

The Maraukians' strength was in-close range combat; enough of them and they could overpower a Vanguard merger. Against regular humans, they were nearly unstoppable.

"All command, this is Ortiz. Support can be called in at the regiment level. If something is holding you down, pass coordinates and hammer it."

This kind of command wasn't simple. It took out the checks that one would make with a normal artillery strike. It also allowed the forces on the ground to react to incoming fire much faster—paint the target and serve them rounds.

The artillery was all rail-based, so they could adjust how strong it fired, allowing them to just barely skirt below where the projector could hit. That meant mostly mortars were being put into use, with the Gorgons providing the greatest amount of close-in support.

Gorgons were holding back in the middle of the trooper formations. Quina saw another wreck as she pushed forward.

"Fuck." Quina dropped to the ground, firing back at the Sharventi that was opening up on her. The Maraukians were just a few seconds later.

Quina was in a small crevasse that was only barely able to fit her body. She felt the pain of a round going in her calf that was still sticking out of the depression she was hiding in.

She couldn't do anything. If she looked up, she would be killed.

"Meija, Jin—bring those fuckers under fire. Get me a reading on their position." She needed to know exactly where they were to get artillery on them.

"Three hundred meters in a depression. Too close, Captain," Meija replied.

"Fuck." Quina fled her armor servos and super structure taking most of the weight as she grit her teeth with the broken bones in her leg grinding against one another. The Maraukians' attention turned as they shifted their fire on those in the regiment who were getting good hits in and claiming lives.

Quina picked where the Maraukians were and fired at them. They were in a natural trench of sorts, between two broken rock faces.

Suddenly, the air filled with silver rounds as Vanguard mergers charged forward. They had flanked through the small natural trench. Their rounds back lit the Maraukians; they didn't know what hit them as they fell under the fire of the M20s.

"Covering!" Dominguez yelled.

"Move it!" Quina tried to get up and run but she'd forgotten about her busted-up leg. It was injected with painkillers and nanites trying to repair her.

She fell down, feeling faint from the rush and blood loss.

"Captain?" Valez yelled out, seeing her go down.

"Got hit in the leg. Fuck." Quina was more pissed at the fact that with this kind of injury she'd be pushed to the back till they could regrow the lost section.

She thought about shooting a nearby Maraukian corpse but angrily hit her fist into the ground.

"Valez, you've got command, all right?" She said the words through gritted teeth, not for the pain, but for the feeling she was letting them down with being injured.

"I've got it, Quina. I'm moving medics to grab you and shift you to the rear."

"Good," Quina said. It showed that Valez was in control already. But still, that inner blame didn't go away, as if she wanted to transcend human abilities.

She couldn't blame the Maraukian. It had been her fault. She knew it was illogical, but it didn't stop her from thinking that way.

A medic slid down next to her, checking on her leg.

"Hey, Captain, going to give you a shot." The medic didn't wait for her to reply before slamming it into her injection port.

"Fucking bit of warning?" Quina said as the pain started to go away.

The medic laughed. "I've treated a few officers before. I know how you lot are. You're going to need time with a printer before you're back out here." The medic confirmed her fears as he moved her around and checked the wound. His supplies came out in a steady stream as he hooked her up to different things and chucked in some clotting agents directly on the wound for good measure.

Quina checked her tactical map. She could only watch as her people advanced.

***

Mark let out a yell as he cut through a Maraukian with the blade in his right hand. He turned, unleashing a burst on another Maraukian nearby. Their head exploded, painting Mark's armor. He was hit by the backhand of a Maraukian and he was thrown sideways.

With a cold smile, Mark pasted their head over their fellows.

He heard the artillery trying to make it to them but they were too close to the projector for plunging fire to work anymore. All of it came into the projector's range.

Mark fired with his left; he kicked a nearby Maraukian. As they stumbled and waved their arms, Mark slid across, using his anti-grav. His sword cut them in two.

A burst went right past his face. He didn't even flinch as another Maraukian dropped. Mark took off an arm and punched another with his M20, putting a hole through their chest.

He fired inside them. The Maraukian that was scratching at his armor turned lifeless. Mark ripped the M20 from their cooling corpse.

He felt his blood boiling, the rage that was building—all of the mergers did. All of their armor was undergoing a change as they started to grow blades on their armor. No longer looking like the simple armor of before, it seemed almost demonic.

They'd left rational thought behind. When shit hit the fan, people stepped up. Their training was there to give them that strength, to know what they needed to do.

Through their training, they had lived and died hundreds of times, becoming killing machines that lived on the battlefield. Some hadn't been able to contain their want for battle and couldn't become mergers. But if they could, and knew when to release it, that made them all the deadlier.

Mark let out a yell. It was raw, fueled by the pain of losses, the anger and frustration of his people, their fear. It turned into white-hot anger.

Anger that drove him faster as he threw his sword, piercing through a Maraukian and nailing a bobblehead to a tree.

His movements blurred as his weapons snapped out. Maraukians were barely outside of the barrels, the Vanguard lines a mess of chaos with intersecting Maraukians.

Something seemed to come from within the depths of the Vanguard, as if they were becoming devils themselves as their armor changed, no longer defensive but a weapon in its own right.

Mark and Ava connected directly, their thoughts as one. The others merged, moving past the rudimentary merge. They weren't people anymore; they were fucking mergers. One organism, one creed: advance.

The Vanguard yelled as one and moved forward. It was chaos but in it, the mergers' actions were cold and calculated, their every action bringing down more Maraukians. They left none behind as they rushed forward.

Even from across the battlefield, they defended one another and assisted.

Mark reloaded on the fly and dodged to the side as a Maraukian cut at him with a blade, bringing him to face a Sharventi.

The pack on his back opened. The Sharventi didn't have time to pull its trigger before the lightning missile shot through its body.

It dropped to the ground with the useless missile as Mark's arm swung upward, hitting the Maraukian that had attacked him in the chin. He pulled the trigger, leaving a line of gore from their abdomen through their face.

Mark used anti-grav to reverse his movement as Dominguez came in, swinging her two hammers. Her momentum was incredible as she took off two Maraukians' faces, crippled another's legs, and drove another into the chest of another. Maraukians were simply tossed back by her force.

Mark moved behind Dominguez and he pushed forward. Mark's M20s moved erratically, firing out small bursts. He and Sarah linked to all of the mergers and one another. Targeting solutions appeared in their minds.

Faulkner and Lindskoy, who had made up his ad-hoc quick reaction force, were cut down by a missile.

Mergers rushed to them, but the two knew they were done for.

Mark read their thoughts before they did anything.

The two of them embedded a case within their armor and reloaded their weapons. Their biological system were already failing.

"Sorry we couldn't do more." Lindskoy's words cut through the anger like a knife as Mark felt his heart was wrenched out of his chest.

Lindskoy shot off, standing beside his brother-in-arms. Faulkner roared as they shot forward.

"Vanguard leads!" His call made Mark's eyes itch and his blood surge.

"Cover them!" Mark's order was hoarse and harsh. It came from a place that was raw.

Another Vanguard died, Xiarhos. His armor didn't pause, following his fellows.

Mark didn't yell, but his anger and emotions were laid bare. All of them felt the emotions, the raging rapids that tore at their hearts and minds of what-ifs.

***

Ortiz worked the mounted M20's actions. The platoon had a few of the modified large weapon pieces supplied and made by the mergers.

He might be a general but he hadn't gotten there by pushing papers. He was up in a weapons detachment platoon that was raining hell down on the Maraukians that were coming from the two valleys that the projector mound intersected.

His NIAI tagged three and then four sets of merger armor shooting through the skies of the valley.

"General!" Trina, who had become his second-in-command, started.

Ortiz checked what she was seeing. His blood went cold. The Vanguard dead once again rose up and shot forward to battle.

They flew just feet above the ground, creating a topless pyramid. They entered the battlefield, skimming above it as they sprayed over the Maraukians and Sharventi. A few sets of armor were so badly damaged they fell from the skies, plowing into the ground. The headless triangle split. There were now three forces: the original that was headed right up the cliff and two more that were headed around the base, right over the Maraukians and Sharventi.

Ortiz gritted his teeth and worked his gun. "Get focused! We only have one shot at this!" Ortiz said to the leadership.

The Vanguard and the merger units only seemed to become more chaotic, taking more risks, but their every action was deadlier.

The seven tanks commanded by mergers exploded with weapons fire, raining down death upon the front lines.

Shrapnel poured down among the Vanguard that could be barely seen as they directly fought the Maraukians.

Something that no human was able to do, they did with ease, tearing apart their enemies and slaughtering the Sharventi.

Then the world seemed to stop as brilliant light appeared around the base and then above it.

The fallen had ignited their cores. The destruction was incredible as it tore at the natural formation of the mountain range, altering it completely.

"Brace!" Nerva's word was barely finished when Ortiz seemed to be punched in the chest by the bomb. He barely stayed in a sitting position. The destruction was hard to believe.

He looked to the Vanguard. As they started to rise out from the debris, he noticed the clouds around them. "What the hell?"

"*It* is *a cloud of nanites.*" Ortiz's NIAI paused, collecting information.

He was about to ask what it did when he saw a Vanguard fire their M20. The round punched into the Maraukian, but it wasn't dead. It took a step before collapsing; its body turned gray and silver before it fell over, nanites corroding it from the inside.

The Vanguard fired across their front. Nanites and part of the rounds exploded and started to cover everything, destroying Maraukians and Sharventi, growing and then moving forward. It created a terrible gray tide.

Mark connected to Nerva and Ortiz. But it wasn't his voice; it was hundreds of voices collected together: "We control the nanites. We will not be able to support them for long as they do not have much power. We must take the base now. Artillery is free."

A chill ran down Ortiz's spine. He hadn't noticed that the projector was gone; too much had happened in just the last few minutes. "Troopers, with me!" Ortiz got up, grabbing his rifle, and ran for the objective.

"Set targets. Artillery, open up!" Nerva yelled.

Ortiz looked over. He saw that Nerva was also running toward the objective, leading a force of troopers he had held in reserve. They were fresh and ready for a fight while Ortiz's people were still trying to organize.

"You go first, we'll follow in once we're straightened out," Ortiz said. Once they had the base, then they needed to just hold tight and hope that their plan worked.

***

Nerva ran with his people. The Vanguard moved forward; in front of them, there was nothing but death. Their coordination had reached a level where they thought and reacted as one entity with multiple independent bodies.

The Maraukians and Sharventi that had been blasted back were nothing in front of them as artillery now came in from the heavens as the projector was destroyed.

Other projectors that were able to see the rounds took those out they could, needing the artillery to adjust. Still, most of their fire was making it onto target.

The Vanguard led the charge forward and up the cliff, firing nearly straight up at the Maraukians above.

"First company, take that pass. Second company, move for that road," Nerva said, marking out different trails and passages that seemed to go to the top.

The Vanguard didn't care for terrain as they flew upward.

Nerva moved quickly up a pass. He reached the top to destruction.

The mergers moved in on the base atop the graded hilltop. They moved across the ground, cutting the Maraukians that lay in wait.

The massive projector was in parts, its silver body now just debris.

The buildings that jutted out of the ground had been ripped apart.

The vegetation was burnt away and the rocks cracked. This was the force of two Vanguards igniting their anti-matter cores.

The other two's armor was damaged, to the point of no return, but their anti-matter cores were still secure.

The mergers advanced on the remains of the compound, killing the Maraukians and Sharventi left.

That gray cloud shot down into the base; the mergers followed afterward.

Nerva gained updates as the nanites reported back what they had found in the base, mapping it out and killing anything that wasn't human inside.

Nerva felt as if he were too late and useless. "All right, I want an all-around defense. We're going to be stuck here, let's get stuck in. First Company, you have the nine till twelve; second, you've got twelve till three. I want watches out there right away and start getting digging. I want strong points and overlapping arcs of fire." Nerva switched to Thomas McDougall.

"I want a tank line in the valleys of either side. The Maraukians and Sharventi are gathering in the center and then flowing down into their valley. You're going to plug up the sides. I want to embed four troop transports' worth of troopers down there with you to beef up your lines," Nerva said.

"Appreciated. I'll see to it," McDougall said.

"Good. I'll be down there for the next bit and Ortiz will command the hill." Nerva wanted to switch out with Ortiz so the other got some rest, also knowing that he was the better gunner and would know how he wanted to place his different strong points and heavy machine guns to cover the valley.

"Ortiz, you're king of the hill. I want you to establish heavy weapons posts all over here. I'm going to give you six forces. I want to have two in reserve to act as a quick reaction force. I want the Vanguard to have a third of their force on the hill and then two-thirds down in the valley in case it comes to close quarters fighting," Nerva said.

"Sounds like a plan to me," Ortiz said after reviewing the situation on his tactical display himself.

Ortiz paused but Nerva could sense he had a question.

"They haven't come out of merge yet," Ortiz said.

"I know." Nerva didn't know what to say, seeing that nanite cloud that destroyed everything in its path and the way they had moved forward after seeing their fellows using their armor to push back the Maraukians and give them the chance they needed to advance and gain a foothold.

Nerva hadn't seen anything like it.

He heard as artillery started to come down overhead, landing on the Maraukians that had survived as the Gorgon tanks that would be the backbone of the valley's defensive line started firing.

He didn't have time to think on it.

***

Mark and the others finally came out from their merge. Using that many nanites at one time was something they could only do when working together. It was a terrifying and exact power. It scared Mark a little bit at how good it felt to have that kind of power.

He didn't have time to think on that.

"Nerva." Mark opened the command channel.

"Mark."

He didn't miss the note of worry in Nerva's voice.

"We're okay. We found it, the ground wire. We're going to need more power, but we've got nanites moving through the hardline connections."

"How long do you guess?" Nerva asked.

"Your guess is as good as mine," Mark admitted. "We spent a lot of juice. We're going to need to get our hands on some more antimatter from the *Moby* before we're in fighting condition."

What Mark said was half-lie, half-truth. Being in someone else's thoughts for that long, being in so many other people's heads at the same time, it was so incredibly strange that he and his people needed time to recover.

The scariest thing was that with them all together, it didn't feel like there was just fifteen hundred Vanguard; it felt as if there were nearly two thousand. With all of their memories, the strange background noise of the net they shared was cleared up.

Their minds, which had merged with those who had fallen, recreated them.

They had fought only with the living, but the dead stepped up to protect their brothers and sisters.

That was a complex bunch of emotions and the Vanguard needed some time to get used to it.

He heard the weapons fire slowly dying down.

"What's going on?" Mark asked. Information started to flow into his mind but he didn't assimilate it, still feeling weirded out.

"The Sharventi pulled back the Maraukians." There was a note of confusion in Nerva's voice. "Never seen a retreating Maraukian. They're either gathering to try to hold the other locations, probably thinking we're going to attack them in series—"

"Or they're mustering their strength for an all-out attack." Mark spoke to the second thought on Nerva's mind.

"Yes," Nerva admitted, not holding anything back.

Chapter Fifty-Five

SLS Rampant

In Orbit Above Velia Prime

Helis System

8/3560

Late to the party, Legate Fidelis watched his screens carefully, absorbing all the information he could with his NIAI. He'd fought with his decision to join the mergers a lot and to follow Zedra out toward the enemy, but he'd always protected Roma and now he knew it had been the right decision.

That day, back in his basic awareness training, he'd met Kaeso, and together they formed a fast friendship. Learning and teaching each other the differences and the way of life, both back when he was first breathing to now the present that faced him. Fidelis was and knew he was a full-blooded killer. He saw the Maraukians as nothing but what needed to be destroyed, and with the technology he had behind him and at his disposal around his region, he had planted and created mayhem for them.

Now, though, he watched as they started to split. Their assault barges dropped to the planet and let loose on the stunning farmlands below them. Velia had always been a rich farming planet. The people there would never have expected this kind of attack, but they'd been ready. They had the best machines to create hell for any invading party and as soon as they knew that's where the Maraukians were coming, that was exactly what they did. Legate Fidelis had flanked the barge, making sure it didn't get any chance to spin off in another direction. They drove it on purpose to this planet and they intended to finish them there. They might not have been able to get through its defenses so well in space, but they would wear them down consistently if they landed.

Fidelis commed for Kaeso. "They've launched. We're counter striking now, but there will be a lot that make it through."

Kaeso's voice came back, sharp and determined. He'd given up the command of his ship to take the lead on the ground. Now his ship and captain would support them, alongside Fidelis's.

"I will be joining you as soon as they're down." He'd not been able to risk dropping with their ship so close and full of fighters and drop-ships. They'd have been picked off even easier. They'd had to wait before they launched a counter strike and were able to drop in where their fellow legionnaires were starting the fight of their lives.

Turning his attention for just a moment, Legate Fidelis watched as one of the other incoming barges erupted in a blast of light, only to darken just as quick.

Admiral Nessa's voice then came through the comms. "We're down to one barge. It's declining quick." She paused. "There's more coming in, though. We are going to head them off. Legate Fidelis, you're now backup for Legate Kaeso. Keep me informed on the progress planetside."

Fidelis replied with a quick acknowledgment and then watched as the battleship started its engines to leave their area of the Hellenic system.

"Once more into the breech," he said, remembering the old saying from Legate Nerva. Most of their ships' captains and fighters had trained and served with him. Fidelis hoped now that all their training and hard work over the years would pay off. It had to.

Chapter Fifty-Six

Drop-ship 428

Moon Base, Gl 829 System

8/3560

Bobbie sent back his confirmation on his newest payload.

He looked at the innocuous-looking containers that were stacked within the drop-ship's hold: magnetically, gravity, and good old-fashioned ratchet strapped to the floor.

"Fuck."

"Are we good to go?" Yu asked.

"If by good to go you mean, are you puckered up so tight that air might not even escape while riding an anti-matter bomb into war! Yes, I'm fine. Let me just get a cowboy hat, sit on top of the drop-ship and yell yee-fucking-haw, all the way through. I don't know—FUCKING lasers, particle thingies of shieldiness, anti-air coil guns! Oh!" Bobbie let out a laugh that wasn't a laugh. "Don't let me forget the fucking war zone filled with *millions* of Maraukians and Sharventi!"

"Hatch sealed?" Young asked, unfazed.

"Hatch sealed." Bobbie dropped into his seat and clamped himself in, staring at the anti-matter capsules and watching for the slightest movement.

Young connected to flight control.

Bobbie talked to them before she could say anything. "Can I get off this ride? I don't like it anymore; Mommy and Daddy are scaring me."

"Uh..." The controller seemed to be at a loss on what to say.

"This is drop-ship four-two-eight, looking for clearance to launch," Young asked.

"Great. Accelerated off a rail. What are we? The fat man tactical nuke launcher?" Bobbie muttered.

"Understood, drop-ship four-two-eight, codename Fat Man, you are cleared to launch."

"*Thank you,* Control," Yu said.

Bobbie couldn't see her but he could feel her glare. He brightened up a bit before the ship moved and he stared at the bombs.

"Why are you staring at them?" Yu asked.

"A watched pot never boils. Maybe watched anti-matter never decides to...you know—interact with nature and turn us into a flaming mushroom cloud!" Bobbie's eyes never left the payload once as he talked.

"I think we should just let him be," Young said.

"There's like four kilograms of anti-matter here. Sorry if I'm a little concerned!"

Yu paused as they were loaded onto the acceleration rail.

"He is kind of right, though," Yu said.

"Fuck off, Yu. *Not* helping!" Bobbie yelled from the rear of the hold.

Young let out a snicker as she started to play a song across the net. "*Allllll aboard! Ha ha ha ha ha.*"

"No, no, it's all going to be all right." Bobbie's eyes went round. "Don't you put those demons on me, Yu! This is not the *crazy train*!"

Yu let out a wild laugh as they shot out of the *Moby*.

"Nice anti-matter, calm anti-matter—she doesn't mean anything by it." Bobbie's voice was almost high pitched as he finished.

"Twenty minutes until we hit atmosphere." Yu sighed, not knowing what to do with his flight crew.

"Four kilos of anti-matter in the cargo hold, four kilos of anti-matter in the cargo hold. Take one out, pass it around; three crew all over the wall," Bobbie started singing.

Yu let out a suffering sigh. "I will mute you both!"

Chapter Fifty-Seven

Projector Stronghold

Moon Base, Gl 829 System

8/3560

All of the Vanguard were tired. Mark had them sleep in shifts. Those who were awake helped with using the nanite vats to create more supplies to reinforce their interconnected strong points. Two or three were watching over the nanites that were moving through the hard lines, first altering them so they could carry a charge to keep the nanites power, and then moving so they could reach out to the other projectors. Their speed wasn't fast but they pushed on constantly.

The base wasn't small, spread out over the mountain region, but the projector was hooked into three different hard lines.

"We've reached the first group of projectors," Ava reported to Mark.

"Nice," Mark said.

"We haven't made any moves to take down the facility and have already started advancing through their hard lines toward the other projectors they're linked to. We should have the system mapped out."

"The power source?" Mark asked. They had found a small anti-matter power cell buried underneath the projector's base. It was entombed in an unknown metal that was even stronger than carbon hendral. They'd checked the design and routed the power to be used for the nanites as the Vanguard waited for the anti-matter power cells to reach them from the *Moby*.

"It looks to be anti-matter again. All of them haven't expended that much energy through fighting off our attacks." Ava sounded frustrated. "Their tech is much higher than ours. I can't help think that something is wrong. We know that there is a home planet, but it almost feels like they're leading us."

"I know. It feels the same way to me, but we can't do anything but follow that signal and try to shut it down," Mark said.

"Yeah." The net went quiet before Ava's voice softened. "How are you? After the complete merge?"

Mark made to talk but paused.

The mergers knew it was possible for them to merge on the level that Mark and Ava had done, but they'd merged to just a level before that, a level where they were all directly linked to one another.

That processing power allowed them to directly take control of a massive nanite swarm that few, if any, people would be able to directly control. Their power had reached levels where it felt like the world was theirs to command as they lost their sense of self and became a part of the whole.

Mark would be lying if he said he wasn't thrilled by it, but also terrified at the thought of losing himself to the merge.

"Shaken up a bit, but good," Mark said. When Tyler and Alexis had died, it had torn at his mind and soul. With the losses, he would give anything to reach that level, but he knew that there was more outside of fighting and merging.

The last two years, he had an actual life for the first time. He had planned for war, but he had been able to go and see the sights; he'd walked around without military people all around him, strapped into armor and with a gun in his hands.

He fought for his brothers and sisters; he lived for those who didn't make it, and for the people in his life.

Even in all of this destruction, the universe was still beautiful.

Mark didn't voice his thoughts but Ava read them from his voice anyway.

"Good." Her voice lost its tension.

"I love you," Mark said, feeling corny as he said it.

"I love you too," Ava said.

"Good. Now get that backside into gear, Captain. We've got projectors to destroy and strong points to make!" Mark said in a commanding tone.

"You just want to watch me bending over when I work." Ava's voice was filled with mischief.

Mark coughed, but didn't deny anything. "I have to go and check on the progress of the strong points," Mark said in a commanding voice.

"Mhmm," Ava said, clearly not missing the subtleties in their conversation.

Mark saw Ortiz as he entered the mess hall and opened his helmet. The hall had been hastily erected, with people coming through, grabbing warm chow and drinks, and getting some face time before they headed back out to their positions.

There were a few of the mess halls dotted around. Just a bit of conversation and food was enough to put anyone in a better mood and help to clear their mind a bit.

"Got to go," Mark said.

"I'll keep you updated." Ava cut the channel as Mark pulled off his helmet and waved to the table he was sitting at.

Ortiz nodded, grabbing a coffee, and headed over.

Mark looked over the mess hall. Even after their losses, the troopers and mergers here were laughing with one another, covering over the pain right below. They laughed, joked, and made fun of one another. In pockets, the losses came up and they would sink into silence and their all to recent memories.

Mark knew those thoughts, memories and second guesses only too well.

Why am I alive? They had so much to give to the world and they're gone. How did this happen? What if I ran a bit faster, or killed more Maraukians? Would we have been able to evacuate them faster?

These poisonous thoughts were right beneath the surface. Just taking a momentary lapse could let them out.

Instead of falling into these thoughts, they would fight even harder, as if to prove to themselves they had done their all and they wouldn't let anyone else die.

"Mark." Ortiz dropped into his seat opposite as he drank with a corner of his mouth, drinking his coffee even with a lip in.

"Ortiz." Mark nodded to him. Mark pulled out a cigar and put it in his mouth. Fire appeared on his finger as he lit it and let out a few puffs. "How are things looking for the troopers?"

"We took a lot of casualties in the push, but now we've got a clear stronghold with trenches and the rest. We can spread out our people, create depth, and bleed the fuckers as they come in. Sure, we aren't attacking, but we hold the high ground. We've got artillery support, albeit limited—I hear you'll be changing that soon enough." Ortiz raised an eyebrow to Mark.

"We've got nanites in the first couple of projectors that are close by. We're already advancing outward and have more nanites creating a network to the other projectors. Once they start going down, then the Sharventi are going to know."

"Makes sense to me. If my power sources started turning into payloads, I'd be a little upset too. Like that reactor all over again." Ortiz sipped from his coffee as Mark coughed on his cigar.

"One fucking time!" Mark sighed.

Ortiz grinned with his fat lip. "Back to the troop deployment." Ortiz's eyes caught Nerva as he walked into the mess and walked straight over to them.

"Gents." Nerva slotted into a seat next to them and pulled out a cigar himself.

Ortiz spat into an extra cup he had brought with him.

"Nasty fuck," Mark said.

Ortiz grinned and the other two laughed. They'd all been through countless battles together. There was a comfort by just being around one another as they knew they could rely on one another for anything and everything.

"What were you two talking about before I got over here?" Nerva asked.

"Troop deployment and battle plan," Ortiz said.

Mark projected a hologram on the table that showed their hill and the valleys that ran into it.

"We've got heavy weapons, mounted repulsors, and M20s up in overwatch positions on either side of the valley and on top of the stronghold. We've got a series of interlinking trenches across the top of the stronghold, giving them good fields of fire down onto the valley approaches. Crisscrossed lines run from the top of the valley, through it, and to the sides of the hill, where heavy weapons had been deployed to face the slope that gave anyone coming in from the valleys a clear path to the top.

"We've sowed anti-creature charges across the battlefield and dialed in the artillery so we know where we're going to hit. Fields of fire have been ranged and checked out. We should be able to hit them from three kilometers out before we start having a severe degradation in accuracy and the surrounding projectors start taking out our rounds.

"Gorgons create the center of our lines in the valleys, their hull down, and have fallback positions. Scouts are out and putting down sensors and setting up positions to shoot and scoot from. It looks like the Sharventi know everything that happens in these hills, so it will be their objective to hit the Maraukian herd commanders and Sharventi to create chaos among their ranks. Taking out the leaders should make them harder to control and if they start charging, then the Maraukians and Sharventi in the rear will just be hitting their own.

"We've got three lines to pull back: defensive lines green, yellow, and red. If we're pushed back to defensive line red, we have pre-targeted the two valleys for orbital bombardment, code named Black Skies. RSDs and drop-ships will be on station to support. We've created ammunition caches across the different lines and we're digging in weapon systems so when pulling back we'll only need to get behind a weapon system, flip off the safety and fire. We don't have time to fuck about," Ortiz finished.

"RSDs are limited but the fleet is working to make as many replacements as fast as possible. Trooper company commanders will be able to call down anti-matter rounds with fire control confirmation. Vanguard platoon commanders can call for anti-matter fire without prior confirmation," Nerva said.

Mark and Ortiz both nodded.

"Intel has it that the Sharventi are gathering all of their surrounding forces and it looks like they're bringing in some kind of artillery," Nerva said. The hologram zoomed up as Nerva linked information to Mark. Troop displacements started to appear.

"We've got roughly three million massing in Valley Alpha, codenamed Death Pass and four million in Valley Bravo, code named Shit's Creek," Nerva said with a straight face.

"Who came up with those names?" Ortiz almost sounded pleased.

"I did," Nerva deadpanned and puffed on his cigar.

"There *is* a sense of humor in there somewhere," Ortiz said with a shocked expression.

Mark laughed and the corner of Nerva's mouth lifted.

"Well, at least the troops won't forget it," Nerva said before continuing. "We've got air defense systems and the Gorgons will beef up our air security if they're bringing artillery to the field."

They fell into a silence as they racked their heads to think whether they had forgotten anything.

"Mark, I'm going to have your people dotted across the lines, with a regiment's worth broken down into platoons to be a quick reaction force," Nerva said.

"Phantom Lords on defensive, Devils as quick reaction force." He didn't want to put Ava in the line of fire, but this was the best break-up of his forces.

"As you said. I'll leave it to you to tell them," Nerva said.

"Just sent a message," Mark said, getting confirmation back. The Phantom Lords began to re-organize and the Devils moved to rear positions, where they could support the front line and react if needed.

"How are things back home?" Ortiz asked. He and Mark looked to Nerva.

Nerva had been updated on the situation but he'd held this information back from everyone else; he didn't want them to be distracted.

Nerva looked away. "You need to speak with Charles." He then looked directly at Mark.

Ortiz raised an eyebrow, but waited while Mark seemed to turn vacant, his thought and chat done at speeds they'd never comprehend. "Do you know what it is they're discussing?"

Nerva shrugged. "Merger stuff is all Charles would say, but that it was very important and he needed to know as soon as there was a real breather in the war."

Ortiz watched them both for a few moments and then asked, "What do you know that Charles will be telling him?"

Nerva met his eyes and he saw pain there. "They're losing."

"Emarl?"

"Both. They made landfall on Tricticus and Roma. They're also nailing other systems. Velia is the worst. They didn't just send in the usual numbers. It's almost ten times the amount."

"Good gods."

Nerva nodded slightly. "Velia is a farming planet on the outskirts of the Helis system."

"What are their chances?"

"They're fighting. They won't let up, just like we won't. But it's not looking good."

"Fuck." Mark returned to them. "Fuck," was all he said again, popping his cigar into his mouth once more.

The three of them shared the silence, the heavy weight of war this time not letting go.

***

"Scouts report that the enemy has reached engagement range," Nerva said. His words woke Ortiz. Both of them were on the line: Nerva was watching Death Pass while Ortiz got Shit's Creek.

Ortiz's armor pumped some chemicals to clear away his forgotten rest. He checked his rifle and stood up from the chair he had gone to sleep in.

Night had descended on the moon as the planet they orbited hung in the sky.

He heard the faraway noise of the artillery as it started to lay fire down along the Maraukian and Sharventi's advance.

"Understood." Ortiz moved to the command table in his bunker, which had been dug out of the ground and formed with cermite. After a quick scan of the map, he moved out of the bunker.

"Won't be long now," he replied to Nerva.

"Nope. Good luck, brother," Nerva said with rare emotion.

"You too. See you on the other side."

The channel went dead. "Amen," Ortiz said.

Across the lines, people were being pulled back from sleep or their chow time or finished up their work on defenses. They just had to hold for a bit longer.

He looked in at the reports on the nanites that were spreading to the other projectors.

So far, they had nanites ready in sixteen different facilities, with each one being connected to three more to make sure they stayed operational. The process was faster with each projector base they reached, with one stream of nanites splitting into two. It looked like a virus as it spread like wildfire.

Thirty-eight more were being invaded and seventy-three had nanites traveling to them. Still, they held off. There were nearly three hundred projectors all over the mountain range, not including the dozens that were all over the main base.

With the anti-matter power sources shipped down from the *Moby*, the Vanguard were once again at full power and they were able to force more power into the nanites, increasing the speed they advanced.

The artillery fire started to descend as rounds landed among the Maraukians.

Ortiz checked on the sniper teams that fired on the Sharventi and Maraukians.

They were quickly located and fired on if they stayed after their shot. The scout snipers learned fast, making their shots count and running.

There were Vanguard mixed up there with them. They'd fire on the move, drawing fire and causing them to go to ground, and escape the enemy guns before they'd reappear and fire again.

The Maraukians were spaced out in blocks shaped into a rough triangle with one point facing their advance. This didn't allow them to bring more firepower to bear, but it meant that machine guns would have to traverse more to catch their targets as they weren't grouped together.

Fuckers.

Ortiz grabbed a pouch from inside his helmet's lining and spat into his spittoon.

His positions were set and his people were ready. They could hear the rumble of fire, the flash of explosions and tracers in the air as fire tore at the hidden positions in the hills.

Just over a million troopers, tankers, artillery gunners, and members of the Vanguard waited in their positions.

"Fire on targets of opportunity. We have the ammunition to spare." Nerva's voice was calm and controlled, easing people's minds. "Remember your training—you're ready for this. Listen to your instincts and your chain of command."

Nerva's words might seem unnecessary, but they focused everyone's minds, made them grip their weapons tighter as a dangerous glint appeared in their eyes.

Ortiz felt his years. He saw the battlefields of the past: forests, jungles, moons, planets, ships. He took in a breath, feeling the hit of nic in the bloodstream as his head seemed to calm down and he felt his blood boil.

"Targets," Mark said on the channel just a few minutes later.

Artillery that had been pre-ranged started firing as the Maraukians made it into their kill boxes.

The Gorgons couldn't see their enemy but through the sensors as they fired, their whole massive body shaking. Death Pass and Shit's Creek was being blown to shit, but the Maraukians and Sharventi were making it through.

"Those aren't artillery weapons—they're close-in portable shield projectors," Nerva said, passing information to Mark and Ortiz.

"Shit," Mark said.

"As long as they have power, then they can clear the skies and bring up more of their forces. It's going to be hard to nearly impossible to kill the Maraukians until we destroy those projectors," Ortiz said.

"It looks like they're limited to defeating Gorgon and artillery rounds. They can't beat small arms fire, unless it's focused on them," Mark said after analyzing the information.

"They're creating a network from their rear to the front. It'll allow their forces to move to support unimpeded." Nerva dropped the bomb.

"Fuck." Ortiz gritted his teeth. Without fire support, this was not going to be an easy battle.

They were outnumbered some six to one, and their enemy showed they finally had some organization.

"I just talked to Charles. He says that while these projectors are a pain in the ass, they shouldn't be able to take a thousandth the damage of the fixed projectors. If we stay our hand on the anti-personnel mines, use them when the projectors are right underneath? Those things *have* to be powered by anti-matter—if we can even just destroy their coverings and the parts of the projector, I'll count it as a win. If we pierce the containment system or cause a back feed in power, ain't going to be pretty."

"I agree. It will also give our artillery and support an envelope to drop fire into. Our Gorgons, if they're facing the Maraukian formations, will still be able to hit them straight on," Nerva said.

"Fuck, I love firepower," Ortiz said as the heavy weapons that were held up in the sides of the valley started to fire down on the Maraukians, opening up their formations as they advanced.

As the heavy weapons opened up, the Maraukians dropped to the ground and started to charge, still remaining in their formations.

"Shit, they're coming in!" Ortiz moved to one of the machine gun nests along the line and slung his rifle over his back as he grabbed dual-mounted M20s. It had been fitted with a butterfly trigger on the rear.

Different sections of the defenses started to engage the enemy. The forces on the hill opened fire as well.

As the Maraukians charged, they covered the ground in blue blood as formations disappeared under Gorgon fire. Weapons fire swept their front, cutting down Maraukians—shredding them, more like.

Repulsors and M20s let out streams of tracers with long bursts.

They were closing the distance quickly. They exited the two separate valleys and joined up with one another, their momentum only slowing; it wasn't stopped.

They could suck up the deaths as thousands were killed.

Artillery fire still tried to pound the Maraukians but they were still dragging those portable shield generators.

Ortiz checked on his feeds as he heard rounds coming overhead. He let out a wordless yell at the universe, his defiance of what was happening in front of him and his powerlessness to stop it.

The Maraukian formations were working together; some of them stood up and pulled out their weapons. They started to give those that were charging forward covering fire. They started using fire and movement, rushing forward, then jumping up and firing.

Ortiz dropped down as he saw a group rising up. "Get down!"

The others in the nest dropped, but one wasn't fast enough. The wave of fire ran over them, directed by a Sharventi. She must've been hit three or four times; her helmet began to deform.

The weapons fire died down. The others in the section looked at their fellow trooper with a wide range of emotions.

"On your guns, troopers!" Ortiz yelled, calling over an ammunition monkey. Their second purpose was to cart wounded and dead back or reinforce the trenches if the losses got too heavy.

Chapter Fifty-Eight

The Core

Sharventi Home System

8/3560

Operator Four was with the other operators as they looked at a screen of information.

"Using tactics of covering fire, our Maraukians are advancing at a hasty speed. Our Sharventi people have been using portable shield generators to get rid of the issues of overhead fire. The first thing the humans did was remove our sensors. We don't know the full extent of their defenses. We believe that it will be a hard fight. We do not know at this time who will succeed. We will hold nothing back. Hopefully humanity has the strength required to defeat us. We don't want to assist them too blatantly, else the Black Guard understand our plan."

"The nanite cloud? No race has been capable of this before," Operator One said.

"That was unseen. As said previously, the merger subspecies creates a great variation in our prediction models," Operator Four said as images of war raging behind him colored the room. "We have begun calling the Black Guard on all frequencies, seeking their aid."

"There is a possibility of less than twenty percent that the humans will succeed, a five percent chance they will not only achieve victory, but have twenty percent of their forces left. With those numbers and according to our prediction of humans, they will look to recover their strength, call up reinforcements and then move forward to attack our home planet," Operator Seven said.

"With them being outside of the predictive models, these numbers relevance is small. If they succeed or only partially, they will call more forces and push forward. They can't not with the pressure now placed on their population centers," Operator Four said. "All of our prepared Maraukian forces are focused on pressuring the humans. If it doesn't succeed, then it will take forty more years for their forces to recover."

The other operators agreed with Four's reasoning. If the humans failed, then forty years was only a short period of time compared to the two millennia it took for humanity to reach this point from when the Sharventi had begun their plan.

"As you said in the last meeting, we will move according to the plan and not alter due to predictions with the limited success the models have had," Operator Eleven said.

The others in the room agreed as one voice spoke for them all.

They rose and departed from the room. The screens showed the losses on both sides, as predicted, as well as the live feeds.

None of them placed interest in these screens as they continued to carry out their tasks.

Chapter Fifty-Nine

Projector Stronghold, Green Line

Moon Base, Gl 829 System

8/3560

"Doi, Song! Your sections on me!" Ava yelled out. She had broken her people down into sections and seeded them across the rear of their forward lines, their purpose to bring back the wounded to be evacuated by drop-ship and provide immediate support where there were breaks in the line.

She rushed forward to where there was a mass-cas report. They had defensive measures in place that were made to deal with incoming artillery and the high-velocity missiles, though they couldn't stop them all.

One had struck a strong point that wasn't built up, taking out most of the section.

Her sergeant and his section followed right behind her, all of them skimming over the ground.

Ava raised her hands as targets appeared. The Vanguard spread out and fired on the approaching Maraukians. They were just a few hundred meters away, using covering fire. They were slower than regular Maraukians, but they had conserved more of their strength as they pushed the human forces into cover.

Ava dropped into the machine gun nest. There were four dead and three wounded; the rest of the section was trying to render aid or thrown into shock.

Even the most hardened veteran, seeing their buddies all killed in an instant, could tear their mind up something fierce.

"Doi, get me some support. Song, get the wounded ready to move." Ava contacted the platoon leader. "I need support in this area. Shuffle the remainder into a new section. They're all over the place. Their sergeant is critical and the master corporal dead," Ava said.

"Understood. Pulling up reserve from the company. I'll shuffle them into a new position," the lieutenant said.

Ava nodded to herself. Having them in the same place that their buddy had died was going to just play mind games with them.

"Ready to move," Song called out.

"Move, then! Doi, I'm with you. We've got reinforcements coming in. Till then, we plug the gap." Ava turned to the section survivors.

"We're going to do the best for your section mates. You're being moved to a new point. Report to your command post for orders," Ava said. It was easier for her to organize things but for the officers in the trooper companies, even with their NIAIs, it took time.

In the end, she just wanted to get them focused on something else and away from the scene.

"All right, let's get moving!" a corporal yelled, pulling his people together before getting them sorted out and heading for the command post.

Ava turned back to the line and started firing on the Maraukians.

A formation popped up and the section she was with came under fire.

A timed Gorgon round exploded in the formation, tearing the Maraukians and the ground apart.

A Vanguard went down, taking a round through their chest. They dropped to the ground and started to self-aid. Their heart had been taken out, but they had redundant systems that were making up for it. With enough time, they could get themselves back in the fight.

Still, the fear, the realization, and shock all came as one, then flowed back into what he'd been taught: recover, prioritize, treat.

It was becoming harder and harder for them to call in fire from the artillery as they were restricted to danger close fire already.

The RSDs had tried a few passes. Their armor was severely stripped away if they got close to the projectors and their missiles were torn apart.

Now flights had their anti-matter missiles removed and were coming in low and at speed so they were in the projectors' range for less time as they strafed the ground with their cannons, leaving spurts of dirt in the air where their rounds struck.

Ava was surprised as Kela updated her on the RSDs and drop-ships that were massing and all of the artillery that was changing its aim.

"Cover! Cover! Cover!" Nerva yelled out.

Everyone across the line ducked, Ava saw through the sensors in the valley.

Rows of charges went off in series, tearing the Maraukians apart and causing the projectors to be dropped.

The RSDs and drop-ships rushed forward, not willing to miss this opportunity. Anti-matter missiles and regular missiles covered the skies, reaching out to the new front of the Maraukians that had been pushed back outside the mined areas.

Projectors that were functioning fought back. They couldn't get them all as the buzz of drop-ships and RSDs' glorious cannons filled the skies.

"Reload. Check your people. They'll be coming right in afterward!" Nerva yelled out.

Ava tossed out her half-used ammunition block and slapped in new ones. She had plenty of ammunition and there were more caches to visit.

The RSD and drop-ships' cannons were focused on the portable projectors that were moving with the enemy force.

The projectors were powerful, but there were millions of rounds in the air. Dozens were knocked out, one after another. The Maraukians shifted their fire onto the ships above. RSDs spiraled, slamming into the ground or the sides of the valley.

The drop-ships were bigger targets. Even with their speed, they couldn't avoid being hit. Their defense systems were pushed to the max but they were still torn apart. The wreckage buried itself in the ground.

"Concentrate your fire!" Nerva yelled. His gun was the first firing as the rest of the line got out of cover and fired on the Maraukians, who had been thrown into chaos.

A shield projector's power core went off, clearing out a section of Death Pass and knocking out three other projectors. Their cores weren't simple and they weren't easy to penetrate.

"*Half of the projector installations have been compromised,*" Kela reported to Ava.

She didn't have time to look into it any further; targets appeared in her eyes. She could barely see them as she fired bursts at them, altering her aim.

With the weight of firepower coming down on the Maraukians, even if they tried to find out who had killed their leaders, it was impossible.

In the Vanguard net, there was only one command: *Kill the Sharventi and herd commanders.*

The herd commanders' deaths and the Sharventi's numbers dropping led to more of the Maraukian regulars starting to go wild and returning to their chaotic instincts. They charged forward, no longer looking to move and cover one another.

The RSDs and drop-ships cleared the valleys and quickly exited the battle space.

Artillery and mortars continued to come down, with anti-matter rounds being mixed in.

They weren't holding anything back.

"*Kela, how much longer do we need to hold for?*" Ava asked.

"Three hours and forty minutes, estimated."

Chapter Sixty

Command Center

Tricticus, Emarl

8/3560

Watching the horde of Maraukians spill forth toward the Skill School had Hael's heart sink. It seemed nothing would stop them. There was a knock at the door but then his wife entered without waiting. She moved to his side and looked out at the mass war zone within their city's grounds.

"Evacuate the rest of the school," Hael said. "If they reach the inner circle, it's over anyway."

"We're coordinating with the others in the new council. A temporary base is being set up less than a mile from here."

"Good. We'll pull back, regroup them here and hold." He glanced at her and saw the worry. "Like nothing we ever expected, are they?"

She lowered her head. "No. Fighting other humans was hard. As an opponent, they were smart, deadly. These *things* aren't smart but fuck they're relentless. Vastly outweighing us in numbers."

"They do." Hael ignored her swearing. He took a different tone. "Thia, it might look bad out there, but we were ready for them."

Hael's eye turned back to the city's fortifications, the lines upon lines of legionnaires and people from Earth. The legionnaires were a fighting force to be reckoned with. Most of them trained for fighting these monsters; some were retired but had volunteered to help protect human cities that weren't trained.

In among these people were the mergers and even those who had not made the merge yet, the best fighters he had seen.

The battle lines surrounding the city were easily defined, but here he had the best view and could watch as the Maraukians shifted in their horde. This was a pattern that meant the testing on their walls and people were easily predicted; couple that with many years of tactical training, and they moved alongside the Maraukians like a mountain river would follow the flow to the seas.

Damus's voice penetrated his mind once more. "Evac called," he said. "All personnel leaving the school now."

Hael saw something then from his position and he moved closer to the window. Placing a hand on it, with his NIAI he focused and zoomed in. With a quick thought, he linked Legate Desialias and Dodger in. It was obvious Dodger was in the thick of fighting.

"Maraukians breached a small section southwest of your position. They are flooding in and flanking around. Move your men at point eighty-one back to meet sixty-four's and we'll bombard them with RSD anti-matter strikes."

It didn't take more than a moment for Dodger to assess his own situation and then come back. "Yes, sir."

Hael could only hope that this would stop them. Losing the school would be a huge loss to them after only just building it all up.

Chapter Sixty-One

Projector Stronghold

Moon Base

Gl 829 System

8/3560

Nerva's situation wasn't getting any better. As the Maraukians advanced, they were bringing their shield projectors that effectively covered them from plunging artillery and mortar fire. He only had the Gorgon tanks, as well as small arms fire, to bring down the Maraukians and the Sharventi, who seemed to live next to the shield projectors, keeping control of the battlefield.

After the mine sweeping exercise that had taken out a number of the Maraukians, they had pulled back out of range and readied their lines again instead of moving forward in chaos.

He had watched with cold eyes. Seeing this kind of organization and command made him think of the worst.

They'd advanced, once again in formation, and lit up the green line that had been reinforced, with the dead and wounded cleared away and sections swapped out here and there.

The Maraukians started with firing and moving. It was slower but more of their forces were making within range to the trenches.

Nerva stood up again, grabbed the repulsor he was manning and fired back at the Maraukians as the group that had kept his area of the line suppressed was now being covered by others.

Nerva's tracers cut through the Maraukians and pinged off in wild directions. They were being pushed and heavily so.

They could hold out for some time, but then the Maraukians and the Sharventi would be in melee range. The Maraukians excelled at hand-to-hand combat against regular human forces.

"All forces, begin moving back to yellow line," Nerva said. They needed to bleed the Maraukians. This was not the line where they had to put all of their strength down and hold the Maraukians back no matter what. They had the depth and the traps; it was better to bleed than hold onto dead ground.

The Gorgon tanks revved their engines as their tracks dug through the dirt and pushed themselves out of the ditches they'd put their tanks hull down in.

Sections started bleeding off from the front line, heading back through the crisscrossed trenches.

Most of the Vanguard moved up to the line. They were the fastest and they could fight the Maraukians hand-to-hand. The Phantoms were split: half of them pushing back to the second line, the other half reinforcing and ready to assist as needed.

Quickly the lines started to come apart as the Maraukians gained more ground.

It was a coordinated retreat and all of their forces were quickly falling back. The yellow line started firing from their overwatch positions to aid the green line. The different sections got into their new positions and readied themselves for the last of the green line forces moving out.

The Gorgons got into their new hull down positions as the last of the troopers flowed out of the trenches.

"Mark!" Nerva said. Staying behind, he would be the last of each of these lines, making sure that all of his people pushed back.

"Vanguard, pull back!" Mark and the other members of the Vanguard used their anti-grav drives and shot into the cover of the trenches.

Nerva ran away from the front line. "Yellow line, green line is evacuated. Fire on targets of opportunity."

Artillery that had been dialed in to the trenches started to rain down from above as the Maraukians had made it past the protection of their supporting shield projectors.

Withering weapons fire now rained down on the Emarl force's old position.

Nerva checked his feeds again. There wasn't anyone left in green line. It was the cleanest retreat he had seen.

This is why we train till we drop.

Nerva was proud of his people. Under pressure, they kept their heads, pulled back and now they were in a new position of strength, ready to deal with the Maraukians once again.

***

"How are we looking?" Mark entered a briefing room with Dominguez, Evan, and Ava.

"Down seventy-three. Forty more are walking wounded and repairing. We've got access to two-fifths of the Sharventi's network at this time. In another twenty, we should have entered the complex at the center of the stronghold," Dominguez said.

Mark's eyes flashed to Ava.

"My people are on the line. I have a company ready as a quick reaction force but are deployed on the front line," Ava said.

"We're good on yellow line. It's tighter and more built up than green line. Not liking how the Maraukians seem to have tactics." Evan shook his head slightly side to side as his helmet allowed.

"None of us are," Mark said. "No change in orders. We hold for as long as possible and then pull back to red line. Get comfortable and be ready to react and move. Once we're back on the red line, we don't have any farther to move."

Chapter Sixty-Two

Base Four Bravo

Moon Base, Gl 829 System

8/3560

Commander Four Bravo reviewed the commands and orders he had spent his entire life memorizing.

Still, he took one more time to look over them before looking at the situation on the ground again.

Operator Four connected to Commander Four Bravo.

"The human forces have been pushed back to their secondary line of defenses. They have not showed signs of moving to attack the other projector positions or attacking the main installation. We have been using formation tactics to improve the Maraukian combat capabilities as well as mobile shield projectors. They have been able to deal with most of these new elements but they are willing to give more ground before locked into a close-quarters fight. What are your orders?"

"Attack the humans. We cannot make it appear that we're holding our strength back. Use what tactics you have to destroy them. If this force is killed, then more humans will come—next time with a better plan than they have in the past," Operator Four said.

"Understood," Commander Four Bravo said as the channel closed.

They weren't just fighting this group of humans; they were fighting all of humanity. The humans had plenty of numbers. If their ships weren't destroyed, then they could pull back into their own sphere, gather more troops and then attack the weakened moon base once again.

The Four Bravo commander started to survey the battlefield: taking in the defenses, the situation on the ground, his resources, their abilities, and the different ways to use them.

"Have the herd controllers move the forces out from valleys seven to eight toward valley five at their greatest speed to reinforce the forces there. Have them build up their forces there and have the forces leading the current assault prepare to move into supporting positions."

His orders were carried out and sent out, the forces on the planet moving according to his orders.

Chapter Sixty-Three

ENS Moby

Moon Base Orbit, Gl 829 System

8/3560

"Sir, I'm picking up a lot of movement on the ground," Francis said.

"Main screen, and explain," Chen said.

The screen showed the mountain range and the different valleys. Three valleys were highlighted.

It zoomed in on one of the valleys as life-forms seemed to appear out of the side of a valley. The image increased in quality as the blur was resolved into Maraukians.

"It looks like in these three valleys, there are Maraukians moving out of their lairs. They're all moving generally toward our forces on the ground."

The bridge was quiet as people looked to Chen.

Do they know about the nanites that have infiltrated the different projector installations? Chen's face was filled with wrinkles as he frowned in thought.

"Forward to the people on the ground, as well as Admiral Hall. Keep giving me running updates on their movements and what they do," Chen said.

Liang and Francis worked to carry out his commands.

Chen privately contacted Maxine. "How are things going with production?"

"Well, we've got every merger who isn't being used for critical tasks making more parts for the RSDs. The supply freighters are working their hardest to secure, refine, and send materials to us. Across the fleet, everyone is trying to make more RSDs."

"Good. Wish that there was more we could do than just sitting here," Chen complained.

Maxine didn't say anything. Chen could feel her agreeing with him.

The rapid support drones were one of the few things that could support the people on the ground with the portable shield generators around.

The drones didn't have a pilot in them. They could move at speeds that made them hard to target, with armor that allowed them to stand up to the projector's particle barrage.

They had cannons they could sow destruction down on the Maraukians. It was a heavy price to pay with the RSDs only good for one or two passes, being stockpiled and ready behind the human lines to be used in an emergency.

"Let me know if there is anything else we can do," Chen said.

"We will. Don't worry, Chen. We might be stuck up here, but we're not out of this fight," Maxine comforted him.

"Thanks, Maxine."

"Anytime." Maxine closed the channel.

Chen's NIAI pushed tactical information into his eyes as he checked over the situation on the ground once again.

The forces that Francis had detected were moving right for the battlefield.

Chen pulled up the estimated time for them to make nanite entry to all of the projector bases.

An hour and seventeen minutes.

"*How long until the Maraukians reach their forward fighting line?*"

"*Forty-seven minutes,*" Chen's NIAI faithfully replied.

Chapter Sixty-Four

Gorgon Hell Raiser

Moon Base, Gl 829 System

8/3560

"Robert, you have command," McDougall said as the Gorgon rocked, another heavy round sent screaming out on its path as the canister shell split apart, cutting down Maraukians.

He closed his eyes and seemed to enter a meeting room projected into his mind by his NIAI.

"All right, it looks like the Maraukians are massing their forces," Nerva said. Information was passed to the different leadership members.

"They're coming in from three other valleys. Instead of joining the line of battle, they're organizing themselves and spreading out. I don't like it. I want to have our people ready to fall back to the red line. We only need to hold out for another twenty minutes and then we can take out all of the projectors and bring down the weight of the fleet's fire onto the Maraukians at our front. When pulling back to the red line, it will give us greater space between us and the Maraukians, allowing our artillery to bring down greater fire on top of them, soften them up before they meet our guns.

"McDougall, the Gorgons will be first. I want you laying down close-range mortars as you pull back. Mark, I want you to take forces up into the hills. Take out as many leaders as possible. If we can take them out, then we won't be fighting the organized groups of Maraukians. Ortiz, I want you to move back to red line with the first troopers, establish command and control so we can all flow into it easily."

"The Maraukians are moving," Ava said.

The images in front of them changed.

"They're just charging straight forward," McDougall said.

"Mother fuckers! Ortiz, start moving your forces now! McDougall, you too!" Nerva used an all leadership channel. "Everyone prepare to fall back by platoon!"

"What's wrong?" Mark asked, just as confused as the others.

"Their front line has stopped. They're up and standing, suppressing our front line. The fresh forces are coming in but they're running on all of their limbs. They can run right under their buddy's fire without issue and get all the way to our line, which is fully suppressed," Nerva said, his mind picking up all the details in moments.

"Yu, get all RSDs and drop-ships ready to move. Mark, get your forces back!"

People disappeared from the room, including McDougall, feeling a sense of fear.

"All Gorgons, this is McDougall. Pull back! Fire mortar tubes all the way. We'll have ammunition at the red line!"

"Boss?" Robert asked.

"Do it!" McDougall yelled as units across yellow line started to move.

The troopers flooded out of their positions. Artillery started to rain down, barrages timed just seconds after one another so they didn't collide with one another as they came down from the skies.

McDougall knew that it wouldn't be enough.

The Hell Raiser's engines came to life. Across the line, the Maraukians' fire increased dramatically. Rounds pinged off defenses, cutting down those who put their heads up and striking the armor of the Gorgon tanks as they came out of their hull down positions.

Their forward weapons continuously fired out anti-missile systems and smoke that lit up their front, trying to confuse the Maraukians.

It made targeting harder for the missiles but the Sharventi had complete control over these Maraukians, with them firing straight forward with little stopping. As they needed to reload, they would take a knee; those behind them stepped forward with a full magazine, marching onward. The force of thousands shook the ground with their footsteps.

McDougall was looking at the overhead sensor imagery from the fleet.

There were gaps between the Maraukians, creating straight lines all the way to their rear.

Maraukians charged forward out of these, their speed already built up.

They pounded forward like greyhounds, unstoppable under the cover fire of their fellows.

"Run the guns!" McDougall yelled out to the Gorgons, allowing them to shoot faster than what they were supposed to for fear of barrel warp and temperature overload.

Chapter Sixty-Five

Stronghold

Moon Base, Gl 829 System

8/3560

Nerva could see it: they weren't going to get all of their forces back before the Maraukians reached them.

They wouldn't even get most of them back.

Mark didn't like his orders but he carried them out as he and a quarter of the Vanguard readied themselves to move back.

Ortiz was already establishing command at the red line, getting people sorted out as troopers flowed back as fast as possible.

It was going well, but the Maraukians were just too fast.

"Quina, Pullo—I need your forces to support the Vanguard until everyone is out." Nerva gritted his teeth. He knew what he was asking: that if the worst came, they would be the rearguard, facing the Maraukians directly.

"When did I get so lucky?" Pullo said in a dry voice.

"You two were legionnaires at one point. You've got most of the veterans with you; they know how to hold a position and bleed the Maraukians, even a Maraukian charge. Have them ready their swords and their shields. I feel that you're going to need them," Nerva said.

"Oh, how I love being more experienced," Quina said.

"We'll hold," Pullo said.

"Yes, we will," Nerva said.

"We? You mean you're staying behind?" Quina asked, shocked.

"Trust me, once Nerva has made up his mind, there isn't anything in this universe that can stop him," Pullo said.

"I don't know if that's a compliment or not," Nerva said.

"Just an observation. I've got to see to my people." Pullo cut off the channel.

Quina did the same as they started to deploy their people across the front of the line so they could cover it all.

Nerva moved to one of the closest groups, checking the mono-blade at his side and the shield on his back before his rifle.

The smoke was starting to clear as people moved to the rear.

Nerva jumped onto a repulsor, staying low so he wasn't caught in the overhead fire.

He fired over the top with the gun blindly. His NIAI linked to sensors; weapons started to fire, to stem the tide as artillery continued to come down.

The Maraukians' fire slowed and then stopped.

Nerva looked overtop. The charging Maraukians were now between the line and their supporting lines, who were marching forward behind them, bringing their shield projectors.

There was seemingly endless Maraukians stretched across the two valleys and the rise that led to the projector stronghold.

"Here they come." Nerva's voice was calm as he continued to work the repulsor, his rounds tearing his targets apart.

They were knocked back and cut down, but there were pockets here and there, rushing across craters or small defilades and were able to escape the weapons fire. They came over the ground, hell hounds with no sense of loss, only seeking death and destruction.

"Vanguard, ready yourselves!" Mark barked. The Maraukians were coming in too fast; they couldn't hold them off anymore.

"Mines live!" Nerva yelled.

The mines under the Maraukians went live. Explosions wrecked their front. Maraukians just disappeared and left openings in their charge.

"Shields!" Nerva's voice made something primal appear in the eyes of the remaining troopers. They grabbed their shields and drew their swords. Their sergeants and officers pulled them into formation as their shields snapped together. Some of them weren't fast enough as the Maraukians came over the top.

"Hold!" Nerva yelled, his shield supporting the top of the defensive position. The Maraukians were redirected by the shields and the trenches, but they were not stopped as they intermingled with those that were pulling back.

"Huh!" Sergeant Laurent called out.

"Ah!" The legionnaires-turned-troopers yelled as their swords shot out, cutting at the Maraukians.

"Huh!" Laurent called out. The gaps appeared in the shields once again and the swords slashed.

Laurent's arm was grabbed and pulled, the Maraukians tearing him out of formation.

"Plug the hole!" Nerva barked as the master corporal stood there, stunned.

"Huh!" Nerva's voice pulled them back together. They didn't have time to think on the loss of their sergeant.

"Step back prepare! Third rank rifles!" Nerva said.

They were plugging one of the trenches that ran back toward the red line with four across and three back.

Selina cried out from the third rank.

"They're behind us!" Master Corporal Yul yelled.

"Rear rank, clear our backs! Forward rank, be prepared to turn and run!" Nerva yelled, pulling grenade bandoliers from those around him.

A hand grabbed his. He looked up and saw Corporal Emmerson. She was a troubled woman, one who had been through the EMF, then the legion, and then finally found her home in the Emarl system.

"You'll need help there, General. Why don't I do this for you?" She pointed to his leg, which had a hole in it.

Nerva's NIAI told him how bad it was. "One isn't going to be enough," Nerva said. "I've lived long enough."

"You and me both." Emmerson laughed and hit his shoulder, shifting her twin repulsors around.

"Groeck, give the general your repulsor!" Emmerson turned and fired at the rear, clearing out the Maraukians there.

"Huh!"

"Ah!"

"Huh!"

"Ah!"

The shields moved backward and slashed out, killing Maraukians.

Nerva grabbed the repulsor, checked it was loaded and slung the ammunition crate over his shoulders, checking the feed lines weren't fouled or turned.

"Grenades!" Nerva yelled.

He saw they were ready.

"Huh!"

They moved their shields and tossed out grenades this time.

The grenades went off.

"Break and retreat!" Nerva barked. He and Emmerson were ready.

The shields fell apart as the troopers ran to the rear, firing and killing what was in their path or fell down into the trenches.

Nerva and Emmerson's repulsors fired. In the contained space, nothing was able to stand up to their firepower.

"Up top!" Nerva yelled. He jumped up; Emmerson took the left of the trench, him the right.

They fired from the hip; they didn't need to aim to hit Maraukians that were coming over the line.

Nerva threw out a couple of grenades into the trenches. Maraukian parts appeared with their explosions but he was already bringing others under fire.

They were taking the pressure off the surrounding groups.

The Maraukians were lost to the battle; their senses drew them to the two.

Nerva took a shot to the gut. He stumbled backward, almost falling.

Emmerson let out a yell, clearing Maraukians. Their bodies lit up from the rounds as they kept coming in close.

Nerva got back into the fight and fired.

Emmerson was shooting one second; the next, her helmet was deformed as she dropped to the ground.

Nerva knew she was gone.

"Rest easy, Emmerson," he said, even as he fired on the Maraukians.

He laughed to himself and a smile appeared on his face. Blood trickled down the corner of his mouth.

"My name is Kaeso Lucillios Nerva, Legate of the Ninth, major of the EMF and general of the Emarl forces. And I'd like to tell you, go fuck yourself!" The Maraukians raised their claws, coming in at him.

Nerva ripped off pull tabs on the grenades with one hand, unstably firing from the other hip.

Nerva laughed, tears in his eyes. He was going to see his brothers and sisters. "Hope you've got a beer for me—I've got one hell of a tale." He laughed. "Ortiz, you have command. Sorry I couldn't do more."

The grenades went off, their successive explosions taking out the surrounding Maraukians.

Fighting raged across the yellow line as people tried to break off their engagement and retreat.

More Maraukians just kept on coming, charging over where Nerva and Emmerson had made their stand.

Just two more people who had died for their people, for their friends. Their deeds remembered by those who were there and the later generations of fighters, but just another name on a wall or broadcast to the people back home.

Chapter Sixty-Six

Projector Stronghold

Moon Base, Gl 829 System

8/3560

"This is fucking it! Our lines have gone to shit and the troopers are being torn apart. If we don't hold the Maraukians back, they're just going to pour into our formations. We will be the one to break them apart! Vanguard, on me!"

Mark charged forward, the Vanguard rushed with him out of their positions, firing as they went, cutting down Maraukians and being cut down themselves.

Their hearts shook with rage and fear—fear for their brother, willing to go to the ends of the universe to protect their fellows.

They rushed through the troopers who were pulling back.

The Phantom Lords on the front line doubled their efforts as their armor changed.

Mark slammed into a Maraukian going for the killing blow on a trooper; his shoulder had a spike in it. Mark let out a yell, tearing the spikes out and tearing the Maraukian's body apart. His M20 didn't even deploy as he fired into the face of another Maraukian; his swords flashed as the Vanguard did what they did best: be the sharp end of the stick.

"All trooper forces, pull back! The faster you do, the sooner we can call in air support!" Ortiz yelled.

Mark saw where Nerva had fallen, watching their rear.

Nerva might seem aloof but he did all for his people. He didn't broadcast what he did or the sleepless nights he went through; that was just who he was.

Mark's head snapped to the side as a Maraukian hit him. Then a Sharventi shot his armor but it didn't penetrate. Mark charged off at an angle, his M20s flaring as he cut down Maraukians.

There was no line, just symbols intersecting one another. More troopers were making it through from yellow line to red line.

Mark came out of the fighting and looked around at the kaleidoscope of death: vibro-blades, mono-blades—weapons of every description were fired and used.

The Vanguard's actions were no less savage than the Maraukians.

All of them were faster than before when they had merged fully. Their abilities had increased dramatically and they were now wreathed in a gray cloud of nanites, their armor silver, revealing their true stature as they formed weapons directly on their armor.

Mark fired on three Maraukians, allowing Vanguard to charge forward. Their bodies were their weapons.

Another Maraukian barreled toward Mark. He was struck by the Maraukian, going tumbling as rounds flew over him.

The Maraukian's blood splattered all over him as he tossed the dead Maraukian to the side.

"No sleeping on the job, boss!" Dominguez helped him up. Through her hand, the nanite glob turned into a blade that pierced through a Maraukian's head.

"Using your own commander as bait? Looking for a pay raise?" Mark fired, taking out another.

Dominguez let out a huff as they faced the enemy together.

"Come on, you ugly fucks!" Dominguez and Mark charged forward, two of the three remaining members of the Triple-Twos.

Brother and sister in every way but blood.

Their actions in sync, their merge turned them into a deadly force.

Side by side, vibro-blades glanced off armor or pierced their armor as they landed a killing blow. Their armor and bodies took the pain as they moved on, never stopping, not pausing. Their M20s flashed as they kicked, head-butted, punched, stabbed, and beat their enemies into submission.

"Mark, blow the projectors! Take them out!" Ortiz yelled.

"We don't have them all yet!" Mark said.

"I don't give a fuck. This is a fucking order, Victor. Blow that shit and I can bring down fucking God and orbital's judgement!"

Sarah flashed him information as he threw his sword, piercing through a Maraukian. He replaced it with a vibro-blade on the ground.

They had reached five power cells in the central cluster of the main base. It would have to be enough.

"Blowing the power sources in thirty seconds!" Mark said across the all hands channel.

Chapter Sixty-Seven

ENS Homeland

Moon Base, Gl 829 System

8/3560

"Admiral, we have a priority. They're going to take out the projectors. Ortiz is calling a danger close bombardment!" Guy rushed out.

"Confirm firing solutions! Weapons free!" Hall yelled, letting weapons operate by themselves. He didn't want anything to slow down the support.

He had been watching the situation on the ground and it was not simple. The line was falling apart, with forces fighting hand-to-hand. There was no escape. The Vanguard had been able to take the pressure off the troopers but with the charge, there were too many of the bastards mustered altogether.

"Firing solution is coming together. ENS *Moby* is assisting. Gunners, hit those fucking targets." Celik's words cut through the ship.

Hall didn't say anything, leaning forward.

"Blast!" Rasalov said as the mountain started to shake viciously.

The man-made earthquake shook the entire continent. Parts of the mountain peaks crumbled and landslides came down. Regions sunk into the ground, revealing craters.

"Fire, you fucking bastards!" Celik barked. The entire fleet seemed to respond to his words: their broadsides opened up and rail cannon rounds punched through the atmosphere, leaving glowing streaks across the planet.

Hall's eyes snapped to the info on the ground. RSDs and dropships that were in support rushed forward, unleashing cannons and missiles across the open area. Destruction covered the Maraukian formations. Their portable projectors that were functioning fought against their incoming fire but they were spread thin with the charge as the RSDs and drop-ships rolled up the Maraukians that had made it to the front lines.

Chapter Sixty-Eight

Projector Stronghold

Moon Base, Gl 829 System

8/3560

The ground was chaos. Dust started to cover everything. The very ground was fighting them. The Vanguard used anti-grav to stay up above the ground so they wouldn't stumble.

"RSDs, orbital—it's all coming in. Move back under their support," Ortiz ordered.

"Vanguard! Move by teams. We're pulling back to red line. RSDs are coming in!" Mark yelled out. He saw Rachel go down, catching a round in the side. She dropped to the side, killing the fucker that got her as she fell. She fired from the ground, working to heal her side. The wound was too big; she needed external aid.

Mark felt Evan close in as he tore through the ranks.

"Drop!" Mark ordered. Everyone did so without hesitation. RSDs shot overhead. Their cannons opened up lines as they looked to overwhelm the projectors and hit them.

Drop-ships rose high and fired down on the Maraukian charge. Their cannons left trails of dead behind, sawing apart all that stood in their path.

The support was close but it wasn't right on the Vanguard. They still needed to break out of their own fight.

"Moving!" Dominguez yelled. "Miles, get Donark. Mark and I will cover!"

Mark and Dominguez bounded backward, dropping down and firing back.

LBMs! They hadn't used them with the projector being able to pick them all out of the sky. Now, with the chaos, the LBMs appeared once again.

Mark's back opened as he fired off lightning ballistic missiles, his full rack followed by others up and down the line. Even as they checked where the missiles would land, the NIAI took care of this as they focused on fighting.

Miles hooked Donark in. "What took you so long!"

"Was trying the slip and landslide! Moving!" He rushed backward, Rachel firing from his back.

"Go all the way," Mark ordered.

"Understood." Evan kept on moving, charging forward as fast as possible. Rachel might be joking but she was just covering up the pain.

The Vanguard disengaged as Mark cast a look over to Ava, who was pulling back with her people.

"Drop-ships, land!"

A few banked away and pushed their engines to the max, putting what distance they could between them and the mountain range. Others came down as fast as possible, taking just a few minutes to let crews get out of the ships and into whatever holes they could find as troopers ducked into their defenses.

"Go to ground! Orbital incoming!"

They dropped once again, firing on the Maraukians as arching lights appeared in the sky.

The hundreds of rail cannon rounds landed like God's hammer. A few had been destroyed on entry, others by remaining projectors. A few were wasted against the portable systems before they started failing, unable to defeat them as the rounds struck. The valleys were targeted, but the destruction reached out farther. It wasn't a wave, but a wall of force mixed with parts of the valleys that ran over the Vanguard, scraping a layer off the mountain region's surface, sending all kinds of equipment across the skies. Drop-ships were picked up like toys and sent flying.

***

Mark pushed the dirt and debris off himself as he stood and looked around, his M20s searching for Maraukians.

His eyes moved to see that Ava's marker was yellow but okay. Dominguez broke out of the ground as well.

The ground started to move more as people broke out and their friends helped them out from under the debris.

People had been tossed all over the place.

Dust covered the valley, as if they were in another world.

Maraukians started to make their way out of the ground as well.

Orbital strikes continued to rain down from above, these no longer directed at the projector stronghold, but moving through the other valleys, killing off the Maraukians and their commanders as they moved closer and closer to the projectors that had been left behind. A number of them were still operating, but some that hadn't even been destroyed in the attack were skewed and unable to properly function. The shield was a powerful creation, but it was a precise instrument; once it was skewed or altered in some way, then the whole shield system would start to fail.

Four-fifths had been destroyed. The main cluster that had been mounted directly over where the signal to the Maraukians was coming from had been destroyed with the anti-matter explosions being the worst there.

Mark fired on the Maraukians that were all beaten up and confused.

It wasn't a fight at all.

Mark's mind and body calmed. It looked as though they had somehow survived again.

"Those who are able to, create a new line and hold. Split up tasks. Half, hold position; the others, help those who are buried," Mark ordered the mergers and then linked to Ortiz.

"How are we looking for med-evac?"

"I've got some ships coming down from the fleet. Crews on the ground are checking what they have to see what's good to fly. I've got about seven or eight who escaped the worst of the orbital strike by powering away from it all. They're circling back around," Ortiz said.

"Understood. I've got one hundred and seventeen wounded needing attention on the *Moby*," Mark said, passing through the names that had been dimmed, another who wouldn't be making it home.

"I'm going to move some people up to you to assist and cover you back to red line," Ortiz said, his voice dull.

"*The signal has stopped coming from the moon base,*" Sarah reported to Mark.

"The signal has stopped," Mark said.

"Once we've got enough ships, we can get the fuck out of here," Ortiz said.

"Agreed." Mark looked at the recovery efforts as the first of the drop-ships that weren't too badly damaged started to power up behind the red line.

***

Ortiz squatted behind a storage crate in one of the portable messes, checking that no one was watching.

Silent tears ran down his cheeks. Memories started to flow back. They'd lost sixty-three thousand people on the yellow line. Too many faces, too many that he didn't know.

Those that he did know pulled at his very being.

He knew that with time it would get easier as the memories faded and it felt like it was a lifetime ago.

Though that wasn't what he wanted. He didn't want to forget them. If he forgot them, then it felt as if he were doing them wrong.

He couldn't explain his emotions. He couldn't forget the people that they were, or think how they might have changed the world if they lived.

In those minutes, he saw the brilliant futures that had laid ahead of them. But war, the Sharventi, had ripped that future away from them.

Ortiz cleaned himself up as he heard someone approaching. He cleared his throat and wiped his face.

"Ortiz." Mark dropped down to sit next to Ortiz.

"Mark." Ortiz let his command mask slip as he sat back down.

"Cigar?" Mark pulled out a pack.

"Yeah," Ortiz said. The two of them had made it, somehow.

Ortiz took a cigar and Mark lit it before lighting his own.

"Bah, don't know how Nerva liked these. Taste horrible." Ortiz chuckled, his eyes still wet.

Mark let out a soft snort and a small smile that dimmed all too soon. "He put us through the ringer a number of times with training."

"Yeah, but we came out better for it." Ortiz didn't know whether he would have survived this long without Nerva's training.

They talked about the people they had lost, different moments that brought them laughter and all the closer to crying.

It was hard to nearly impossible to cover up the tears.

Their people were being rapidly evacuated. There were few Maraukians or Sharventi left now. Ortiz didn't know where they were going next. None of them did.

Chapter Sixty-Nine

Command Center

The Yard, Emarl

8/3560

Jerome watched on as what was left of his space fleet pounded the Maraukian insertion barges. But they were getting too close, too often. This was beyond dangerous for them, and their ships were taking a battering. He was surprised that Emarl had any of their fleet left. The fighting was brutal, and seemingly unending.

Jerome called up Captain Grild. "Pull back to the Ark. Reload."

Grild's voice came back to him, thick with emotion. "If we pull back now, they'll *all* land."

He knew this. He also knew they were out of options. These creatures—no, monsters—were swarms more than they'd ever encountered, and it looked as though they were here to wipe out Emarl for good.

"Aaron," he said, his voice a lot calmer than he expected it to be. "There's nothing more you can do. You get any closer, they'll destroy you. Move to the Yard, reload, and get artillery supplies to the planet. They'll need more support there now. Your job in space is done."

Esamai entered the room and moved to his side. She watched with him as their fleet pulled back from engagement. Jerome could see in the dim light of the room how frail and tired she looked. None of them had slept properly since this all started; none of them had eaten well enough, or taken care of themselves. The worry for her pained him, but he turned to the screens. Life in Emarl was being extinguished.

"Tricticus?" She stood beside him and leaned her head on his shoulder.

"They'll hold." Jerome kissed her forehead, trying to ease her pain. Though he felt the same as she did. This loss of life so very difficult to bear.

Esamai took his hand in hers and squeezed it. "Hurry up, Mark," he heard her whisper.

They were his exact same thoughts.

Chapter Seventy

Medical Center

The Ark, Emarl

8/3560

Pela lay on the table while she was examined by a doctor. This was a little old-fashioned for her, but it seemed to make Lucus happier.

The doctor looked at him and finally announced, "Everything is fine."

Pela breathed out a sigh of relief. Their baby girl hadn't made much of a show for him, but he was in awe, watching her moving around inside Pela.

"You can stop gawping at her now." Pela laughed, finally tugging her shirt back down.

Lucus leaned over and kissed her. "I'm allowed to look at the two most beautiful things in the world right before me."

The doctor laughed a little and Pela punched him in the arm. "Stop it, or I'll not let you come next time."

Lucus's face fell, and Pela knew it was because they'd been separated. "Sorry," she said. "I didn't mean it."

"It's not looking good for Tricticus." He frowned.

Pela sat up. "What do you mean?"

The doctor moved away and left them. Lucus sat on the edge of a chair while she finished putting her clothes back on.

"Tell me," she said.

"They're being overwhelmed. They defeated a lot of the insertion barges in space, but several more came into the system. They're in huge numbers. They're struggling."

Pela burst into tears, and within a moment, Lucus was holding her. "Hey, hey, shhh..."

"I can't stand them. I can't stand the fact that the mergers are out there fighting with everything they have and we're sitting here doing nothing!"

Lucus brought her chin up so she had no choice but to look him in the eye. "We are doing something. We're making sure that humanity still survives, that there's another," he patted her stomach, "generation after us. That's what we have to do, keep moving forward. The mergers will be all right. They're the best fighters ever."

She couldn't help the tears, thinking of Rachel, such a vibrant woman, giving everything. But Lucus made sense. They were fighting so that they could live. She snuggled into his shoulder. "I want to call the baby Rachel, is that okay?"

"Anything you want, my love. Anything you want."

Chapter Seventy-One

ENS Moby

Gl 829 Inner System

9/3560

"It's confirmed." Liang looked to Francis and the engineering team.

The whole room seemed to drop.

The losses had been severe. Nearly three hundred thousand of their people had died. Another one hundred and seventy were walking wounded or still under the medics' care.

They hadn't even had the time to properly send off those who were lost.

"What do we do?" Maxine asked.

"We tell them." Charles looked to have aged ten days in as many seconds.

Charles got up from his chair, the movement and the chair returning to its position the only noise in the room. "I'll do it." He walked out of the room, feeling the weight of the information on his shoulders.

He passed people in the halls.

They nodded to one another but there were no smiles, no laughter. The losses had been too great for them to try to brush it off. All of them knew the people who had been lost and although it was a victory, it didn't feel like it.

Charles knew that the information he held wouldn't make it any better.

He finally reached his destination. He entered a big bay. People were moving around quietly, all of them Vanguard. They were playing games here and there, trying to look past the losses. It was hard and it would take time.

The bunks where the dead had stayed were empty. People kept on glancing over before being filled with emotion.

Their crates had been moved out.

When they returned to the Crucible, they, too, would be added to the ranks of the fallen.

The others greeted Charles with their eyes, some saying hello as he passed and made it to where Mark's office was. He knocked on the door.

"Come in," Mark said.

Charles opened the door and looked at Mark. For a second, he paused, seeing how similar Mark was to Nerva. Charles's gut twinged before he closed the door and took a breath.

"It must be bad to get you all the way down here," Mark said.

"There's a new signal. We've tracked it to the BD+00 4810 system. It looks like it's the Sharventi's home system," Charles said, in a rush, wanting to get the words out as fast as possible.

Mark's eyes darkened, an expression of pain on his face. He sat back in his seat, looking tired. "Thanks, Charles. I'll report to higher. You got anything else?" Mark sounded as if his spirit had left him but he pushed on with sheer willpower.

Charles sent him the information that he had.

"Thanks. I'll pass it out to the others," Mark said.

Charles nodded. He opened his mouth but he didn't know what to say. He closed his mouth and left the room, heading back to his workshop.

When he got there, he slumped into his seat.

People were working to make replacement parts or repair different items. They all looked tired. Not physically but emotionally, as if their soul had been dragged out of them.

He didn't have words or ways to say what he was feeling, as if it would cheapen those raw emotions and those attachments he had to so many people who hadn't made it back.

He didn't know how or when but at some point he just started crying. His shoulders shook with the frustration at being unable to help them, being unable to affect the fact they were dead. There was no going back; there was no stopping. They had to push on.

Chapter Seventy-Two

ENS Moby

Gl 829 Inner System

9/3560

Mark looked out at the mergers lined up in formation.

They were in the main flight deck to fit them all.

There were more people in the rafters and on the catwalks. Opposite them, there were crates lined up, standing and looking back in their own formation.

The Vanguard all wore their armor as Mark stepped forward to the podium and took off his helmet.

He looked out to the people in front of him and then looked to the crates. "Today, we are here to commemorate and say good-bye to our fellow mergers." Mark's voice carried through the flight deck as he looked out upon his Vanguard, the pilots, the tankers.

Their fallen each had their own way of being commemorated: The Vanguard their armor crate. The tankers, a round with its charged removed and their name on it with their tank's call sign. The pilots, an oversized flight helmet they had used in training and was the last flight helmet they had ever used, with their name carved into it.

They stood among one another, one formation facing outward.

"We come from all walks of life and we have reached here through different means. We do not know how we will go out of this life. When we started this journey, we didn't know the people who stand together with us on either side on this path. For some, their path has ended. We will continue on that path, but we will not forget one of those who stood with us."

Mark felt their eyes burning into his, the promise that lay there.

"No one can express what their loss means in words and no one should need to try." Mark coughed, clearing his voice as it became hoarse. "Here we leave our brothers and sisters to rest, but not forgotten."

Mark looked over to Dominguez. "Regimental Warrant Officer, roll call." Mark's voice was firm, but his stomach plummeted as those in the room stiffened.

"Private Rendeer!" Dominguez's voice carried through the room.

"Here, Regimental Warrant!" A Vanguard member came to attention.

"Private Henderson!"

"Here, Regimental Warrant!"

"Corporal Lindskoy!"

There was no noise as Mark clenched his teeth and felt water gather at the sides of his eyes.

"Corporal Steven Lindskoy!"

Again, there was nothing. He was with them, but his crate was empty.

"Corporal Chung!"

"Here, Regimental Warrant!" Another came to attention, their voice deep to stop their voice from breaking.

Dominguez snapped off names, the normal routine now turned grim in those periods of silence.

Mark stopped his tear ducts from working, as did the other mergers who weren't wearing armor. They still couldn't hide the way their faces moved and the emotions that were clear for anyone to see.

Some still weren't able to stop themselves as they held back their crying and allowed tears to fall. They didn't move to clean their faces. This parade wasn't for some general or officer showing off and being meaningless. This was their friends' parade and they would do them fucking proud. They would put on their greatest parade, suck it up and carry this out with dignity as their buddies deserved.

Mark stood there with Ava, Miles, Thomas McDougall, and Yu at his back.

Dominguez officiated as rows of people stepped up to the first line of crates, rounds, and helmets.

Vanguard opened their armor and people took a knee in front of their friends' markers.

There were a lot of mergers but they had all gotten to know one another in passing over the last three years.

The first group moved to the second row of markers as a new group moved up to the markers.

Mark could see the pain in their faces, could hear the murmurings as they talked to the markers, their promises, the recalling of some event they shared, or something they remembered from them. They touched the markers and some left a piece of something important for them.

When they finished, they stood back together and saluted the fallen before marching out of the flight deck.

Finally, it was the leadership's turn.

Mark, Ava, Polwell, Evan, Dominguez, and Rachel—just released from the medical ward—stepped up as one. They snapped off a salute as one to their fallen, to their troops.

Mark moved forward and took a knee. Everything he had been holding back came out of him.

Dominguez, who had been calling out those names as if any other day, shook as she cried.

Mark looked up at them and right back down, shaking his head and holding his forehead, asking himself why, why this had happened and why these brilliant young people had been taken from him. He had been one of them, someone at the bottom of this great big machine. He had been with people from all ages; he had survived and today he was saying good-bye to more people.

He moved from person to person, leaving none of them alone; the entire command staff did.

Taking their time to say good-bye.

They were old warriors now, sending younger ones on.

They came to the end of the deceased and turned around, tears down their faces and eyes red with the pain and loss.

They snapped off a salute and marched off.

Mark shared a look with Dominguez. They didn't need to say anything as they both looked to Polwell, Rachel, Ava, and Evan. They had taken losses before, lost friends, but losing someone under your command, unless you were some detached bastard, those emotions only increased as you took on a figure meant to look after them and guide them.

The Vanguard and the mergers in general were a close group. Mark knew that it was going to be incredibly difficult for them all.

They just didn't have the time to focus on it. There was the next fight and he needed his people to get their heads right, repair, rearm, and ready themselves for their next battle. They only had three months until they reached the BD+00 4810 system to try to find out what waited for them there.

Chapter Seventy-Three

Royal Palace, Crisidium
Tricticus, Emarl System
10/3560

It had been two more long months of fighting. High King Hael Desialias sat now in his office, his head in his hands. There hadn't been and probably wouldn't be a reprieve. Ever.

Malazar Skill School had fallen to the Maraukians a month previous. Their retreat to Crisidium was intense—so much death.

Now it felt like there was just this, nothing but this. He looked to his 3D holo of his city. Crisidium was holding, yes, but each day they held seemed an eternity. The Maraukian forces on the ground outnumbered the residents inside by a thousand to one. Their only hopes of ever surviving this was their drop-ships, the constant supplies and work from the Yard and the Ark, and the refineries and miners that were still churning out weapons, ammunition, and food.

He waited today, as he had every day since they landed, for news from Mark and the mergers. But as much as they were in contact and also fighting it out in the far distances of space, there'd been no recent news and no telling as to if they'd ever complete their mission and kill the Maraukians where they originated from.

General Orbel's link in was surprising. He accepted the communication. "Report." He expected news. Bad news. It always was.

"All strong points are holding, but..." Orbel paused and then let out a sigh. "It seems the Maraukians have a cycle, just like we would: they hold, wait it out, then push forward."

"Any predictability to the way they do this?"

Orbel laughed. "That's the point. They're building, it seems, to rally against 187."

Point 187 was where his son was, overseeing the far corners of the city, where the Maraukians had again and again been bled in, and then pushed back out.

"The Vanguard?" Hael asked.

"Spread out on the south side at present. Strong points are also holding."

Hael brought up the views he had of the walls and mounted defense. The Vanguard and mergers showed in slightly different colors than his own men. This made tracking their places easier, but in the hundreds of thousands that were out there, it was a lot to absorb.

"You think Point 187 won't hold?"

Orbel was a seasoned general, involved in all of the times Hael had fought, from their first Maraukian invasion to now. He trusted him. He also didn't answer. Julieus was in command of the force at 187 now, after moving in from the Skill School. The whole west side was his. But if he needed help, would he ask for it?

Hael pushed a few other spots on his holo; the computer systems responded, bringing up strong point 187. Orbel was correct. The fighting there was quiet. They were bolstering their numbers in the background. Herd commanders moved and shifted in the waves of the enemy, but they were too easy to spot now. Hael knew their patterns.

"Link me with Julieus, Dodger, and Phillips."

It took a few moments for the three other men to join him, Dodger obviously in the thick of the fight on the south walls.

Hael gave them the details.

Dodger came back. "We can't move, barely holding here. They're pushing forward faster now. With higher numbers. Wearing us down slowly. But they are wearing us down."

Figures didn't lie. Though the Maraukians were being beaten all the time, they kept on pushing.

"Solution?" he asked the others.

Julieus answered, a little more personal than he should have. "Father, trust me."

"It's...not that I don't." Hael realized now that he couldn't help but worry. Julieus, however, was right.

"We'll bolster our numbers with those from 186 and 188. They won't get through."

Chapter Seventy-Four

ENS Homeland

BD+00 4810 System

12/3560

"Transit!" Yeltsin said as the *Homeland* entered the new system with the rest of the fleet.

Rasalov was on the sensors. All of the sensor operators were to find out about this new system and look for the new base.

"Sir." Rasalov paused before continuing. "It looks like this system was inhabited at some point. I've got a bunch of derelicts across the entire system. It looks like whoever was in this system was a greater power than the Union based on the different systems, the drifting ships, and infrastructure across different planets."

Information started to come in. The main tactical net showed things as the light reached the fleet and then updated as the ship's own sensors started looking at them, getting greater detail but taking longer than the light that was already on its way to them.

Hall looked over the system. There were stations at all of the major points in the system. All of the planets and even some of the moons had stations. The planets were uninhabitable or they were undergoing massive terraforming. They were simply a place for these stations to be held. The asteroid belts had been mined extensively and there were dead processing stations there.

It looked as if they had entered some kind of apocalypse. There didn't seem to be anything living in the systems. It seemed to be just one giant junkyard of forgotten stations and systems from an empire that had fallen long ago.

"We have signal lock on. It's on a main planet," Guy said.

"On it," Rasalov said.

Soon they had a new image in front of them as they looked down at the planet.

There were mega towers and the whole planet looked like a metropolis, except for a sphere that came out from it all.

That was where the signal was coming from.

There were ships moving around the dome but compared to the rest of the planet, it was incredibly small.

"All of this and they live in a dome on the planet?" Celik muttered.

Hall was thinking the same thing.

"We're clear out to ten light-minutes," Rasalov said. People started to relax. "I've got ships that are moving. They're non-military."

New icons appeared on the tactical map.

"Looks like freighters, bigger than even ours," Rasalov continued.

"No weapon signatures?" Hall asked.

"Nothing. But it looks like the thing has a shield. I'm betting the place on the ground does as well," Rasalov said.

"Guy, call a meeting. Ask M if he is available to join us. I want to hear what he has to say," Hall said.

"Yes, sir," Guy said, passing word. Guy felt he had done nothing but plan and hold meetings while other people were forced to do the real fighting. Ever since the Harmony War, he had stopped taking a back seat and put time into being a warship captain, instead of just the guy ferrying people to the battlefield.

Now, he felt useless if he wasn't doing something that might change the conditions on the battlefield.

***

Everyone joined in on the briefing—including Moretti, all the way in the Hellenic system—working with all of humanity to see whether they could survive the coming tide of Maraukians.

Hall quickly shared his information to all of them, not sure whether they had the time to review it themselves.

"Does anyone else have any other information?" Hall asked.

Maxine cleared her throat and raised her hand. Hall indicated for her to speak.

"We have been working over the signals and we noticed that there was another signal. We've been decoding the Sharventi lexicon and we were able to find their message. They are calling out to a group called the Black Guard. We don't know who or what they are, or if they exist or not. Though they seem to be saying that we are the attackers and that we are pushing them back and we're about to wipe out their race." Maxine looked thoroughly confused. "I don't understand it myself, but maybe someone can make sense of it."

Moretti raised his hand, not hidden by anything as he trusted everyone here. "I think that charging forward would be a bad idea. So far, we only have information from one source. Nothing has been confirmed. If all of these stations are dead, their memory banks should be fine. If we can pull information from them, we should be able to build up a quick picture of what the hell is going on there."

Hall's eyes widened as he looked at the others.

"Moretti's reasoning makes sense to me, but we all know who would be making entry to those stations," Ortiz said, looking to Ava and Mark.

"We've got it. Get us on station and we'll pull out every shred of information from them," Mark said.

"Well, looks like we have a plan. Now we need a target. Which station looks the best or should we roll for it?" Hall asked.

"Next you're going to be in the corner with a cardboard box, rolling dice," Yu said.

"Or playing Dungeons and Dragons," Ava said.

"Only the noblest of pursuits!" Charles said, raising a finger.

Hall was about to ask how Ava knew of the famous game, but it seemed Charles was once again the answer.

"I want to launch the offensive as soon as we can, within six days if possible. If this Black Guard is a thing, I don't think I want to run into them," Ortiz said.

His words cut through the banter and people quickly started to depart.

***

Ava looked over their target. It was a massive station. It dwarfed the Aegean Gardens and it was only a drop-off point for freighters that dropped off goods, received others, and moved on.

Even across different species, they had similar needs.

There were still freighters docked at the station, forgotten.

The station was not only a freighter drop-off point, but also a place where people could stay; it included different living quarters. These two things made it a prime target.

The freighter station was civilian made, so its security should be less. It had good sensors to guide people in and to watch the situation going on around it.

The freighters must have come from other locations, holding different information in their memory cores.

The housing would also allow them to see how the Sharventi live and, if anything had been left behind, they could check between their different sources to see whether any of it was correct.

Ava drew on Mark's chest. They had been training the entire time they approached the station and moved deeper into the Sharventi home system.

They were both broken and feeling their losses but they didn't let it drag them down.

Mark pulled her closer with one arm and wrapped her up in a hug so she was on his chest, kissing her head.

"It's time," she said, half-question, half statement.

"Yeah," Mark said.

She kissed him on the lips, giving him a small smile before they disentangled from each other and got up, moving to put their Pluto armor on.

"Don't take any risks you don't need to," Ava said to him as she grabbed her helmet.

"You too." Mark smiled at her. Even now, Ava couldn't help but let out a small smile. They completed each other and whenever they were apart was hard.

Mark wasn't a man of many words. Thankfully Ava didn't need to hear many to know what was going on in his head.

She pulled on her helmet, leaving his room and heading over to her regiment.

The mergers were all gearing up, checking their ammunition blocks, their weapons and armor.

Groups moved off, out of the barracks.

Ava moved through them. Everyone knew what to do.

She joined those heading out and passed through the ship, reaching the flight deck that was filled with drop-ships being rotated out of storage and Vanguard loading up before the drop-ship was sealed and placed into a rail launcher zone, ready to be accelerated out at their targets.

Ava moved to her assigned drop-ship.

"Polwell, comms check," Ava said.

"Hearing you just fine," Polwell replied.

"Looks like everything is going smoothly?" Ava turned the statement into a question. Even if things looked calm on the surface, she knew that it might be a complete shit show in reality.

"For once your NIAI isn't lying to you. Everyone's loading up fine," Polwell said.

"Launch in five!" Mark's voice rang through everyone's helmets.

"Nice. Just enough time to get plugged in," Polwell said.

"I'll leave you to your tunes," Ava said.

"Thank you, ma'am," Polwell said, coming off the channel and starting to listen to music.

Ava sat back in her seat. Her mind started to run with the what-ifs. She pulled up a movie and started watching it to distract her mind, even if only barely.

"Launch!" the flight commander said as the first flight of drop-ships were fired and released.

Ava checked the situation. The RSDs were deployed and providing a screen for the drop-ships.

Ava's ship was loaded and then fired out of the acceleration rails. Ava's body, with Kela's help, adjusted so she only felt a slight push. She looked over the target once again.

It looked like a multi-layered sandwich with toothpicks stabbed throughout it, holding it together.

The metal shone in the system's sunlight, glancing off the freighters that were docked at different levels of the station.

Ava's tension climbed as they got closer. The drop-ships were already bobbing and weaving in case weapon systems came online.

Nothing happened as they pushed onward: no weapons fire, no shielding, nothing as the drop-ships flared their thrusters and the Vanguard were raised up.

They were fired out from the ship. Using their gravity drives, they landed in a perfect defensive coverage.

"First forces have made entry. No enemy contact," Ava reported to Mark and higher.

The second round of drop-ships came in, dropping Vanguard from their belly as well as they rushed off.

The Vanguard moved forward, using the first drop as a firebase to hold the landing zone. They moved to make entry into the facility.

It was Ava's turn.

The seats moved away and they were all picked up as the doors under their feet disappeared.

The red light on the side of the craft turned to green as from the front of the drop-ship to the rear, they dropped in silent sequence.

They landed on the ground below. Ava's M20s were up and scanning the area. There was still no movement.

Ava moved up with the sections that had been in the craft with her.

The toothpicks that went through the station were actually massive skyscraper-looking buildings. Some were one hundred meters by one hundred meters, with the largest central tower being three hundred meters by three hundred meters.

These were the targets of the entry teams. They grouped up on the different towers and pushed into the openings they could find.

She checked on the scans and reports. Nanites were already in different computer systems.

"I want a casualty collection point here, extra ammunition and supplies in here." Ava tagged two different rooms in the tower her regiment was supposed to assault and clear.

"I can handle that. You're going to want to see this." Polwell gave her a location.

She followed the bouncing ball to a room. It looked like some kind of command room that looked over the freighter docking area.

Nothing was alive on any of the consoles.

"What am I looking at here, Sergeant?" she asked the section leader in the room.

"Ma'am, it looks like this station doesn't have any power at all. It's just derelict. We've got a call out to get power sources to get these systems online and see if we can recover anything," the sergeant said.

"Good work. I'm going to make this my command post for now."

"Yes, ma'am." The sergeant nodded and got back to work with his people.

She called up Mark. "I don't think that there's anything alive in here."

"I have the same feeling but we'd best keep our people active and push out a sensor net. Don't want anything sneaking up on us," Mark replied.

Ava grunted and checked her connection.

The sergeant got his power sources online. The different systems on the bridge started to come online. Instead of trying to use them, the different members of the section poured nanites out from their suits and started to decode what the stations were even for and trace where the memory cores of the station were.

"Got firm connection back to the *Moby* and to Moretti," Ava said.

"Good. Keep me updated," Mark said.

Ava closed the channel, checking on her people's deployments and what they were doing.

Chapter Seventy-Five

Outpost 187, Crisidium
Tricticus, Emarl System
12/2560

Shawna watched on as the Maraukians advanced. This time around, they pushed forward in much higher numbers than she'd seen before. She sucked in a breath and listened as the barrage of incoming fire from their Bellonas struck with impeccable force.

She shivered. There was no way they'd be able to hold this point anymore. Since the Maraukians had surrounded the city, since they'd managed to dig in, it was a pure waiting game. It seemed the wait would soon be over. Their enemy came in cycles: they pushed forward, were painfully taken down, and then they pulled back. Only to wait and then try again. All they could do was cannibalize everything possible and defend each attack with everything they had.

Their only hope was that something would turn this inevitable death away. That something—that someone—being Mark Victor and his mergers. With everything they'd already expended, and with more wounded succumbing to their injuries, she hoped for just that one miracle. Now watching the line, she hesitated, knowing Dodger was in deep talks with command.

Almost within seconds, the surge of Maraukians rushed forward once again and her heart sank. *There's just too many of them.*

She wanted to hold this section. Without it, the enemy would overrun this side of the city.

The war raged on before her, and the sounds of it would have deafened the strongest of humans. Here now, she almost felt nothing, heard nothing. *Too used to it.* She knew someone came up behind her, but she didn't take her eyes from the battlefield. Rounds exploded and she smiled as their enemy's bodies were splattered everywhere. She liked this side of death. Seeing them die meant everything, that they were indeed still fighting.

"It's not making a dent...none of it," she said to him, though. "They just keep coming!"

"We are, and we're holding," she heard Dodger reply.

Shawna shook her head, watching on her HUD as she saw one more of the Vanguards' readings blinked and went dark.

So much death. So much pain for Dodger, and all those connected to the net.

Feeling a hand on her shoulder, Shawna turned to look into his eyes. His sad yet very unwavering eyes.

"Phillips has sent in reinforcements. They'll be here imminently. We will hold the line."

She looked back to where the Maraukians flooded in: their manmade traps, their city, everything was being overrun now. There wasn't anything else to do... There could never be a retreat. Do or die.

"One eighty-seven," she said over the net to all of them. Her voice didn't waver. There would never be any complaints, or anyone to pull back without their say-so. Shawna's determination to help them more flooded her veins. "Hold. The. Line."

Her M20s formed quickly and with Dodger by her side, they ran forward in the hopes that ground reinforcements would be there in time. If they had no more ammunition to use, then it was down to hand-to-hand, and they would go down fighting. All of them would.

Their air assaults were good for now, and the loud explosions ahead sounded great. But they, too, wouldn't last forever. Everyone was struggling with ammunition, and personnel.

Another voice came through on the net. Shawna recognized it but then didn't quite understand why it was so clear till she saw it for herself. Coming from the west side were those reinforcements. There weren't many, but the mergers didn't need many. Their seven-strong force spread out and backed up 187's side with nothing but a couple of nods. As extra firepower now sounded out against the Maraukians, hers echoed with it. It didn't slow down the enemy advance but there were now more enemy's bodies starting to litter the path. For the first time in a while, Shawna grinned. They really would hold this line.

Chapter Seventy-Six

The Core

Sharventi Home Planet, Sharventi System

12/3560

Operator Four was once again addressing the others in the room.

"There has been no response from the Black Guard. The humans have entered the system. Instead of directly coming at the Core, they are located at one of the extraneous stations that we abandoned when gaining our purpose and having our emotions removed. It is unknown what they are doing." Operator Four was unperturbed.

"We did not think they would defeat Four Bravo. Their abilities with their nanites are powerful," Seven said.

"Indeed. We have included this threat with the assessments we've made," Operator Four said.

"Do we know the purpose of them visiting the station?" Operator Ten asked.

"We do not know for sure. It seems they might be trying to gain information on our weaknesses or a way to combat our capabilities. All of these increase their potential threat, even if outside of normal parameters."

Chapter Seventy-Seven

Unknown

Unknown

12/3560

Systems started to flicker and come alive.

A pod opened as a gray and silver creature climbed out. Many would be shocked to see the Maraukian that came out of the pod. This one, instead of looking crazed, had a calm look in its eyes and was smaller than the ones that the Sharventi controlled.

Its eyes glowed as it walked forward. The systems came on around it.

It looked young, its fur fresh and clean, but its eyes seemed ancient, as if they had seen eternity.

They moved to a station. They laid down on a bench as a harness held them in position.

The Maraukian closed its eyes. After a few minutes, it opened its eyes and then started pressing controls. The stations around it started to come alive as more pods were opened.

"Commander," a Maraukian said, standing next to the first.

"The Black Guard moves once more. The Sharventi have contacted us." The commander seemed to age in moments.

"We must pay for our previous actions. I do not know the extent of the Sharventi's actions but they did not leave the lower races behind and even found our genome and created mindless warriors to fight for them." The commander's voice was monotone through it all.

The one beside him showed a flash of anger before the heat in his eyes retreated, as though he were too tired to be angry anymore.

"We'll clean up our mess personally this time instead of sending drones," the commander said.

Others started moving to their stations. They had heard his orders and carried them out.

Chapter Seventy-Eight

Command Center

Roma, Hellenic System

12/3560

Moretti was reviewing the information as it came in from the Vanguard. There was just so much of it, it took time to separate it all down in to what was useful, what might be useful, and then go over it in detail. Thankfully he had mergers assisting him so the process was sped up greatly.

"The fuck?" Moretti's face changed and continued to get darker as he directly contacted Mark.

"There won't be anyone on that station. I need you, Ortiz and the others in a meeting as soon as you can. I'm still reviewing here, but I can tell you that the information that you had before is only half accurate."

"I can get them," Mark said.

Moretti was still reviewing information when all of the different leaders were connected together.

"The Sharventi were one of three races that ruled over everything and they made something called the Boundless Council. There were four races in the beginning, but the fourth race raised them up, helped and groomed them and then they seemed to disappear. They had an issue: they loved to fight. As such, they made themselves unable to reproduce. A group of them went into seclusion as their race died. Very much like the Shadow Legion, they were there to support the council and assist if needed.

"The Sharventi were empaths. They could feel the emotions of their own race. They were peaceful creatures. With little war and advances in medical sciences, they lived longer and their numbers exploded and they were unable to be around too many of their own kind.

"It was a massive problem as with so many voices in their head, it was possible for their young to be brain dead from when they were born.

"The Black Guard appeared and they remove the empathic abilities of the Sharventi, much like how they had made themselves infertile.

"The issue was that as the virus stopped them from having empathy spread, the Sharventi started to realize how vital it was as their people turned into robots. The entire race had their empathetic traits removed. Their emotions didn't develop as they had no way to express themselves. Instead, they had a mission from those that saw the loss of their emotions: call back the Black Guard and get them to return their emotions and their empathic abilities. It was the beginning of the end." Moretti took a deep breath, his face grave.

"Roles were created off the other races' history and information they had found. They created a military; they created a structure and rules.

"If one died, then another would be born to fill their role. They were picked at random, raised from the time they were born to be a janitor, a teacher, an engineer. They were just pieces to carry out tasks and push forward this great mission. The race died out as they had no interest in creating more of their people.

"The other races wanted to help, but the Sharventi didn't care for them. Their plans moved on how to bring back the Black Guard. The Guard said they would come back if the council was in danger. The Sharventi needed to create some of that danger.

"They built a fleet of warships and nearly wiped out the two other races, twice. This Black Guard appeared and they saved those that were under threat and disappeared.

"Now, the records end up to there, but there is still information in the station. We know that the Sharventi created the Maraukians.

We know they seeded our people across different planets. I think that it was to get us to attack them."

"The fuck?" Ortiz said what everyone was thinking.

"Look, they took a large group of our people, threw them in every type of environment, seeded in some Maraukians and waited. Only when we reached a certain point did the Maraukians appear. That was the first stage. We advanced weapons tech, and the Maraukians were only slightly behind. Or, when there was a change in the forces, then the Maraukians would adapt. I think they were using the Maraukians to temper and raise us into a force that could fight them effectively. As we freed planets, we would get reinforcements, greater production. Look at the signals: it was hard with our previous technology; with the merger technology, we could find it, and it directed us right to these three locations, all the way to the Sharventi home system. They gave us a map and they've tested us the whole time. Now they're calling out to the Black Guard, looking to be saved."

"That is some seriously skewed thought process," Mark said.

"They're aliens." Moretti shrugged.

"So how can we deal with them? This Black Guard might show up, but here's the facts: the Maraukians are on their way or are already among humanity's planets and systems. It doesn't matter what they want; the fact is that we need to destroy that signal to stop the Maraukians," Hall said.

Moretti had a queer look on his face.

"The other thing: the Black Guard last showed up some seven thousand years ago."

Expletives came from those in the room. None of the different stations showed any signs of wear as they had been in space this entire time. Humanity had only moved into recorded history the last three and a half thousand years.

"It explains why they pulled people from all kinds of different groups and generations," Mark said.

"As you said, even though this is good to know, there isn't really anything that we can do." Ortiz looked at Moretti in confirmation.

"No." Moretti shook his head.

"Strip the station of useful materials, feed them into the supply ships and we move toward the planet?" Hall asked, looking at Mark and Ortiz.

"The only plan that we've got so far," Mark said.

"Maxine's confirmed that there are shields on the dome where the signal is coming from," Mark said.

"Well, we'd best get to work," Hall said.

Moretti could see the fatigue in them all, the pain that lay in their eyes. They didn't want to fight, but they would—till the end, if necessary. Just like they were in Emarl and the Hellenic system. It seemed it was all or nothing. Moretti hoped it wasn't for nothing.

Chapter Seventy-Nine

ENS Moby

Inner Sharventi Home System

1/3561

Yu, Young, and Bobbie were looking over their drop-ship, merging with it, and checking every system down to their basic components.

Bobbie was checking the ramp door while Young was up in the cockpit and Yu was checking underneath the belly of the beast.

The interior of the flight deck was filled with people working on their ships, RSDs being assembled, and fabbers working around the clock.

They had torn apart what they could of the station. The already processed materials were of great use to the forges to turn into the much-needed machines, weaponry, and ammunition for the fleet.

"*Something has transited into the system*," Yu's NIAI alerted him. All of the people on the ship dialed into the information as it was coming.

"Fuck," Yu spat.

"All units, this is not a drill. Prepare all weapons and move to battle stations!" Admiral Hall's voice rolled through the ships as weapons started to come online and people woke up to don their armored suits.

Yu put back the system he was working on and slapped the hatch back into place before kicking out of the other side of the drop-ship. Young was running the start-up on the drop-ship. Bobbie threw Young's suit from the rack into the cockpit and then Yu's as he rushed into the bay.

Yu grabbed it and triggered the ramp. "Get us combat loaded!" Yu's NIAI connected him to Young as he donned his suit.

The calm maintenance of earlier was being disrupted as everyone was scrambling to put things away and clear the decks.

Launchers were being readied and RSDs as well as drop-ships were being readied for launch.

"RSDs are getting priority—we're being put into storage!" Young yelled, jumping out of her seat and pulling on her suit. Her fatigues, made from nanites, turned to silver, connecting to the suit. She only had to step in it and it would do the rest.

Yu pulled his helmet on, connecting to the extra displays and processing center. He grabbed the bar above his seat and jumped into his chair. In his eyes, he saw the system. He let out a cold breath as he looked at the *fleet* that had emerged from nowhere.

"Maraukians?" Yu couldn't help but say.

The ships coming in looked like Maraukian insertion barges.

They were a kilometer long, made up of multiple ships interconnected together.

Yu checked their weaponry. Still, the information wasn't updated. They were too far away; the imagery was crap and the systems didn't look familiar.

"It looks like it, but that design, their speed—those are generations ahead of what the Maraukians have," Bobbie said.

Young jumped into her seat as their cradle was picked up and moved out of the way.

"Going RSD!" Yu sat back in his seat. Across the fleet, the RSDs were being scrambled. This was a new force; it might even be the Black Guard that was talked about in the records they had found.

They didn't know their capabilities, so they had to check everything.

All of the ships were broadcasting back home. In case they were destroyed, then they would know more about their enemy.

Yu felt his heart in his throat as he connected in to an RSD that was loaded and then fired out. All of the ships had moved in closer to defend one another, the RSDs on station to assist or react as needed.

"All right, your move." Yu looked from the planet to the thirty or so ships that had appeared.

***

Chen and the entire engineering team pored over the new information coming from the ships. He was trying to find out their weaknesses, their strengths. So far, he didn't have much to go on but the design and the build for the Maraukians ships, which looked incredibly similar.

"Transfer! They're just five light-seconds from us!" Francis yelled.

"Weapons are online and ready," Travestki said.

Chen nodded, his face cold. "Be ready to merge." Chen's voice rang through the ship.

"They only sent five ships," Francis said as the information cleared up.

"Share all of the scans and try to get as much information as possible," Chen said.

"We have a message coming in from the ships," Liang said, looking to Chen.

"To us directly?" Chen asked, getting his NIAI to send a message to Hall.

"Yes, sir," Liang said.

"If they're sending a message to you, open it," Hall replied to his question directly, overriding the communications officers.

"Let's see what we're up against," Chen said. Everyone tensed, their eyes cold as they all looked at the main screen. There was no noise on the bridge as Chen sat there in total command of his ship, his people united as one.

The screen changed and a bridge appeared on the other side. Maraukians lay on benches, their hands moving over different command consoles.

"They've sent an information package," Liang said.

"Decode and check it over," Chen said.

The Maraukians on the other side didn't seem bothered at all to wait on-screen.

Chen linked into sensors so he could see that the ships weren't moving at all. They weren't showing their broadsides either. Still, with them having weapons all over their body and coming out of nowhere, he wasn't going to just stand down.

The mergers on the ship all put their processing power into the information package.

In just a few seconds, Liang looked to Chen. "It is a translation package," Liang said.

"Very well. Translate this." Chen cleared his throat. "My name is Captain Chen of the Emarl Navy. I must ask who you are and what your intentions are."

The Maraukian on the screen seemed a bit surprised. It didn't open its mouth but modulated words came back. "We are Black Guard. We have come with the Sharventi calling for aid," they said back. Their voice had an odd tone.

Chen looked to Liang.

"*Is it just me or does it sound like they slowed down the speed they talk at?*"

"*Maybe—don't know how fast they talk normally.*"

"*Remove the speed filter. Allow me to speak at normal speed.*" Chen looked back at the screen but kept his mouth closed.

"What are your intentions toward the Sharventi?"

The Maraukian leader's eyes seemed to show some light and the others on the Maraukian bridge looked up with confusion.

"We are the ones that placed them in this condition."

"You are the ones that removed their emotions and now they have been fighting and killing my people over hundreds of years. What are your intentions with the Sharventi?" Chen demanded.

"We are going to give them what they ask." The Maraukian's voice sped up with every word.

"What they ask?"

"We will give them back their empathy."

"What will that mean?"

"It means they will once again experience one another's feelings."

"They have committed war against my people. They will need to be punished," Chen said.

"Punished—we also agree. What do you propose?"

Chen paused.

"We have sensed that you are not simple biological creatures. What are your alterations?"

"I am not at liberty to say." Chen's face hardened.

The Maraukian's expression changed; Chen's NIAI told him that the Maraukian was showing pity.

"Such advancements, all for war. We did not wish for this. We hoped for peace to continue, but our actions were too severe and they turned the Sharventi into what they are today. Learn from us, mergers." A massive amount of information started to flow into the *Moby*. The different mergers started to break it down, merging together as they distributed it through their network. It was the history of the Boundless Council, the "Maraukians" or Black Guard as they fought one another, advancing through their greater technology until they reached space, eventually turning into half machine and organic until they were able to suppress all the violence. They had to kill off all of their race to stop them from pushing forward and destroying everything they set their eyes on. They made it their duty to watch over the Boundless Council and make sure it, and no other race they found, fell into depravity like that.

They had existed for thousands of years, being woken up only to deal with problems and then sent back into sleep.

Chen's face softened. All of the mergers softened as they understood these Black Guard more completely.

"*Send them back our history.*" Mark's voice came out of the mergers. With his words, the others rallied.

They gathered together their memories and sent it to the Black Guard.

It was their turn to go blank-eyed as they reviewed the lives, the information that spread through their minds.

Minutes passed by but to the two groups it felt as if it were lifetimes.

Afterward, they both looked at one another. Their hard and cold expressions started to feel a bit more familiar.

"Seems that we are more alike than I would have thought," the Maraukian commander said.

"It seems that the Sharventi knew a bit of you guys, enough to make us follow your path in order to look like a threat and confuse you. They didn't know you would see through it all so easily," Chen said. Knowing who they were now, he wasn't so scared. The Black Guard was made to protect. As long as humanity didn't cross their line, they wouldn't act.

"We are deciding the Sharventi's punishment," the commander said.

A few moments later, the Maraukian commander looked back at Chen. "They will regain their memories, but they will also be given your memories. We would like for a delegation of your people to come with us to render judgement. This is optional," the Maraukian said.

"I'll go." Mark's voice rang in Chen's head.

"I will too," Ava said.

"Me too," Carla said.

"We'll need some other people there," Charles said.

Quickly, a group volunteered to go.

"Well, you'll need a ride over there," Yu said.

"We'll have to talk to higher before agreeing," Chen told the Black Guard.

"We will wait." The Black Guard didn't stop the connection and simply went back to what they were doing.

Chen quickly opened a chat with Admiral Hall and General Ortiz, sending them a file on what had happened.

Hall and Ortiz called him back up.

"I don't like it, but I think it's a risk that we need to take. Assaulting that planet is going to be a nightmare and we've got war all over humanity's planets. We need to end this," Hall said.

"I trust Mark. If he wants to go over there, I'll trust him to end things," Ortiz said.

Chen pulled himself together. "Understood." Chen closed the channel and messaged the volunteers from before.

"All right, you're all on the shuttle. Take your gear." His voice was brusque. He didn't know whether he was handing them over to the devil himself. They had gone through one another's memories, and although they were edited so that the other side wouldn't get a tactical advantage, they didn't know who these people were fully.

They only knew they were kind of similar and they might have the power to end this meaningless fight.

"We have a delegation ready," Chen told the Black Guard commander.

"Very well. We have sent docking instructions."

Chapter Eighty

Drop-ship 428

Inner Sharventi Home System

1/3561

"Well, let's go and say hi to the neighbors," Yu said as Bobbie confirmed that the rear hatch was closed.

Young and he shared a look and a smile.

"One more time." She sighed, opening a channel to flight control. "Flight control, this is drop-ship four-two-eight. We are ready for launch."

"Understood, flight four-two-eight. Launch in five," the flight officer said.

The rail accelerated them out of the ship as they took a lazy arc toward the massive Black Guard vessel.

The distance had closed down to one light-second, so everyone got comfortable, talking about this or that, relaxing back.

"Kind of feels like Masoul and Osdal." Yu sat back in his seat.

"Yeah," Young said, her one word filled with memories and a tinge of sadness as they looked back on the good times and missed the people who they'd shared them with.

"Well, the ship can look after itself. Why don't we go back and shoot the shit for a bit?" Yu said.

If this was going to be the end, then he wanted it to be with his friends.

They didn't know these Black Guard fully—they might be running into an ambush—but they'd face it together. It was a risk, but the payoff, if it worked, might end the war.

"You got any of that jerky?" Mark was asking Bobbie.

"Well, only a full pack." Bobbie laughed and pulled out a bag from a hidden compartment.

Ava shook her head as she talked to Carla and Charles. “Look, I’m not saying that a mage is weaker than an archer—just the fact that a mage takes time to cast magic, an archer is faster.”

“Nerds,” Young said, but mysteriously went over to them with glowing eyes, excited.

Yu pulled out a cot and strung it up on the rafters and got comfortable.

“Jerky!” Mark tossed the bag over; Yu caught it and grabbed a few pieces before passing it to Ava.

“Cards?” Yu asked.

“Sure,” Bobbie and Mark said. The three of them started up a game of twenty-one.

“Come on, he has to have the damn queen,” Bobbie said to Yu. The two of them looked at Mark.

“What is this? Mutiny?” Mark said indignantly.

“Drop-ships, not ground and pounders,” Yu said proudly.

Mark complained about the unfair rules of the game. The time passed and although they smiled and laughed, there was that underlying tension as they knew they might be going toward their deaths.

We’ve done it so many times, it’s almost a familiar feeling.

Yu put his queen down on Mark’s two of spades.

“Come on, dude!” Bobbie put down his king of spades.

Mark laughed as Yu simply shrugged, the corner of his mouth pulled up in a sly arc.

Chapter Eighty-One

Command Center

Roma, Hellenic System

1/3561

Dozens of the assault barges had landed on Roma; artillery fired on them. Their defensive fire was impressive and nothing could get close to them. The amount of ammunition it took to overwhelm their defense system was astronomical.

Still, it meant one less assault barge and they had ammunition to spare. They had been preparing for this battle for hundreds of years.

The assault barges were disgorging Maraukians in the thousands. There were already thirty million of them on the ground and rushing out, looking for the different defensive cities and structures that the people of Roma lived in.

Artillery worked to weaken their forces and thin their numbers. With their ships in orbit, they still had a good idea of where the Maraukians were, bringing down direct fire on them.

The acceleration tubes and artillery cannons fired through their armored hatches, their crews working around the clock.

Damus looked away from the information on Roma and turned to the reports coming from across the Union.

Maraukian barges were showing up all across the alliance.

Already, the quick reaction forces had been deployed. The fleets and ships that were over Roma were preparing to move to assist, their battle done in the Hellenic system.

Squadron One and Two would remain on the station but the rest of the Union were being beaten back.

Unlike Roma, only a few of their planets were built for war. Most of them had defenses and they had been building ever since Gilese, but this was a full-frontal assault, making it incredibly hard for the different systems and people to support one another.

Damus could only move more of his legions around and hope they were enough support to the people on the planets and moons so they were able to hold out.

Once planets were cleared, then their forces could be relocated to support others.

Chapter Eighty-Two

The Core

Sharventi Home Planet

Sharventi Home System

1/3561

"The Black Guard have ordered us to present ourselves and they will give us the cure." Operator Four's voice was the same as it had always been.

"There is a craft from the fourth race moving toward their vessel," Operator Seven said.

"The mission has been accomplished. There is no need to worry about the other races. Do we agree to end our mission?"

"End it once the Black Guard have allowed us to regain our emotions," Operator One said.

The others agreed as they looked at the Black Guard fleet.

It easily moved through the crowded system with micro transfers, heading for the Sharventi home planet.

The Sharventi continued their jobs, changing nothing about their routine.

Chapter Eighty-Three

Drop-ship 428

Inner Sharventi Home System

1/3561

The drop-ship became tense once again as Young and Yu needed to return to their stations.

They expertly flew the ship. The Black Guard ship was massive. One of the bays was open. Inside, there were lines of fighters, row upon row. They were spherical, with shield projectors, rail weapons, and hatches for other weaponry.

"Damn, they don't go light," Yu said. The weaponry wasn't something that the mergers could compare to.

They came down at an open area. The Black Guard waited for them. They didn't wear helmets even though the area wasn't pressurized.

The drop-ship came down and started to shut off its engine.

"Ramp opening," Bobbie said once they were settled down. Yu watched as Mark walked off first. He was in full armor with Ava on one side of him, Carla on the other. Charles and Bobbie followed afterward.

Yu and Young took off their harnesses and followed them out.

"Now you have arrived, we will move toward the Sharventi system." The Black Guard commander's voice was transmitted to them via their NIAIs before he moved to exit the bay.

They followed him into the ship.

There were pods stacked everywhere but not many people were actually moving around.

"What are in the pods?" Charles asked.

"Black Guard ready to be awakened if they're needed. We're just moving between systems so they are not needed unless for battle," the commander said.

Charles started to ask more questions; each time, he got answers as the ship transferred.

Yu and the others looked at one another and then the commander.

He sensed their gazes.

"We are going through a number of micro transfers toward the planet. You may look at our logs directly, if you want?" The Black Guard commander's openness shocked the others.

"Why are you letting us see so much?" Carla asked.

"We are alike. We have fought a lot and we are tired of war. We fight if we need to, not because we want to. We have needed to kill off the rest of our race. Death is something of a relief to us. We have nothing to fear in death. If we are killed, the others will avenge us. With the power of the Black Guard, there are no known forces that would be able to stop us at this time." The commander was neither gloating nor proud; it was a simple fact to him.

This chilled Yu's blood as they continued to the bridge where Black Guard manned their stations.

"*It's so strange being around what look like Maraukians but they can talk and they're not attacking us,*" Ava sad.

"*I know,*" Mark said, the two of them confused and feeling odd as they shifted around, ready to fight if they needed to, but making no moves to.

"We will arrive in seven of your hours. You are welcome to watch from here." The Black Guard commander resumed his position in the middle of the command center.

"So, do you have herd instincts like the Maraukians?" Charles asked.

"The Maraukians were based off our genome. They were brought forward, though the Sharventi created a version that was basically brainless slaves they could easily control. It is our duty to remove them and the threat they are. This was the purpose of the Black Guard originally."

Yu shook his head. For peace, they had killed off the rest of their race. Still, they stood here, hoping to create a future for some race. For it to end in failure with the Sharventi, he didn't know what that would do to their state of mind.

They watched as they continued forward.

Carla sent back messages to the fleet, updating them on their condition and what they saw in the ship.

Chapter Eighty-Four

Black Guard Flagship

Sharventi Planet Orbit

Sharventi Home System

1/3561

Those seven hours were some of the longest.

They were all shocked at the speed of the Black Guard, but still it seemed insane.

When they reached the planet, the ship came apart, with the module they were in moving toward the planet.

They passed through the shield and the defenses of the planet easily.

They were looking at the dome. It was covered in shield projectors as well as all kinds of anti-air batteries.

The other positions were to ignite the fighting intent to the humans. This was to stop them.

Ava felt a chill looking at those defenses.

Still, they passed through a docking bay to meet a group of Sharventi.

They all stood there, not moving in the slightest.

The Black Guard commander stood up and he received a gray solution in a capsule. He noticed the mergers' eyes on him. "We, too, use nanites when needed." He moved away.

They all followed him. It didn't take long for them to leave the craft.

"Black Guard." A Sharventi came forward.

"You wish for the cure." The Black Guard looked over all of them.

There were thousands of them, row upon row, with myriad clothing. They were all organized into their own subgroups, even the children. None of them moved.

It was eerie and creepy.

"The Black Guard has understood their failure and will reverse the empathy change. Turn off the signal to your fighting forces and destroy the system," the Black Guard said.

There was a muffled explosion and shaking.

"Done," Operator Four said.

Ava almost didn't understand how far these people would go, just to recall these people and gain back their emotions.

The Black Guard pressed a button on the capsule he had been handed.

Nanites sprayed out of the can and they spread out, entering the bodies of the Sharventi.

Nothing happened after a few moments. Then the Sharventi started moving in place.

***

Operator Four was in front of the Black Guard commander, so he was one of the first to receive the nanites.

It started to assail his senses and he was left in a state of confusion.

The Sharventi were all shocked as their emotions started to come back. It was as if they were newly born again. Everything was so raw. They could feel one another's emotions. They were excited they had completed their goal. They celebrated. Everything was worth it.

"We did this in order to save you from a life of pain. We did not know what would happen, nor the destruction that you would bring down on others."

The Sharventi were brand-new to their emotions and didn't fully understand. They looked, confused, at the Black Guard leader.

He looked over to the mergers and to Mark.

Operator Four noticed this all. His emotions were complex but he felt something in his gut, an uneasiness.

"Mergers." Mark's word passed from the Sharventi home world all the way to the Emarl system.

Mergers of all creeds merged into one. Those in front of the Sharventi looked directly at them. Even the ghosts of the net, the mergers recreated through the other's memories, were there, lurking in the depths of their glowing eyes. Thousands looked back at the Sharventi.

"What are you doing?" Operator Four asked.

"Judging." All of the mergers spoke together, their voices one and distorted with the others.

Nanites shot out from their bodies, as they withered.

The nanites shot out to the Sharventi, who were confused.

Then it started to hit Operator Four: emotions. The emotions, the thoughts, the dreams, hopes and beliefs, images, memories, lives. These were the memories of the living as they thought of those who had died under the Maraukians, under the Sharventi.

The Sharventi's recently awakened emotions were being torn apart as they lived through the lives they had destroyed.

They collapsed on the ground, letting out moans, asking for it to stop even as the pain grew. This is what they had done, what they had done for generations.

The nanites were passed on; just like the genetic alteration, none of the Sharventi were left out.

The mergers all looked tired as they disconnected from one another.

***

Mark stumbled, Ava helping him. He felt as if his soul had been scoured.

He reached out for her hand with a smile.

His eyes turned to the Sharventi. They had seen the humans as only a pawn. Now they were living through thousands of lives, seeing the deaths of millions who had perished, living through the emotions of those who had died, and those who had lost their loved ones.

There was nothing to be done for them now.

"What will you do now?" Mark asked the Black Guard commander.

The Black Guard commander turned to Mark. "There are another eleven races that were being used by the Sharventi. We will look to help them, destroy the Maraukian threat as you call them. We have turned off the signal, which will turn them into nothing but roving bands of animals, with no ability to use weapons or build ships." The Black Guard's casual words stunned the other mergers.

"Eleven more races? So that means there are fourteen in existence that we know of?" Charles asked.

"Correct," the Black Guard commander said. "You mergers are good mediators and unlike us, you find better solutions to issues. Your power isn't as high as ours, but it would be beneficial if we worked together."

Mark looked to Ava. In front of them laid eternity. He didn't know what would come or where that path would go.

He just hoped that he would be able to set down his rifle and his armor and live. Live life to the fullest for those who hadn't been able to.

He felt her squeezing his hand as he squeezed hers back.

"I don't know about the universe—I just want to protect my family." He was an old warrior, from fighting his way out of the orphanage on Earth, to stepping on alien planets, no longer human, but something else.

His eyes steeled. "I have one more duty, my final one." Mark's voice quivered slightly.

Chapter Eighty-Five

Command Center

Roma, Hellenic System

1/3561

"Emperor, Legate, we have something strange happening," a sensors officer said to Damus and Cassius, who were looking over the newest report coming in from the Emarl assault fleet that had gone chasing down the Sharventi.

"What is it?" Damus demanded.

"They're, well, I think you should see, sir." The communications officer sent him a link.

Damus shared it with Cassius. They looked through some of the optical feeds on the front line of battle.

The full weapons fire of the defensive structure was tearing into the Maraukians, destroying them, but still they were crawling forward, simply too many of them for the guns to kill off.

Different sections of the wall were hit with explosions and damaged with missiles and coil gun rounds.

Then something strange started happening with the Maraukians. They stopped shooting; they stopped moving forward.

It lasted only a few seconds but thousands were killed off.

Then the Maraukians seemed to figure out where they were again, and they started running, not toward the defenses but in every other direction they could find.

"What the hell?" Cassius asked.

"They're retreating, sir." The communications officer sounded as if he didn't believe it himself.

"Fuck." Damus looked to Cassius.

"They might have done it." Cassius looked back at him, the two of them hoping but they didn't know for sure.

"We have a message from Admiral Nessa. It's a video," the communications officer said.

"Send it," Damus said.

Damus was greeted by a sensor plot showing Maraukian insertion barges moving through the Yeali system for the planet Grasu. The barges were firing on the different defenses. Then, suddenly, their weapons fire declined; only their automated systems fired. Their engines kept firing, but they didn't make adjustments to their course. They just kept on moving forward, being greeted by weapons fire from the defensive orbitals.

The insertion barge was being pummeled but it didn't turn; it wasn't turning toward the planet.

They continued on their original course, actually hitting the planet's atmosphere on the wrong angle. The ships started to come apart. The Maraukians didn't adjust; they didn't release their assault barges.

The feed cut to another Maraukian fleet that simply entered the system and didn't fire back as weapons fire rained down on them.

"Maraukian herds that were engaged in fighting are now turning away from the battle and retreating," the communications officer said. This scene was happening all across the Union.

"We need to capitalize on this. Corral them with artillery fire and destroy them. We don't know if they'll start to regain control of themselves," Damus ordered. They needed to hit now that the metal was hot.

"Yes, sir!" The communications officer started passing on the orders immediately.

Chapter Eighty-Six

The Crucible

The Ark, Emarl System

3/3561

Drop-ships returned to the Crucible, coming down like wasps, dropping off a group of mergers. With them, there were crates—some pitch-black, others with a helmet or shell embedded in them.

They departed. The ranks of mergers and the crates created a line at the entrance to the Crucible itself as more drop-ships came down.

Mark and the mergers stood, releasing the crates as the drop-ship's doors opened.

They exited, each group of mergers marching with a floating crate between them.

The air lock cycled. Once passing through the air lock, the sound of marching could be heard.

There were rows of mergers from all branches.

They all filed in, following one another, accompanying their fellows on their last journey.

There weren't holes in the walls. Instead, the walls had been cut back, revealing an open area on one side of the hallway.

The floating crates came to a halt at their different resting places as the merger next to the wall marched to fill the gaps.

Mark and the leaders of the mergers turned around as one, looking at the merger looking at them, the crates to their side, between them and the wall.

Row after row, they kept on coming. The mergers flowed behind those already there, standing three ranks deep behind the crates.

"Le-ft, turn!" Mark yelled. The mergers faced the crates and the wall.

He paused, as they all looked upon those crates.

Four hundred and fifty-three mergers who hadn't made it home.

"To the fallen!" Mark and everyone snapped their right fist to their heart.

The crates slowly turned and moved backward. They threaded through those who were there already. From the back wall, they locked into clamps in the ground. It was as if the fallen were standing at attention, looking back at their friends, their section mates, and fellow mergers.

Looking upon them all, it was powerful. Mark took a deep breath in through his nose and released it slowly.

"Release!"

Fists snapped down to their sides.

"For*ward* face!"

The mergers turned to look down the hall. Mark felt all of the mergers at his back.

"For*ward* march!"

Their boots shook the hall as they moved forward as one.

***

Evan knocked on Mark's office.

"Come," Mark said.

Evan opened the door and looked at Mark. Dominguez was there as well.

He made to salute when Mark looked up without raising his head.

"Major." Evan's arm came back down.

"That's Mark to you." Mark sat back in his seat. Likewise, Dominguez was relaxed in her seat.

Evan felt that something was weird, seeing the two of them sitting back. He had barely seen them relax ever. "You wanted to see me?"

"Effective immediately, Major Dodger, Regiment Warrant Officer Dominguez, Captain Desialias, and I are retired." Mark threw Evan a cigar box. Something moved around in it that wasn't a cigar.

"Sir?"

"Open the box," Mark said with a tired smile.

Evan opened the box to find a rank tab for a major.

"You are now the major of the Vanguard." Evan got a big information file. "That is everything that you need," Mark said.

"But, sir, you're Mark Victor," Evan said.

"And you're Evan Miles," Mark said.

Evan looked Mark in the eyes, really looked him in the eyes—no merge between them, no difference in rank. He saw Mark's unguarded self.

He didn't see the warrior, the leader he had followed into battle. He saw the man he was willing to stand beside. He saw how truly broken he was.

He looked to Dominguez and Mark. The two of them had shouldered so much, lost so much. He didn't have the words to say anything as Dominguez and Mark stood.

"If you need anything, we'll be around. I wouldn't be giving you this if I didn't think you deserved it." Mark walked past and headed out the door.

Dominguez was shorter than Evan and patted his arm. "You're not bad, kid. Don't fuck it up." She laughed.

Evan smiled, feeling his heart being pulled on and tears in his eyes, as if he were seeing the end to a legend.

The two old warriors walked out the door together. Evan brought himself up to salute: not a legionnaire salute, or a merger salute—a trooper salute.

"Attention!" His word rang out as he gave off the best salute he could. They had taught him so much. His eyes itched as his jaw worked.

Mark and Dominguez drew themselves up and saluted him back.

He lowered his hand and the two of them started to walk away down the hall.

"Hah, look at him—all grown up. He can even salute now." Evan heard Mark's voice, the pride and the barely contained emotion.

Evan felt tears on his cheeks. "Your watch has ended," he said softly.

***

Mark heard Evan's words like a shot to the gut as he let out a hot breath. He looked to Dominguez.

"He's not bad," Dominguez said, the two of them with tears in their eyes.

"We have some people to put to rest." Mark pat her on the back as they walked down the corridor.

The word passed; mergers appeared as they walked out of the Crucible, lining up and saluting.

These were the people they had trained.

Dodger and Ava joined them. The four of them walked, two behind the others. Their emotions brought them to the edge. They held out as they reached the entrance hall.

They halted and turned. Dodger and Ava stepped out to either side of Mark and Dominguez. They saluted the crates there and the tears fell as they looked over those men and women.

After some time, they continued on their way, out of the Crucible, leaving behind their legacy.

Chapter Eighty-Seven

Tricticus

Crisidium, Emarl System

4/3561

Mark sat on top of the mountain overlooking Crisidium. The city state had changed a lot. Towers rose out of the sand, with growing turrets and shuttle pads stretching as far as he could see. This hadn't shocked him, it was Ava's reaction to it that had. He looked to her now, her calm exterior didn't belay any fears, but he felt as she did. Unsure, and he loved her for it.

Mark squatted down, looking out over it. Behind him, Yu, Bobbie, Young, Dominguez, Jerome, Ortiz, and Pullo were wearing cloaks against the breeze. They all waited on him.

Mark squeezed his arms. Two familiar twin blades appeared in his hands. Everyone knew those blades.

"They aren't actually fully solid," Mark said into the wind. "They're hollow inside. When someone died, I added a bit of ash from something they owned into the blades. I reforged them and had another opening made, adding a bit of who they were to my blades." Mark's words were soft, but their effects were punitive.

Mark looked at the two blades. He'd had them with him for so long. Even if he lost them in battle, he searched till he found them.

When he had become a merger, he hadn't dissolved them; he'd placed them inside his arms for safekeeping.

"It's not a bad place. The view is a lot better than back on Earth." Mark laughed, his words not for those around him, but they still smiled.

They all looked at those blades, different emotions being churned up.

Mark took the blades and pierced them into a rock on the hill. His nanites moved over the rock and started to build a small pillar around the rock and those blades. On it were names. Too many names.

Mark's finger passed over a few, feeling the indent. Faulkner, Shaw, lingering on Nerva, Alexis, then it stopped with Tyler.

"Rest well brothers and sisters."

Mark rose, an old warrior, aged by the battles and the losses. His features engraved into his body through experience, his eyes tired.

"To the fallen!" Mark's voice even forced the wind to listen. "Salute!"

Everyone's hands snapped off in a perfect salute, not the uniform, but to those that wore it. Slowly they lowered their hands as one.

Mark pulled his duster up against the wind. He met Ava's pained gaze with his. Then looked back at the others, his people, the survivors.

They weren't related by blood, but they'd walked the path to hell together and would do so again.

There wasn't a way to explain the understanding they had between them. They knew one another better than themselves; they shared a bond that couldn't be described as friendship or brotherhood. It was much more.

They walked away, leaving the pillar in the swirling sand.

The End

Thank you for reading! If you like the book, please rate and review! It really does help get the word out there and allow other readers to find this book!

From the Authors

Michael Chatfield

You can check out my other books, what I'm working on, and upcoming releases through the following means:

Amazon: http://www.amazon.com/-/e/B00WCAOQME

Website: http://michaelchatfield.com/

Twitter: @chatfieldsbooks[1]

Facebook: Michael Chatfield[2]

Goodreads: Goodreads.com/michaelchatfield[3]

Thanks again for reading! ☺

Dawn Chapman

Dawn Chapman has been creating sci-fi and fantasy stories for thirty years. Until 2005 when her life and attention turned to scripts, and she started work on The Secret King, a 13-episode Sci-Fi TV series, with a great passion for this medium.

In 2015, Dawn returned to her first love of prose where she revelled in the world of The Secret King, Letháo and First Contact, as an epic prose space journey over three generations.

This year her experience of working with others expanded. From Drama, Sci-Fi, Action, to LitRPG/Gamelit. Dawn's built a portfolio of writing, consulting and publishing.

Website - https://dawnchapmanauthor.com/

You can follow Dawn on any of her public pages.

Author Facebook —

https://www.facebook.com/kanundra

1. https://twitter.com/chatfieldsbooks
2. https://www.facebook.com/michaelchatfieldsbooks/?ref=hl
3. https://www.goodreads.com/author/show/14055550.Michael_Chatfield

Twitter Link —
https://twitter.com/kanundra
Amazon —
https://www.amazon.com/Dawn-Chapman/e/B014A0RUBC
Many Thanks

Don't miss out!

Visit the website below and you can sign up to receive emails whenever Michael Chatfield publishes a new book. There's no charge and no obligation.

https://books2read.com/r/B-A-MXIG-DOHX

BOOKS 2 READ

Connecting independent readers to independent writers.

Also by Michael Chatfield

Emerilia

The Trapped Mind Project
Benvari Mountains
For The Guild
New Horizons
This is Our Land
Stone Raiders' Return
Time of Change
Beyond All Expectations
Of Myths and Legends
The Pantheon Moves
Empire Burning

Maraukian War

On The Warpath

Ten Realms

The Two Week Curse
The Second Realm
The Third Realm

www.ingramcontent.com/pod-product-compliance
Lightning Source LLC
LaVergne TN
LVHW020702110826
845149LV00012B/2083

* 9 7 8 1 9 8 9 3 7 7 0 8 6 *